Sweet Baklava

Debby Mayne

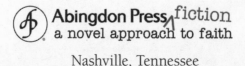
Abingdon Press fiction
a novel approach to faith

Nashville, Tennessee

Sweet Baklava

ISBN-13: 978-1-4267-0870-1

Published by Abingdon Press, P.O. Box 801, Nashville, TN 37202

www.abingdonpress.com

Published in association with the Hartline Literary Agency.

Cover design by Anderson Design Group, Nashville, TN

Library of Congress Cataloging-in-Publication Data

Mayne, Debby.
   Sweet baklava / Debby Mayne.
      p. cm. —
   ISBN 978-1-4267-0870-1 (pbk. : alk. paper)
   I. Title.
   PS3563.A963877S94 2011
   813'.54—dc22

                                                        2010054491

Printed in the United States of America

2 3 4 5 6 7 8 9 10 / 16 15 14 13 12 11

To my daughters
Lauren and Alison
and to my granddaughter Emma.

I love y'all more than all the baklava in the world.

Acknowledgments

I'm thankful for my pals Sandie, Paige, Tara, and Tamela for friendship, fun, and loyalty through this amazing journey.

Thanks to Barbara Scott for being such a fabulous editor, who sincerely cares about all her authors.

Tamela Hancock Murray gets a double nod for being my smart, gorgeous, and supportive agent.

Note to the Reader

What is baklava? According to Dictionary.com, it's a dessert made of paper-thin layers of pastry, chopped nuts, and honey. Oh, but it's so much more than that. One bite of baklava can send a dessert connoisseur into sugar orbit.

This delightfully sweet dessert with questionable origins has been claimed by many, including the Greeks, who have made it a staple in some of the best bakeries in the world. Really, who cares if it started in Assyria, Turkey, or Greece? It's the perfect finale to a meal of spanikopita and lentil soup or Greek-style beef stew. Or for the health conscious, start with a Greek salad and avgolemono soup and erase the guilt of finishing your meal with a triangle or square of baklava.

1

*N*othing like the aroma of authentic Greek food to stir a woman's injured soul. Paula Andrews had to walk around toys scattered on the front porch. She inhaled deeply and knocked on the door of the large, two-story, wood-frame house. Nestled among other old Tarpon Springs, Florida, mansions, the Papadopoulos family home overlooked the Anclote River's Spring Bayou. She heard the bustling and scurrying inside the house as she stood and waited. A wave of nostalgia blended with the smells coming from the house and flooded her senses. The only thing that trumped chicken fried steak on her taste buds was Greek food cooked by one of the Papadopoulos women.

"Don't knock!" someone yelled. "Just come on in!"

Tentatively at first, she pushed open the door a few inches. When she was certain a small child wasn't smashed up against the other side, she shoved harder, making the heavy wooden door squeak. As she entered the grand two-story foyer, she spotted a familiar petite figure standing on the top rung of a ladder, her arms stretched to their maximum, fussing with the end of a piece of crepe paper.

"Hey, girl," Paula called up to her best friend. "What can I do to help?"

"Hand me that streamer." Steph Papadopoulos pointed to the table beneath the ladder.

Paula grabbed the first one she came to and passed it to her friend. "Nick will love this." She surveyed the room, and her eyes rested on the banner. "But why does it say 'Welcome home, John Smith'?"

Steph smoothed the tape over the streamer and chuckled as she stepped down off the ladder. "Remember that old family joke? Nick Papadopoulos is the Greek version of John Smith?"

"Yeah, that's right." Paula grinned. "I do remember. And this is so you, Steph! Nick'll be beside himself when he sees all this."

Steph snorted. "Nick's so full of himself, that's impossible."

A couple of children scampered past them. Steph hollered, "Slow down, or you'll break something." She shook her head. "I don't know where my brothers are, but they're obviously not watching their kids."

"Young'uns. Gotta love 'em."

Steph grinned at her. "You always did have a way with words."

As if on cue, a shrill scream emanated from the other side of the wall. "Stephie! Joey put gum in my hair!"

"Did not," the little boy yelled back. "That's yellow gum in your hair. Mine's blue."

Steph groaned and rolled her eyes, but Paula noticed the spark of amusement on her face as she rounded the corner and placed her hands on her hips. "Okay, you two. Enough of this craziness. Get me the scissors, Cleo, and I'll get that gum out of your hair."

"No way." The little girl giggled. "I'll get the peanut butter. That's what Mama always uses."

Steph quirked an eyebrow. "This is obviously not the first time your hair's been tangled with gum." She plucked another streamer from the table and held it up. "Sometimes I think I'm better off than my brothers."

"Not so much," Paula said. "At least they're married." She nodded toward the child who was still in Steph's grip. "And they have you to watch their little angels."

Cleo stuck her tongue out at Paula.

"Yeah, I know, they're all happily married and everything, but in my fertile family, kids follow shortly after the wedding, and the only time they're quiet is when they're sleeping. What do you think?"

Paula contemplated making a face back at Cleo as she studied the decorations for a few seconds then thought better of it. "Want my honest opinion?"

"Of course."

"When they're your own kids, their noise is like music." She rolled her eyes. "Or so I hear."

Steph made a face. "I was talking about the streamers, goofball. Do you think we should put silver or gold with the blue?"

"Nick used to fancy silver." Paula lifted one of the silver streamers, held it up against the blue, and studied it. "But I'm not sure now."

Steph gave her a look of annoyance. "Just tell me which one you think he'd like so I can be done with it."

Paula paused only for a split second. "Silver. Definitely silver."

"Then gold it is. We don't want Nick to think we put too much thought into his homecoming party, or he'll accuse us of trying to make him feel guilty for leaving."

Paula snorted.

"What's so funny?" Steph moved away from her work and took a long look at it. "I'm serious."

Paula had known the Papadopoulos family for sixteen years. Since she didn't have much of a family herself, she was happy they didn't seem to mind her hanging around. But not so much lately. Her business, Paula's Natural Soap and Candle Shop, consumed most of her waking hours.

"Paula?" Steph waved a hand in front of Paula's face. "Are you in there?"

"Oh, sorry." Paula gestured around the room. "Why are you doing all this now? I thought Nick wasn't coming until Saturday. It's gonna wilt in all this humidity."

Steph shrugged. "You know my family. They like to turn everything into a holiday, and they always start early for holidays." She held out her hands and shook her head. "Mama says that's the Greek way. Who am I to argue?"

"Best not to argue with a Papadopoulos," Paula agreed as she looked around the room again. "Okay, so are we still on for the outlet mall tomorrow?"

Steph nodded. "Yeah, that's why I'm trying to knock out my share of the work around here. Mama wants everyone to do something . . . you know, carry our share of the load and all?"

"I know. I should help out too since y'all have as good as adopted me."

"Yeah." Steph smiled and nodded her understanding.

Paula helped Steph finish hanging the streamers. The room looked like a high school gymnasium before a pep rally, but that was the whole point. The gaudier the decorations, the more welcome Nick would feel.

"Ophelia!"

The shrill voice of Steph's aunt reverberated through the house, making Paula jump. Steph contorted her mouth, bugged her eyes, and clicked her tongue. "We know who that is."

Paula bit her bottom lip to keep from bursting into laughter.

"Whaddya want?" A middle-aged Greek woman with shoulder-length, gray-flecked black hair trudged out of the kitchen carrying a silver tray and tea service. "Oh, hi, Paula. You'll be here for Nick's homecoming celebration, right?" Without giving Paula a chance to answer, she yelled, "Whaddya hollerin' for, Phoebe? I'm right here."

Another group of kids ran past. "Slow down!" Steph shouted after they'd left the room and trotted out of hearing distance. "C'mon, Paula, let's go outside where we can talk. This place is a zoo."

"Don't be rude, Steph," her mother barked. "Let me talk to Paula before you take off with her." She put down the silver tray and offered Paula a sweet smile. "Will you be able to make it to the party? We have enough food for all of Tarpon Springs and half of Tampa." She lowered her chin and looked at Paula from beneath very bushy eyebrows. "Nick'll be pleased to see you."

"I . . . uh, well . . ." Paula widened her eyes and shot Steph a look for help.

"Of course, you're coming. You can't stay away from Nick." Without missing a beat, Steph's mother took a few steps, grabbed her sister Phoebe, and pulled her toward the stairs. "You should see how I fixed up Nick's room. It's a sight, I tell ya. Football posters, football statues, and football pillows everywhere."

"Don't forget the sponges," Steph added. "Once a Sponger, always a Sponger."

"I told Arthur he'd better bring home some sponges." She hesitated then added, "The biggest net he can find full of sponges—the best ones in the lot."

Steph gestured toward the front door. "Let's get outta here while they're not looking."

As soon as they escaped to the outside, Paula stared back at the house. "Why is Nick staying here instead of at his parents'?"

"He's getting passed around." Steph snickered. "They drew straws, and Mama got him first."

Nothing had changed for Nick. Everyone wanted him. "Must be nice."

"Huh?" Steph shot her a quizzical glance.

"Oh, never mind. I tried calling your cell phone, and you didn't answer so I figured I'd just stop off on my way home from work to see if you were still coming with us to the outlet mall. Looks like you're busy, so I'll let you get back to your . . . work." She paused before adding, "Unless you need help, that is."

"Nah, I'm good."

"Okay, then. I'll see you tomorrow."

Paula stood up to leave, but Steph yanked her arm. "You are coming to the party, right?"

"I'm not sure, Steph." Paula felt her shoulders sag as the memory of her failed romance with Nick flooded her. "It just seems so . . . I don't know . . . desperate?"

"That's not true. You and Nick never really broke up. You even told me so yourself."

Paula widened her eyes and bobbed her head. "In case you haven't noticed, Nick isn't exactly beating my door down. As soon as my back was turned, he took off and joined the Army."

"Air Force," Steph corrected.

"Whatever. We have completely different lives now. He probably doesn't even want me at his party."

"He doesn't know he's having a party." Steph shook her head. "Don't give me a hard time about this. You're coming, and that's the final word."

"The final word was when he didn't even say good-bye when he took off for the Army."

"Air Force."

Paula shrugged. "Okay, Air Force. If he wanted me around, he would have called."

"You could have called him just as easily," Steph said. "Besides, it's not like you haven't both gotten on with your lives. You can be friends now." She narrowed her eyes. "You are over him, aren't you?"

"Yes!" Paula said a little too quickly. "Yes, of course I am. I'm just saying . . ."

Another group of younger cousins chose that moment to run out of the house screaming, so Steph had to go quiet them down. Paula stood on the front lawn, waiting and thinking about Nick's homecoming.

Steph obviously didn't get it. Maybe Nick had gotten on with his life, but Paula hadn't. She didn't think she'd fooled Steph. After college she returned to a town where she didn't fit in anymore—but she never really fit in anywhere—and opened the shop on the docks, half-dreaming about, half-dreading the sight of Nick Papadopoulos when he returned to grace the town that had always belonged to him.

Back in high school he'd been a superhero on the Tarpon Springs Spongers football team, while she'd barely won a spot on the school newspaper. She'd zeroed in on Nick the second she spotted him in the school hallway, standing in the midst of a group of his ardent admirers. It wouldn't have been a big deal if he hadn't glanced up and caught her standing there with her mouth hanging open. She'd been ready to run in shame, but he winked and grinned at her.

The next day she pointed him out to Steph Papadopoulos, her best friend since seventh grade. Steph had howled with laughter. "You've got to be kidding," Steph said. "That's my dorky cousin Nick. He's a junior. And he thinks he's Elvis."

Steph went on to tell her how she'd caught Nick making Elvis faces in the mirror. That intrigued Paula even more. When she pushed for more information, Steph brushed her off, saying Nick was two years older, and they'd just gotten out of middle school.

It was obvious Steph wasn't going to be any help at all, so Paula had to come up with her own plan. At the time she thought it was pretty crafty. Now that she looked back, she cringed with embarrassment over how transparent she'd been. But it worked.

She wanted to find a way to be around Nick, so she spent her first week of school scoping out all the possibilities. It was too late to be a cheerleader; besides, she wasn't perky enough. Then there was the newspaper staff. Since all the athletic boys were on the football team, her only competition to be a sports writer was some wimpy guy who couldn't have cared less about following around a jock who towered over him. She asked for the position and got it by default.

The whole setup was easier than she'd expected. Nick was the football star. Paula was the sports reporter, so she interviewed him after all the games. He loved being on the front page, and she didn't mind putting him there. It had been a match made in high school heaven from the get-go.

Steph teased her at first, but by the end of her freshman year, Paula and Nick were an item. Her plan had worked. Classic matching of the hunk and the geek.

When people had asked Nick what he saw in her, he let them know that he wondered what she saw in him. After all, she was the smart one. Steph told her that when she wasn't around, he bragged about how he'd caught the smartest and prettiest girl in school.

The shrieking of children snapped her back to the present. She waved at Steph. "Since you're busy—"

"Don't go yet. I'll be right there," Steph called out. "Let me get this game started so we can talk."

After Steph got the kids settled in a quiet game of duck-duck-goose, she rejoined Paula. "This whole thing would be easy if we didn't have so much distraction. So what did you decide? You gonna come to the party and show Nick you've moved on with your life, or are you gonna hide out and let him think he got the best of you?"

Paula flinched. "Now that you put it that way, I guess you're right. I don't see that I have a choice."

Steph grinned. "Good. Now what time are you picking me up tomorrow?"

"Nine. Oria said she'd open the store for me, so I can leave early."

Another of Steph's aunts came to the door and waved. "Hey, Paula. Coming to the party?"

With Steph's blistering gaze on her, she didn't have a choice. "I'll be here."

"Good. Steph, we need you in the kitchen."

Steph took a step back toward the house. "Gotta go. Baklava's calling."

⁓❧

Two more days, and he'd be home. Nick was more than ready to see his family. He left the office and headed over to his barracks, where he shed his uniform and slipped into some gym clothes. What he needed was a mindless work-out to keep him from counting the seconds until his leave kicked in.

He'd served two four-year stints in the Air Force, and it hadn't been half bad. The lure of new faces in exotic places had called him a couple of years out of high school—right after Paula went off to college. He thought he could bide time while she was gone, but mostly he felt like jumping out of his own skin, thinking about her away at college and doing exactly what he'd told her to do—date other guys to see if what they had was real.

Someone needed to knuckle some sense into his head. What had he been thinking?

The intense love he felt for Paula was real. There was no doubt about that. As young as he was, he'd had experience with girls, and no one came close to Paula. But he wasn't so sure about her feelings. They'd met when she was a freshman, even before she could date. His cousin Steph had her over to the house quite a bit, and he just happened to be there most of the time, until his aunt shooed him away.

He'd never forget when her mother gave her the go-ahead to go on a real date. For the first time he could remember, he was nervous about meeting a girl's parents. After days of rehearsing answers to questions he figured her mother would ask, he arrived at her house with sweaty palms and wobbly legs. But Paula had been waiting at the door for him. Alone. Her mom had left with instructions not to let him in. As anxious as he was, he couldn't imagine his own parents being gone if a girl came to see him.

The instant he focused on Paula, he lost his breath, she was so beautiful. Her eyes sparkled as she greeted him at the door. "Ready?" Her soft, sweet voice had charmed him the first time he heard her speak, and now it carried a melody unmatched by anything on the radio.

"Hey, Sarge!" His buddy's voice startled him back to the present.

Nick forced a smile as he spun around. "What's up, Brock?"

"Wanna go to the NCO Club?" Brock, the guy who bunked across the hall, arched an eyebrow. "They've got two-fers during happy hour. And if we're lucky, we'll see some hot girls who like their men in uniform."

"No thanks," Nick replied.

Sergeant David Brock chuckled. "I was just hoping I could lure you over to the wild side."

"Not a chance." Nick squatted to tie his sneaker. "I don't want to make life any tougher than it already is."

"How tough can it be for you?" Brock shook his head. "You made rank faster than anyone I know, you've managed to save most of your money, and you could have any girl on base if you stopped long enough to let one of them catch you."

"I don't know about that." Nick straightened and gave his friend a two-finger mock salute. "See you tomorrow, buddy."

A couple more days and he'd be home. He wondered if he'd get to see Paula. According to his mother, Paula's business had been picking up lately. He grinned. Her shop was on the sponge docks. Yeah, he'd see her.

❧

As Paula drove across the Sunshine Skyway Bridge leading to the Ellenton Outlet Mall, she half-listened to her friends' chatter and half-daydreamed about seeing Nick again. Would he be happy to see her?

She did a mental forehead slap. Why should she care if he was happy to see her? He'd made her miserable by leaving before she got back from college.

A finger snapping in her ear startled her. "What's up with you?" Steph asked. "Normally you can talk the paint off the wall, but today you're, well . . ." She lowered her voice to finish the sentence. "Pensive."

Paula nodded. "I have a lot on my mind."

"It's Nick, isn't it?"

Suddenly the chatter stopped. Paula glanced over to the passenger seat and saw Steph staring directly at her. She wanted to deny that knowing she'd see Nick was getting to her, but she couldn't do that and be truthful.

"Well, yeah, sort of. It's weird, you know?" She lifted one shoulder and let it drop, trying to act casual. "But that's not all. Business is picking up, and I'm a little worried—"

"You've got a good life, Paula." Steph shot her friend a glare. "With all the online orders you're getting, you can pretty much do whatever you want and your business will be fine. Jake at church has the biggest crush on you I've ever seen, and I'm sure there are others we don't even know about. Don't let my cousin mess with your mind like that."

"I'm okay," Paula said with a smile. "Really."

"None of us can believe he just up and joined the Air Force without any warning. Aunt Ursa was so distraught she lost ten pounds that first month." Steph snickered. "Not that she couldn't afford to let go of a few pounds, but, well, it was stressful."

"Like I said, I'm fine. Let's drop the Nick thing, okay?" Paula forced her voice to sound normal, and that made it squeak. She cleared her throat. "I just hope I can keep up with the orders—at least through the holidays."

"It's barely September," Charlene piped up. "So why are you worrying about it now?"

Paula tugged at her seatbelt and shifted so she could see in the backseat. "This is retail we're talking about. Everything is a season ahead."

"I'm just finishing up tax season for late filers," Charlene moaned. "That's why I'm so ready for this shopping trip."

"We could all use some retail therapy—the kind where we're the customers and it doesn't involve us having to sell anything," Steph agreed. "I need something cute to wear to Nick's homecoming party tomorrow. You could stand to get something new too, Paula." She caught herself and covered her mouth as she offered an apologetic glance at Paula. "Oops! Sorry, I forgot."

Paula shrugged and forced a smile. "Enough with the apologies. I'm fine. Y'all don't have to walk on eggshells."

She could tell Steph was staring at her and sizing up her true reaction, so she lifted her chin, never dropping the smile from her face. Paula was glad when they finally pulled into the mall parking lot.

"I've been looking forward to this for a long time," Charlene said as she patted her messenger bag. "I've been saving all my clothing allowance just so I could pick up a few designer duds."

"Aw, how cute!" They didn't miss a step as Steph pulled Paula and Charlene by the arm. "You give yourself a clothing allowance."

"I'm an accountant. It's all on the balance sheet."

As they perused their favorite outlet stores, Paula wondered what Nick would be like after being away for so long. He'd come back home for several visits, and she'd seen him a few of those times. But this was different. He'd be in town for six weeks.

Paula picked up a coral necklace to go with her ecru knit sweater set because Steph said it brought out her golden highlights. Okay, so she wanted to impress Nick, but she needed to try not to be so obvious.

2

*N*ick arrived at the airport several hours ahead of time and managed to get on an earlier flight that wasn't full, but he didn't tell anyone back home. He wanted to surprise them.

"Going home to see your girl?"

He turned to the woman beside him. "No, just taking some time off and chilling with the family."

The elderly woman's expression instantly registered disappointment. "Oh." She fidgeted with the edge of her sweater for a few seconds. "I don't like to fly, but my daughter didn't want me driving."

She reminded Nick of his mother. "Are you visiting your daughter?"

The woman nodded. "She moved to Tampa with her husband seven years ago."

"Do you have grandchildren?"

Her face lit up. "Yes, two granddaughters and a grandson." She reached for her handbag on the floor, but she paused for a moment, dropped it, and glanced away.

Acting on a hunch, Nick asked, "Do you have some pictures? I have a bunch of nieces and nephews, and I sure do miss 'em."

A grin slowly spread across her face, warming Nick's heart.

"I have pictures." Once again she reached for her bag and dug around until she found a small photo album. She hesitated for a second. "Want to see them?"

"Yes, of course."

Nick settled back in his seat as his new friend, Mrs. Cooper, shared experiences that reminded him of his family, which made his flight more enjoyable than it would have been if he'd remained silent. When she wrapped up a story about how she'd missed the birth of one of her grandchildren, her eyes glistened with tears.

"I miss them so much."

He wanted to hug her, but he resisted and patted her arm instead. "At least you'll see them soon."

"Yes." Mrs. Cooper turned to look out the window, leaving him with his own thoughts.

Nick managed to get lost in his own daydream until Mrs. Cooper turned back and studied him for a moment, her lips turned downward but not in a classic frown.

"What are you thinking?"

"I just realized that all we did was talk about me. I don't know much about you."

"There's not much to tell."

"I'm surprised you're not married, a handsome sweet boy like you."

Nick shifted in his seat before turning to her with what he hoped was a comical face. "Looks can be deceiving."

"Are you thirty yet?" The directness of her question caught him by surprise.

"Uh, yeah, I hit the big three-oh last month."

"It's time," she said. "You'll find a nice girl soon. Don't wait too much longer—at least not if you wanna have kids.

You'll want to be young enough to enjoy them." She sighed. "Children can bring such joy."

He paused before slowly nodding. "I'll keep that in mind."

After they landed at Tampa International, he asked if she needed help with her baggage. When she said she had everything in her carry-on, he walked her to the pickup area and waited until her daughter arrived. Then he went back inside, gathered his things from baggage claim, and arranged for a van limo. Mama would be hurt he didn't call for someone to pick him up, but after being on the sterile base, he needed that extra time to decompress before arriving home where he was sure to be swamped with well-meaning but overbearing family.

He stepped outside and inhaled the humid, salty air then smiled as he slowly blew out his breath. There's no place like home.

Since Nick was one of two passengers in the limo, the driver took them across the Courtney Campbell Causeway over the bay from Tampa to Clearwater, where they dropped off the other person. As they headed up Highway 19, where traffic flowed heavy but steady, he rubbernecked the whole way. Some of his old haunts were gone, but new businesses took their places along the main artery that ran north and south through Pinellas County. He flipped his cell phone open and called his mother. After her voicemail kicked in, he speed-dialed his cousin Steph, who answered on the first ring. They chatted for a couple of seconds before she asked, "Are you here already?"

"I'll be there in a few minutes. I got a limo."

"You weren't supposed to—" She stopped. "Never mind. See you in a little while."

As the limo turned onto Tarpon Avenue, Nick felt a settling in his soul. Only a few blocks away from the insanity of chain stores and restaurants, the Greek life flourished on either side of the tree-lined street. Some streetscaping and remodeling had been done, but his hometown still maintained much of the old-town flavor.

They passed the shoe repair shop and an antiques store that had been there as long as he could remember. A small café he'd never seen before was next in line, but it still had the same look as the other businesses along downtown Tarpon Springs—weathered and worn but loved.

His mother had informed him that she expected him to attend at least one service at the Greek Orthodox cathedral with her and that he was staying at the old family home his first night back. Ever since he could remember, when visiting relatives came—whether from Greece or Michigan—his family drew straws to see who got to play host first. He chuckled as he thought about his aunts and mom, all huddled in the kitchen, studying the tips of the straws that stuck out above the ribbon, each of them hoping to get the longest straw.

A sudden thought slammed him in the gut. At some point while he was gone, he'd been relegated to being a visitor.

His vision blurred as he tried to wrap his mind around being a guest in his own hometown. Every once in a while the limo driver took a quick peek at him in the rearview mirror, and this time he did a double-take.

"You okay, man?" the driver asked as he slowed to a stop at the traffic light. "You don't look so good."

"I'm fine." But he wasn't. This was his home. He was born in Tarpon Springs and played first string for the Spongers football team, for crying out loud. But now he was a guest.

Next time the driver looked at him, he forced a grin. "Tarpon Springs hasn't changed much since I was last here."

"How long's it been?"

Too long. "Not long. About a year or so." *Actually closer to two years.*

The driver's shoulders shook in what appeared to be laughter. "A year . . ."—he looked in the mirror and shook his head—". . . or so can seem like forever." He paused for a few seconds before he continued. "I know. I've been there. Back in the day, Sharon—she's my ex-wife—didn't want me to go off to Nam. But I told her . . . it's like this. Sometimes a man's gotta be a man. Know what I mean?" He looked at Nick in the mirror again.

"Um . . . yeah." Nick wasn't in the mood to have this conversation with someone he'd never see again, but he didn't want to be rude. "So how's the weather been around here lately?"

"You're kidding, right? Hot and humid." He clicked his tongue. "Gotta love this place to put up with all the sweat."

Nick popped a Tic-Tac before he realized the driver was watching. The man's eyes crinkled. "She must be special."

"What?" Nick asked. "Who?"

The driver tilted his head back and roared. "So you haven't let her catch you yet, huh? Don't wait too long, or she'll get away before you know what happened."

What was up with these people who wanted him paired off? Did he look over-the-hill or desperate?

When they arrived at Aunt Ophelia and Uncle Arthur's place, the old family mansion, the limo driver blew out a low whistle. "No wonder you're all homesick. Your family's got some bucks." He snorted. "I didn't figure you for the rich type."

Nick handed the driver a wad of bills that would more than cover his fare. "It's my family's money, not mine. They just let me stay here when I'm in town."

"Thanks, man. Call and ask for Roger when you wanna go back." He opened the back of the van so Nick could get his bags. After he slammed the door shut, he lifted his hand. "See ya. Have fun." Then he got back into the van and zoomed off.

Nick stood on the front lawn and looked around. Nothing had changed, but everything seemed so odd. And still. His antenna went up. It was too still and quiet. Something was going on.

He lifted both bags and got halfway up the walk when he spotted some movement behind the edge of the shade in the room facing the street. Yep, something was going on in there, and he had a feeling he knew what it was.

Nick braced himself for a lot of commotion as he trudged up the front porch steps. The second his foot hit the top step, the front door flung open.

"Surprise!"

"Opa! Hey, everyone, Nick's here!"

"C'mon, Nick, get the lead out! What's taking you so long?"

"You got a lot of stuff? Want me to send Zeno out to get it?"

"Opa! *For he's a jolly good fellow* . . . c'mon, everyone! Sing!"

Nick scanned the crowd until suddenly everyone became invisible but *her*. There stood Paula, all five-foot-seven of the woman he'd loved since the first time he saw her. Her hair was shorter . . . and lighter? She had a line or two on her otherwise perfect, heart-shaped face. But in his mind she hadn't changed a bit. His radar would have picked up on her if she'd been within a mile of him.

Her lips quivered before they stretched into a smile. He tried to smile back, but someone was pulling him into a hug.

"Aunt Ophelia! Thank you for doing this, but you shouldn't have."

The woman flapped her hand from the wrist and waved him off. "Of course I should. We miss you, Nick."

A manly slap on the back caught his attention, and he turned. "Uncle Arthur. How's the sponge business? I heard Dad had a little accident."

"He's fine. Can't keep a Papadopoulos man down long, son. So tell me. How's the Air Force?"

Nick grinned. "Still flyin' high, I guess."

"So I hear." Uncle Arthur chuckled.

"Hey, Nick, over here!"

The instant Nick turned, a flash went off and momentarily blinded him. He blinked and lifted his hands to shield his eyes. "No pictures, okay?"

Zeno laughed. "You know better than that, Nick. We gotta have pictures."

Aunt Ophelia lifted her hands over her head and clapped them frantically. "Okay, everyone, you'll get a chance to talk to Nick, but give him some space. He needs to put his things away, so make room and let him freshen up. I got more food in the kitchen, so everybody grab a pan and give me a hand."

Within minutes the foyer cleared out and Nick stared out the front window trying to process his feelings. He glanced off to the side and spotted Paula standing there watching. Waiting. Looking at him then turning away when their gazes met. His lips went dry.

∾✑

Paula swallowed hard. She'd followed a couple of the Papadopoulos cousins toward the kitchen when Steph suddenly stopped, grabbed her shoulders, nodded toward Nick, and turned her around to face him. She didn't have time to glance away before he caught her staring at him.

"Paula," he said softly. His gaze lingered on hers, and she took a step back. Whoa, buddy. The room felt like it swayed. "You look great. How's business?" Nick made a face, frowned, and laughed. "That was a stupid thing to ask. Mind if I start over?"

∾ *28* ∾

"That wasn't stupid," she replied. "Business is good—sometimes too good."

Unexpectedly, he took several long strides toward her, bridging the gap between them. Her heart hammered. *Lord, give me the strength.*

Nick touched her face with his fingertips then pulled back quickly, as if she'd burned him. "Is there anyone . . . I mean, are you involved . . ." He didn't finish his question, but she knew what he wanted to ask. His lips pursed, and he closed his eyes. "Sorry about that. I'm not doing this right."

She wanted to say *Yeah, there's someone. A husband, a kid, and a baby on the way.* Paula shook her head. "No, there's no one. I'm so busy with the store, I don't have time—"

Suddenly, a Papadopoulos army charged through the swinging door leading from the kitchen, everyone carrying a pan, platter, or serving bowl. Steph's mom took the lead, with Nick's mother right behind her. When they caught sight of Nick and Paula standing a foot apart, face-to-face, they halted in their tracks.

Steph's mother spoke first. "You two probably have a lot of catching up to do. Why don't you go on outside and take a walk around the block or something?"

"No, that's okay." Paula spun around. "I want to help."

"We don't need your help," the woman said.

"But—"

Mrs. Papadopoulos tilted her head and grinned. "Everything's already done, Sweetie. All you and Nick have to do is grab a plate and fill it." She looked at her nephew and winked. "Maybe you can go for your walk after you eat. You'll need it if you so much as taste the baklava. Phoebe really outdid herself this time."

"You gotta try the spanikopita," one of the aunts said. "I used my secret recipe."

Within seconds, the clattering of spoons against chafing dishes echoed through the dining room and spilled over into the foyer. Once she had her plate filled, Paula found herself herded toward the sunroom, along with Steph, Alexa, Nick, and a half dozen other cousins around the same age.

"Hey, Nick, you do the blessing," Steph urged.

He contorted his mouth and lifted his eyebrows. "Why me?"

"You're the guest of honor," Alexa replied. "Just do it so we can eat."

Nick put down his plate, reached for the hands of those on either side of him, winked at Paula, who stood across the room from him, and lowered his head. As he thanked the Lord for the blessings of family, friends, and the wonderful food before them, Paula knew his faith was as strong as ever, and she was relieved.

Paula didn't need to say much. The Papadopoulos clan did enough talking to mask her silence, which was fine with her. Only Nick seemed to notice, but he just smiled at her between bites. Occasionally Steph cast a questioning glance her way, but otherwise Paula was off the hook.

When they finished eating, Alexa grabbed Paula's plate, and Steph took Nick's—leaving no doubt they'd done some planning. Alexa stabbed her finger toward the backdoor. "Go now," she commanded. "Before someone comes in here and starts something."

Nick laughed as he swept an exaggerated, low bow. "After you, Madam."

Paula hesitated for a second, but Steph nudged her with her elbow since she had her hands full of plates and silverware. "Do what Alexa says. Hurry."

"Better listen to them," Nick said. "I've learned that my girl cousins are generally right . . . at least, I let them think that. It's easier to do what they say the first time, or . . ." He turned and grinned at Alexa, who pretended to scowl at him, cutting him off. "C'mon, Paula. I know a great spot where we can chat."

Nick took her by the hand and pulled her across the massive back lawn. They cut through the neighbor's backyard and continued down the street.

"Where are you taking me, Nick?" Paula asked, out of breath.

"You'll see."

Within a few minutes they came to a small field where no one could see them. Nick turned her around to face him.

"So tell me," he said softly, never taking his eyes off her. "What's really been going on around here?"

Paula tried to think of one of her clever quips, but her brain failed her so she just gave him a straight answer. "We've all been very busy lately."

Nick nodded impatiently. "Yeah, I know. Everyone's business is doing well, and you don't have time for anything else." He twirled his finger in the air and rolled his eyes. "Busy, busy, busy. But what's *really* going on?"

She made a face and shifted her weight as his gaze made her increasingly uncomfortable. "Nick, I don't know what you want from me. Your family is still the same. Everyone is either in the sponge business, works in a restaurant, or is a baker. Nothing's changed. They're all fine. They're all happy." She lifted her hands and dropped them to her sides.

"I mean with you, Paula. What's going on with you?"

His dark-eyed gaze was hot and questioning, and Paula's throat went dry. She looked at him in silence.

"Look, Paula, I know there's some unfinished business between us. I wish I could snap my fingers and make everything crystal clear."

"I think the business between us has been finished for a while." She shook her head. "Even so, nothing will ever be crystal clear, I'm afraid."

He took her hands in his. "Maybe not, but I'd like to find out why I feel the way I do."

She tilted her head, lifted one eyebrow, and met his gaze. "So tell me, Nick, how do you feel?"

He blinked and slowly turned his head from side to side. "It's strange. When I'm not here, I almost forget this place exists, except for occasional moments when I think about you."

"What do you think about?" Now she lifted both eyebrows as she waited for an answer. She wasn't going to let him off without some explanation. After all, he was the one with the big idea of talking.

"I don't know." Nick closed his eyes and lowered his head. When he opened his eyes again, she felt as though she'd been transplanted to another time—but she couldn't let him know that.

Paula looked down and shuffled her feet in the grass. "Well, you started this."

He grimaced. "Yeah, I did, didn't I? Okay, I remember all the fun times you and I had."

She glanced up at him and smiled. "We did have some good times."

Nick let out a little laugh. "Remember the night cruise on my uncle's boat?"

"How could I forget? We wanted to go on that dinner cruise with the rest of my class, but my mother wouldn't give me permission until it was too late to sign up."

Nick gently caressed the back of her hands with his thumbs. "But we had our own cruise."

"Yeah, on a sponge boat." Paula crinkled her nose as if the air smelled bad, but she wouldn't have traded the fishy smells for a whole night of the class cruise.

He feigned shock. "You got a problem with sponges? That's what made my family what it is today."

"No, Nick," she said softly. "Your family is wonderful, loving, caring, and considerate. It has nothing to do with sponges . . . or their smell before they're cleaned up."

He smiled down at her. "You're right, it smelled disgusting. But I had a great time on our private cruise—fishy smells aside."

"Yes, it was nice." In spite of Nick's obvious desire to reminisce, Paula needed to change the subject. It served no purpose, since he was still in the Air Force and obviously had to return. And it made her stomach hurt. "So when do you go back?"

"Six weeks. I accrued some time off."

"Your family is very happy to have you here," she said. "I'm glad you didn't let 'em down."

Nick tightened his grip on her hands. "How about you? Are you happy I'm here?"

She swallowed hard. "It's very nice to see you again."

"That doesn't sound like you, Paula." He dropped her hands and raked his fingers through his hair. Their gazes locked, and he sighed. "Let's go back."

When they returned to the mansion, all eyes riveted on them—but only for a couple of seconds. Steph studied Paula and Nick then diverted her family's attention by sticking her fingers in her mouth and giving a shrill whistle. "Okay, everyone, how about a game of charades?"

Amidst a few groans, Nick held up his hands. "Since I'm the guest of honor, I get to be a team captain. Who else wants to be one?"

"Nick, since you're such a wise guy and want to be in charge," Alexa said, "why don't you pick the other captain?"

Nick glanced around at everyone until his gaze settled on Paula. He lifted his eyebrows as if to ask if she was interested. She shook her head no, so he scanned the group again. Finally, he pointed to Alexa. "Okay, Miss Smarty-Pants. Why don't you be the other captain?"

She bobbed her head. "Only if I get to pick first."

Nick rolled his eyes and laughed. "Women!" He took a step back and swept out his hand. "Okay, you go first."

Alexa grinned, looked toward Paula, and pointed. "I want Paula."

A few people gasped, but Nick didn't seem fazed. "I want Aunt Ophelia."

Alexa pointed again. "Steph."

"Mama."

And so it went until all the adults and kids who were old enough to play charades were on a team.

At first Alexa's choosing her confused Paula. She thought part of the plan would be to have her on Nick's team. However, shortly after they started playing, the reason became evident. Nick was competitive, but he backed down for Paula.

After Team Alexa won, she high-fived Paula and Steph. Nick didn't waste any time making his way over to enemy territory. "You've been practicing while I was away."

Steph laughed as she planted a fist on her hip and shook her head. "You're kidding, right? Do you think all we do around here is play charades, waiting for our cousin to come home?"

"Well, don't you?" Nick teased.

"Not I," Alexa said.

"Me neither." Steph pulled Paula to her side. "And neither does she. In fact, Paula is so busy we hardly have time to talk, let alone play games."

Everyone, including Nick, turned to see her reaction. Paula wished Steph and Alexa weren't so obvious, but they were who they were, and she loved them anyway.

"I think it's been established that we're all busy," Paula agreed.

Steph scowled at her then mouthed something Paula couldn't understand.

"I'm sure," Nick said. "At any rate, I'm ready to crash. This welcome-home party is exhausting."

Paula lifted her hand in a wave. "It has been a long day. Thanks for inviting me, Steph."

She hugged everyone, including Nick, who held her an extra second or two. Paula made her way into the kitchen, where all the aunts congregated. "Thank you so much for including me, Mrs. Papadopoulos. I had a wonderful time."

Steph's mother smiled at her and looked at Nick's mother, Ursa. They both turned toward her with grins. "No thanks necessary, Paula. You'll always be like family around here."

Paula thought she'd slip out the back without having to see anyone again, but she was mistaken. She'd barely gotten to the bottom step when Nick came around from the side of the house. "I'll walk you to your car."

3

After being around the noisy, rambunctious Papadopoulos family, her house seemed eerily quiet and still. Her ears still rang from the sounds of adult chatter and children's shrieking laughter.

Paula's tiny house had been a fixer-upper when she first bought it. It took a couple of years of painting, repairing, and shopping thrift stores to get it the way she wanted. Last summer Steph and Alexa helped her lay sod in the yard. As she parked her car in the driveway, she looked around at the place she called home. A little mulch and some flowers would make it her dream cottage.

With a sigh, she got out of her car, walked up the sidewalk to the tiny front porch, and let herself into the house. After turning on a few lights and tossing her handbag on the floor of her bedroom, she walked through her dining room on the way to the kitchen.

She stopped in front of the sideboard her grandmother had left her. Opening a drawer, she pulled out a photo album she had stuck away after she came home from college and learned that Nick had joined the Air Force.

As Paula turned each page, she saw the steady progression of their relationship, from her shy smile in the beginning to her comfortable posture with his arm draped over her shoulder while they posed for pictures on one of his uncles' boats. The Papadopoulos family accepted her as Steph's friend first and Nick's girlfriend later. They went out of their way to make her feel like one of them—and that hadn't changed.

Her mother was in some of the snapshots. Paula stared at one of the pictures with just her and her mother. She thought about her own family and how confused she'd been by her parents' divorce. Her father made a few feeble attempts to contact her, but her mom was so angry he gave up. He could have tried harder.

Paula understood both sides, which made it especially difficult, since she lived with her mother, who took one low-paying job after another whenever someone offered her a quarter-an-hour raise. She kept talking about how she'd be rich one day and buy the car of her dreams and wear the finest clothes—clothes that didn't come from thrift stores or sale racks.

She closed the photo album and placed it on top of the sideboard before turning around and closing her eyes. This had been an emotionally charged day—one she'd remember forever.

Seeing Nick was both good and bad. He looked great—better than ever, in fact. And based on the way he looked at her and some of the things he said, he felt the same way about her. Her mother said she glowed whenever she was with Nick. Until they met, Paula never saw herself as pretty, but his soft, caressing gaze made her feel like she'd just been crowned Miss Alabama State Fair.

The sound of the doorbell jolted her back to the moment. She leaned forward and looked through the peephole. What was he doing here? It hadn't even been an hour since she left Nick's homecoming party. With all her "spies" in the Papadopoulos family, someone should have called and warned her.

After unbolting the lock, she flung the door open. He stood there grinning at her, a flower in one hand and a small pastry box in the other. "Hi."

"Hi yourself." She took a step back and gestured toward the room. "Wanna come in?"

"Sure, if that's okay." For the first time in their history, he seemed tentative as he stepped forward. "Your place looks nice. Very you."

"Of course it's me. I live here." She paused. "Alone."

"Yes, I knew that." He shuffled for a moment before thrusting the flower toward her. "I hope you still like white roses."

Paula took it and smiled. "Love 'em. Thanks." She glanced down at the box in his other hand. "Did you bring me something to eat?"

A playful grin spread over his lips. "Yeah, I sort of remembered the way to your heart—with the help of Aunt Ophelia that is. And I pulled you away before you had a chance to eat your favorite dessert." He held out the box.

"Baklava! You brought baklava!"

Nick belted out a belly laugh. "Some things haven't changed."

"Not when it comes to dessert. Let me go stick this in the fridge."

He feigned a hurt look. "You're not going to ask me to join you for dessert?"

"Oops. Sorry. Want some baklava?"

Folding his arms, he shook his head. "Not a chance. No way will I come between a woman and her baklava."

"Your mama didn't raise a fool."

As he followed her to the kitchen, he glanced around at her décor. "I recognize a few of these things from your mom's place. How's she doing?"

Paula shrugged. "Fine, I guess." She opened the refrigerator and moved some items to make room for the prize in her hands. "I don't see her much now that she's remarried."

"How about your dad? Is he still in Alabama?"

"Are you kidding?" Paula straightened and looked Nick in the eye. "He's not going anywhere. That man's not about to leave his grits."

"He can get grits here."

She shook her head. "It's not the same. Daddy always told me he loves the South, and in his mind Florida is not the South. It's a relocation camp for Yankees."

Nick burst out in laughter. "He has an excellent point. How about you?"

"I like it here. Obviously." She leaned back against the counter and tilted her head. "So now that you've buttered me up with a flower and baklava, wanna tell me what you're doing here?"

"You still don't mince words, do you?"

"Why should I? Do you want me to be like everyone else?"

"No, one of the things I like about you is your directness."

"Okay, so when are you going to give me the same courtesy?"

Nick hooked his thumbs in his belt loops and glanced at the floor before looking her in the eye. "I wanted to talk about some things that have been on my mind lately."

"Yeah? Like what?"

"Like church and your shop, and . . ." He took a tentative step toward her. "And us."

Paula opened her mouth, but she couldn't think of a retort, so she clamped it shut.

"Sorry. I guess that was too abrupt."

"No, I asked for it. Why don't we start with the first thing and work through your list, one item at a time."

Nick smiled and nodded. "Sounds good. I'd like to pick you up for church tomorrow."

"What makes you think I still go to church?" Her eyes held a playful gleam.

"Don't forget, I have informants."

"So your cousins are double agents. It's that old blood-is-thicker-than-friendship thing. I get it." She moved toward the kitchen table, and he followed. They both sat down.

"So answer me, Paula. Could I pick you up for church tomorrow?"

"Okay, sure, that's fine. But I've been going to Sunday school, and I don't want to miss."

"That's cool. I like Sunday school."

"Anything else you wanted to discuss about church?" Her question was a challenge.

He sighed and shook his head. "Steph told me when you and that . . . sorry, can't remember his name . . . the associate pastor you were seeing . . ." He twisted his mouth and snorted. "I feel like I'm back in high school."

Paula leaned back and howled. "You're acting like it too. No, Drew and I broke up shortly after you reenlisted."

"Just my luck. I might have stuck around if I knew you'd be available."

She lifted her hands. "Whoa. Don't blame me for anything you do."

"No, that's not what I mean. I came here hoping you might want to . . ." He sucked in a breath and slowly blew it out. "This isn't going very well."

"Sorry. I think I broke your train of thought."

"So what time do I need to pick you up for Sunday school?" he asked.

"How about eight-thirty? The class starts at nine, and I like to get there early."

"So you can get a seat front and center, right?"

"Yep. I don't want to miss anything." The softness in her eyes defied the set of her jaw. He'd always loved Paula's blend of strength and vulnerability.

He shook his head. "You've never been one to miss anything, Paula."

"And I don't intend to start now," she replied, sounding more flippant than she felt, considering how her knees suddenly started wobbling. "Did you need anything else, Nick? There's some stuff I need to do, and, well . . ." She glanced around and tried to come up with something that wouldn't be a lie.

"Okay, I get the message. I'll be here at eight-thirty."

After Paula closed the door behind Nick, she leaned against it and slowly slid down until she sat on the floor. Hoo-boy, that man sure did make her heart gallop. She thought she'd be over him by now, but obviously he still could get her all charged up.

❧

Paula didn't need an alarm clock to wake her up for church. She hopped out of bed, threw back the curtains, and held her face up to the sunlight, smiling. Seeing Nick had renewed her excitement.

Then she remembered he was leaving in six weeks. This was just a vacation for him. And then what?

Her smile faded, and a sense of dread washed over her. *Lord, please don't let me fall so hard I can't get up.*

She rushed through the house getting her coffee, dressing, and tossing things into a closet so he wouldn't see her mess. A glance at her hands made her cringe. She should have taken Steph up on her invitation to get a mani-pedi.

Nick was five minutes late. The second he knocked, she opened the door.

"You must have been standing right there," he said.

"You're late."

"Um . . ." A grin spread over his lips. "Guilty as charged."

"Do they let you get away with that in the Army?"

"Air Force," he corrected.

Why couldn't she keep that straight? "Air Force, whatever. I thought the military was into punctuality."

"They are." His smile turned into a frown. "Somehow I get the feeling you're angry at me."

"No, Nick, I'm not mad. It's just that I've been a little stressed." She left out the fact that she started feeling that way as soon as she heard he was coming home.

"Wanna talk about it?"

"Maybe later. But now we need to go to church." She grabbed her sweater and handbag from the table by the door and nudged him outside. After she locked the deadbolt, she nodded toward the Town Car at the curb. "Nice wheels. Whose is it?"

"Uncle Arthur's."

"Yeah, I figured. I can't see any of your cousins driving a land yacht."

He laughed. "You're still the same old Paula."

Tilting her head to one side, she cast a teasing glance his way. "Of course I am. Who else would I be?"

4

So tell me," Nick said with a wry grin on his face. "Is that associate pastor you dated still at the church?"

Paula stifled a laugh. "Yes, and he's still pining for me."

Nick's jaw went slack. "He is?"

"No, silly." She didn't know if she was more annoyed by Nick's reaction or the fact that she'd caused it. "Drew and I are just friends. We discovered that a couple of months after we started dating."

"Maybe that's just what you think. He really might be pining for you."

"I don't think so. He didn't waste any time finding someone else."

Paula saw the rise and fall of Nick's chest as he sighed. "Does that bother you?"

"If it did, I wouldn't have introduced them. She was one of my new customers at the shop. When she told me she was lonely and wasn't seeing anyone, I thought she'd be perfect for Drew."

Nick rubbed his chin and shook his head. "You're one of a kind, Paula."

When they arrived at Crystal Beach Community Church, Paula started to open her door, but Nick reached over and took her hand. "This is a lot harder than I thought it would be."

She blinked. Nothing had ever been hard for Nick. What was he talking about?

"I've been looking forward to seeing everyone at church, but not knowing what's going on with you and me, well . . . I feel sort of lost."

"Nick, honey, we're all lost, so get over yourself."

Nick grimaced then chuckled. "You won't let me get away with anything, will you?"

"Not on your life. I've known you long enough to see what you're doing."

He snorted. "Okay, so stay there and let me at least put on a show of being a gentleman."

As he got out, Paula thought about what a gentleman Nick actually was . . . always had been. His mama and daddy had done a nice job. If he weren't so Greek, he could have gone anywhere in the South and blended right in.

The instant they walked into the Bible class, Nick was swarmed with old friends. Paula stood back and watched him work his magic. Even Drew hung on every word Nick said.

"So when are you coming home?" Michael asked.

"What are you talking about, Mike?" Drew said. "He is home."

"I mean for good."

Nick shrugged and cut a glance toward Paula. She folded her arms and pretended not to be fazed.

"Still trying to decide," Nick replied softly. "There are a lot of factors to consider."

"Been overseas yet?" another guy Paula didn't know asked.

"No, not yet."

"If I were you, I'd do another stint and put in for someplace in Europe or Japan. Do some traveling while you can."

Feeling flushed, Paula crossed the room and poured herself a cup of water. She felt Nick's eyes on her the entire time, but she tried not to let him know the effect he had on her.

After another fifteen minutes of chatter—all about Nick—Michael instructed everyone to find a seat. "We have a lot to cover, and we're already running late, so I'd like to just jump in. Let's read the verse silently, and then we'll talk about it."

During the entire Bible study, as they discussed the analogy of fishing on the sea and being fishers of men, Paula felt Nick's frequent glances at her.

When the last prayer and *amen* had been said, Nick remained seated with his head bowed. Paula sensed something bothering him, so she left him alone and joined the others by the refreshment table.

Drew's girlfriend, Molly, approached her. "He's very cute."

"Yeah," Paula said. "He is that."

Molly leaned against the wall and stared at her then laughed. "Why do I sense something you're not saying?"

Paula grinned. "Maybe because you don't have the sense to leave this one alone?"

"Paula, I've known you for a while now, and I can tell something's up. Drew already filled me in on your history with Nick. He even said that was why you weren't into the relationship with him, which I'm thankful for, by the way."

"So what else did Drew tell you?"

"Don't be so defensive. There's no shame in liking Nick. What's not to like? He's cute, smart, and nice."

"Everyone loves Nick." Paula couldn't keep the sarcasm from her voice. "But that's not the point."

Molly widened her eyes. "Maybe that *is* the point."

Nick left the group of guys who'd surrounded him and walked over to Paula. "Ready to find a seat?"

"Sure." Anything to keep from talking. Communication was highly overrated.

All the front pews were taken up by the family of a new member being baptized.

"Looks like we're gonna have to sit in the back," Nick said. "I know how you like the front row."

She shrugged. "Not when someone's getting baptized."

Steph and Charlene walked into the church, waved, and continued on toward the other side, where some of their younger family members sat. "I wonder why they weren't at Bible study this morning," Paula said.

"Aunt Ophelia needed some help with the kids. Adam and Marissa cut out last night, and they won't be back until tonight."

"They have some mighty spirited kids."

"Yeah, why do you think Aunt Ophelia talked Steph into sticking around?"

"I hope the peanut butter got the gum out."

"Huh?"

She laughed. "Ya had to be there."

"I guess." Nick glanced around and waved at some people he recognized. "I can't believe what I'm seeing."

"What's that?"

"Stan Margolis."

Paula leaned back to see Stan. "Why do you seem so surprised?"

"I know God can do anything, but Stan's the last person I expected to see here."

Paula chuckled. She thought about something her mother once said. "Being here doesn't make him a Christian any more than standing in his garage makes him a car."

Nick burst out laughing. "I remember your mother saying that once, and she was right."

After church, Nick guided her toward the parking lot and the waiting land yacht. "Wanna go see Aunt Ophelia?"

"What? And get roped into helping chase after Adam's kids?"

"I'll take that as a no."

"Oh, I didn't say that. I wouldn't miss this show for anything in the world."

"Good," Nick said, smiling. "I promised Aunt Ophelia we'd entertain them for an hour or so."

"You got me good this time, Nick. You're going to owe me big time."

He gave her a look that used to melt her insides all the way to her toes. "And I plan to pay my debt."

For once, Paula was speechless. She reached over and turned on the radio. The sounds of Big Band music filled the car.

"Uncle Arthur," Nick explained. "Turn it to something you like."

Paula folded her arms. "What makes you think I don't like this?"

"Nothing." He smiled as he steered the Town Car out of the church parking lot.

He'd barely pulled up at the curb of the house when Joey and Cleo zoomed out of the house like it was on fire.

"I bet Aunt Ophelia will be glad to see us," Nick muttered.

Ophelia popped her head out the door. "Did you see where they went? I told them not to leave the yard."

Nick took off running after the kids while Paula walked up the porch steps and joined Ophelia. "Thanks for inviting me to the party, Mrs. Papadopoulos."

The woman flapped her hand. "Don't be silly. Around here, you're family. You're always welcome."

Nick came from around the house with each hand on the shoulder of a child. "Look what I found."

"We weren't doing anything wrong, Yia Yia," Joey said. "Hey, Paula. Yia Yia made you some more baklava. She said it was the way to your—"

"Joey!" Mrs. Papadopoulos shook her head but wouldn't look Paula in the eye.

"What?" Joey said. "I didn't do anything wrong."

Nick laughed. "Joey, you got some lessons to learn about how to behave around women."

"Since when would you know how to behave, Nick?" Paula asked.

"Yeah, you're right. I could use some lessons myself since I've never really grown up."

"You don't have to grow up," Paula reminded him. "Just know how to act like you have."

Mrs. Papadopoulos cleared her throat, reminding them she was still there. "You kids want some lunch? I made some avgolemono soup, and it's still hot."

"Yes, of course we want lunch." Nick took both kids by the hand and led them to the door. "Right, Cleo?"

"What about me?" Joey piped up.

"All depends. You gonna behave?"

"Cleo started it."

"Yeah, right. She made you run off into the neighbor's yard, huh?" Nick tossed a wink over his shoulder toward his aunt. "One of these days you'll learn that even when it's the girl's fault, you gotta take some of the rap. Otherwise, you'll never get anywhere with 'em."

"It's not my fault," Joey insisted.

"I didn't say it was your fault, but you still have to take some of the blame."

Mrs. Papadopoulos placed her hand on Paula's shoulder as they hung back. "I wonder if any of Nick's advice will stick with Joey."

"If it does, you'll be chasing girls off with a stick very soon."

Mrs. Papadopoulos broke into broad grin. "That'll be Adam and Marissa's problem, won't it?"

They walked into the kitchen still laughing as Nick stood at the stove scooping soup out of the largest stockpot Paula had ever seen. "What's so funny?" he asked. He took one look at his aunt. "Never mind. I don't think I wanna know."

↬❧

Nick couldn't remember ever seeing Paula look so pretty as she was right this minute. He'd always been attracted to her, but maturity made her even more beautiful. And to top it off, she'd grown into her wit that showed wisdom beyond her years. But there was something different he couldn't put his finger on.

After he placed the soup down in front of Joey and Cleo, he pointed to the chairs. "You ladies have a seat, and I'll serve you."

"No, that's okay—" His aunt scurried toward him.

He gently took her by the arm and walked her to the table then pulled out the chair. "Have a seat, Aunt Ophelia, and I'll bring the soup to you."

Paula nodded and sat down next to her. "I don't mind being waited on."

Aunt Ophelia fidgeted for a moment before shaking her head. "I guess it's not a bad thing."

"No, it's a very good thing, Aunt Ophelia." Nick placed the first bowl in front of her. "I'll bring the bread after I serve Paula."

"You should have given Paula hers first, Nick." She leveled a motherly look at him.

"Oops." He offered an apologetic grin. "I'm still learning about manners and stuff."

"At least you admit it," Paula said.

Aunt Ophelia looked stricken until he winked, then she smiled. "Nick, your mama and papa are coming over in a couple of hours. I told Ursa to bring some rice pudding."

"Are you trying to make me fat?" Nick asked as he carried two bowls of avgolemono to the table, setting one in front of Paula and the other where he was going to sit. "Bread?"

"Over by the stove," Aunt Ophelia said.

Once he sat down, he bowed his head, and the women followed. He offered a blessing before they started eating.

"This is yum!"

"Thanks, Paula. It's Arthur's mother's recipe. She gave it to all the girls who married her sons, just like we do with our—"

"Um, Aunt Ophelia," Nick interrupted. He shook his head as Paula's spoon stopped midway to her mouth.

"I should check on the shop pretty soon," she said. "I have my part-timers working, and I need to make sure they have enough cash for change."

Nick grabbed at the change of topic. "Stephie said you're doing a big Internet business these days. How's that working out?"

Paula gave him a rundown of how she'd started selling wholesale to shops all over the country after a small chain store owner purchased some of her natural soy candles and soap. He knew she was rambling to prevent Aunt Ophelia from sticking her foot in her mouth again, but he was happy to hear all about her success.

"Want me to drive you over there?" he offered.

"If you don't mind, I'd like for you to take me home so I can get my car, in case I have to stay at the shop."

Nick knew better than to argue with her. Joey and Cleo were so busy eating, they didn't say a word until they finished.

"I want some baklava," Cleo blurted.

"It's not for you," Joey reminded her.

"But I really want some," she whined.

Aunt Ophelia jumped up and scrambled over to the tray of pastries on the counter. "Let me get these boxed up for you to take home, Paula. I made them just for you."

⁓෨⁓

Paula carried her bowl to the sink and glanced at the baklava on the counter. "That's way too much sugar for one person. Why don't you keep some here for the family, Mrs. Papadopoulos?"

"Oh, but you love baklava, and I wanted—"

"I know, and I appreciate it, but really . . ." Paula rubbed her belly. "I can only eat so much."

Mrs. Papadopoulos nodded. "Okay, you kids can each have one small piece, but you have to promise to behave the rest of the afternoon."

Paula noticed Nick trying to hold back his amusement as his aunt handed her a plastic container filled with pastries. "Ready to take me home?" she asked.

"Let's go."

They'd almost made it to the curb when a full-size van pulled up behind the Town Car and some people from the Bible study group piled out. "Nick! Hold on a sec! Where ya goin'?"

5

*P*aula groaned inwardly as Michael headed toward her and Nick. "Your mother told us there was plenty of food, and we're starving."

"My mother?" Nick placed his hands on his hips. "Where did you see my mother?"

Steph came around from behind the van. Paula glared at her, but she wouldn't look Paula in the eye.

Nick turned to Paula. "How important is it to leave right this minute?"

Paula took out her cell phone. "Let me call Oria and see how things are going at the shop."

As she stepped away from the noisy group around the van, she felt Steph staring, but when she glanced up, Steph was never looking directly at her. *Ooh, that girl is in deep swamp water.*

"Everything's fine here," Oria said. "Business is steady."

"Do you need change or anything?"

"Nope. Most transactions have been credit or debit."

Paula thought for a moment. "So do you need me at all this afternoon?"

"Not really, unless you *want* to come in," Oria said. "I know how you can't stand leaving things alone here, but this place practically runs itself."

Something about the way she said that bothered Paula, but she tried to ignore the feeling. "Okay, then. I guess I'll just leave you alone, unless you need me. I have my cell phone."

"Paula, why don't you relax and try to have some fun on your day off?"

That's what she got for hiring the sister of one of Steph's childhood friends—advice. "I'm relaxed. In fact, I'm so relaxed I have to hang up before the phone falls on the ground."

She flipped the phone shut to the sound of Oria's laughter. What was it with people, all thinking they knew what she should be doing?

Nick didn't waste any time when he spotted her walking toward him. He held up his finger to pause the person talking to him and was by her side in a flash.

"Everything okay at the shop?"

She nodded. "I don't have to go in."

"That bothers you, doesn't it?"

Paula faked a smile. "Of course not. Why would it bother me?"

"You say that enough times, you might start believing it."

She was about to make a snippy comment when Steph broke away from the group on the Papadopoulos lawn and started moving toward her and Nick. Her hesitation let Paula know she was up to something.

"The guilty always return to the scene," Paula whispered to Nick. "Don't look now, but your cousin is about to make a confession."

Nick glanced over his shoulder then back at Paula. "Why don't I let you interrogate her while I show everyone inside?"

She was about to blast him for leaving her to do the dirty work when Steph replaced Nick on the sidewalk. A tiny grin played across her lips.

"What's this all about? Are you conspiring?" Paula cleared her throat. "Scratch the last question. I know you're conspiring. Just tell me the plan now. I hate surprises."

Steph held up both hands, but she had guilt written all over her face. "I'm innocent. We ran into Aunt Ursa, and she said there was still a ton of food left from Nick's homecoming party, and if we were hungry there was no reason to go out to lunch, and . . ."

"You're doing way too much explaining," Paula said.

"I have a clear conscience."

"No, you just have a bad memory." Paula snickered. "Whatever. If everyone's hungry, this is the place to be. There's food all over the house." She suddenly remembered something. "When your mother cooks avgolemono, how much does she normally make?"

Steph shrugged. "Enough for whoever is coming."

Paula figured as much. "I don't know how you do it, but your family is amazing. I'd hate to be an enemy of the Papadopoulos family."

"We don't have any enemies."

"That's because y'all feed everyone in town!"

"You got a problem with that?" Steph challenged.

"Of course not."

"Then why are you mad?"

Paula softened when she heard her friend's tone. "I'm not mad, Steph. Maybe a little perturbed about all the scheming."

"I'll take perturbed over mad any day." Steph linked her arm in Paula's. "C'mon, we have a lot of people to entertain."

"Just don't make me sing."

Steph snorted. "Trust me, I won't. I heard you singing on the way to Ellenton."

Paula pulled away and feigned hurt. "Are you trying to say I don't have a beautiful singing voice?"

"I never said that." Steph tried not to smile, but she couldn't stop the chortle that escaped.

Paula rolled her eyes and shook her head. "Okay, just checking. Did y'all bring the whole Bible study group?"

"They were invited," Steph admitted, "but we couldn't get them all in the van." She glanced at her watch. "Billy and Thomas can't come, but the rest of them should be here soon."

"You people really take the cake."

Steph stopped and turned Paula around to face her. "But you take the baklava."

Paula groaned. "This is going downhill, and fast. Let's go party."

Once inside, Paula noticed that Nick was the center of attention again—no surprise. It was like he'd never left town. He chatted with old friends as if he saw them every day, and he treated new folks like he'd known them all his life. The only difference now was he kept looking at her, almost as though afraid she'd bolt.

Steph's mother was in her element—feeding family and their friends. Nick's mother arrived, arms laden with even more food.

"This is like a soup kitchen for starving Christians," Paula whispered to Steph.

"Some of them are always hungry, and none of them will turn down a free meal."

"I noticed."

Nick pulled away from the crowd and joined his cousin and Paula. "This is cool. Thanks for doing this, Steph."

Nick was glad Paula stuck around. Yeah, he was happy to have his friends here, but more time with Paula was like the cherry on top of a bowl of his mother's rice pudding.

He did everything he could to entertain his friends while staying close to the woman he'd never stopped loving. It wasn't easy with people tugging at him and wanting to talk about everything from sports to military life—and, when Paula wasn't listening, about their relationship. Paula always seemed interested in whatever the topic was, but as time wore on he wanted to focus on nothing but her. How pretty her hair was. How beautiful she sounded when she sighed. How soft her skin was. How wonderful she smelled. All the things he'd dreamed about for the past ten years. Being away from her made being here even sweeter.

No matter what he'd done to get his mind off her after she left for school, nothing worked. Other women never measured up. They might be pretty, but they couldn't talk about everything under the sun like Paula could. Even the same perfume smelled different on other women.

He'd been avoiding his parents' house ever since he got back. As soon as he was behind closed doors with his dad, he knew he'd get a lecture about joining the family business. Sponging had never appealed to Nick, but now he was starting to think he'd be willing to do it if it meant he could be with Paula for the rest of his life.

The problem was would she want him back? He sensed so many things lying deep beneath the surface with her, he wasn't sure if she'd be willing to make their relationship work, even if she wanted to.

"Nick! Wanna go toss a football?"

He glanced at Paula, who nodded, before looking back at Michael. "Sure. Let me go put on a T-shirt and some shorts, and I'll be right out."

❧

Paula knew that when Nick came downstairs in his T-shirt, all the women would swoon. They always had. He looked good no matter what he wore, but he was at his best in athletic wear.

Steph's mother crooked a finger and motioned for her to step closer. "I'm getting ready to put the food away. Do you want me to set anything aside for you to take home later?"

If Paula hadn't known Mrs. Papadopoulos would do it anyway, even if she said no, she wouldn't have even thought of taking her up on it. "I love the soup, and a little bit of the bread would be good."

"What did you do with the baklava?"

"It's in the car."

"Why don't you go get it, and I'll put it in the refrigerator so it won't spoil."

Paula nodded. "I'll go get it now."

As she passed the oversized kids—the guys from the Bible study class—she could tell Nick was watching her. Suddenly, she heard a thud and "oomph!" Paula spun around in time to see Nick lying on the ground.

She ran over to check on him. His eyes were closed when she first approached, but after a few seconds one eye opened, and then the other one. A slow grin spread across his face. "So you do care." He hopped up and brushed himself off. "I'm getting you back for that, Drew. I don't care if you are clergy. That was a cheap shot, taking me down when I wasn't looking."

"Serves you right for looking at a pretty girl." Drew grinned at Paula then looked back at Nick. "Ready to get back in the game, or do you wanna call it quits?"

"One more play and we can call it a day. I'm not a kid anymore."

"Could've fooled me." Steph giggled. "But you're a Papadopoulos man, so I don't think you'll ever grow up." She turned to Paula. "What did Mama want?"

"She told me to bring the baklava back inside so it wouldn't spoil."

"You're not still mad at me, are you?"

Paula stopped and turned to face her best friend. "Now why would I be mad at you?"

"For this." Steph gestured toward the crowd, which had grown by two more carloads and a few of the neighbors.

"If I got mad at you for . . ." Paula waved her hand around, ". . . this, I'd stay mad at you all the time."

"True." As they walked toward the car Steph spoke up again. "So how'd Nick talk you into not working today?"

"He didn't. You did."

"Huh?"

"He was about to take me home when y'all pulled up in the church van."

"So who's minding the shop?"

"Oria."

"Good. You'll need to replenish stock soon. When that girl helps Mama out in the bakery, we blow through the pastries."

"Yeah, she definitely sells a ton of candles."

"So you're saying your store does just as well when you're not there."

"Sometimes," Paula admitted.

"So when was the last time you had a day off like this?"

"When we went to the outlet mall."

"Okay, so before that." Steph stared at her.

Paula stopped by the car door and shielded her eyes from the afternoon sun. "So what are you getting at?"

"No one should work twenty-four-seven. It's not healthy." Steph planted her fists on her hips and tilted her head as she stared Paula down. "Everyone needs some rest."

"I get plenty of rest."

"When?"

Paula shook her head as she opened the car door. "You're not gonna let up, are you?"

"What kind of friend would I be if I didn't say something about you working yourself to death?"

❧

No matter how hard he tried to keep his mind on football, all Nick could focus on was Paula, and how she was deep in conversation with his cousin over by the car. He kept fumbling the ball.

"Hey, man, you gotta concentrate on the game or you're gonna get hurt," Michael said as they had another turnover.

"We're not supposed to be playing tackle," Nick argued.

"Maybe not, but I don't wanna throw the game away, just because you can't keep your eyes off Paula."

"Can you blame me?"

"Nah, but you gotta decide what you wanna do right now, dude—play football or be with your girl."

"Good point." Nick jumped up and caught the football before the intended receiver from the other team could get to it. "This'll be my last play." He took off running for a touchdown then threw the ball hard at the ground. "I'm done for the day."

A few loud whistles and cheers came from the guys on his team. "Why didn't you do that earlier, Nick?"

"I didn't want to show off." He waved and headed off toward Paula and his cousin.

Steph turned around when she heard him. "Who won?"

Nick folded his arms and quirked his eyebrows. "Who do you think?"

"Don't be so full of yourself, Nick."

"I am not full of myself. Those guys are tough competitors."

"I'm sure." Steph took a step back and lifted her chin in a nod. "One's a pastor, one's a techno-geek, and one's . . . I'm not sure what that new guy Zach does, but I don't think he's a jock. Good job, Nick. I'm going to go see if I can round everyone up and call it a day."

"Good luck with that," Nick said. "Your mother is in the house concocting something else to feed the animals."

"Then I better hurry." She turned and jogged up the steps to the house, leaving Nick standing there alone with Paula.

"So what's going on?" he asked. "Sorry I abandoned you."

The instant he said those words, her expression changed. "Nick, I've got to go home now."

"Did I do something wrong?" He sensed that something in Paula had snapped.

❧

Paula shook her head. "No, Nick, it's just that . . ." How could she explain how conflicted she felt with him looking at her with those big dark eyes, his face inches from hers? Everyone she had ever loved took off and left her alone. Even Nick. "It's been a very long day."

He pursed his lips and nodded. "Okay, I'll take you home."

Steph's mother started to argue with her when she said she was leaving. But after a glance in Nick's direction, she scrambled to get some food packed up for Paula to take home. He must have gestured or mouthed something, but at this point Paula didn't care what it was. She needed to be alone. Nick obviously sensed her instant panic, and just like he used to, he gave her the mental space she needed—without filling it up with chitchat.

All the way to her house, she thought about Nick's choice of words. Yes, he'd abandoned her—so had her dad the summer before middle school. Her mother never let her forget it either.

Sometimes Paula wondered when she'd stopped being the daughter and become a parent to her mother. It had happened so gradually she hadn't seen it coming. Every time her dad was even mentioned, Paula's mother took advantage of it and made a verbal jab at his character. She knew her father hurt her mom deeply, and she never wanted to make it worse. Even after all these years, Paula didn't dare mention her dad to her mom.

Paula's mother had tried to fill the void with material things—mostly from thrift stores—and their tiny house had become packed with stuff they didn't need. She said she deserved everything after all she'd been through. Paula understood her mother's bitterness over her dad being unfaithful, but it seemed like she wasn't willing to put any of those feelings behind her—not even for the sake of her daughter.

A couple of blocks from her house in Palm Harbor, Nick pulled over and stopped. "Paula, I don't know exactly what happened back there, but if I caused you to be upset, I'm sorry."

She hung her head as she stared at her hands—the hands that had worked so hard to stay busy and keep her mind off the fact that she didn't have any family of her own. Most of the time she could banish it from her thoughts, but every once in a while it hit her—hard.

"You didn't cause anything. It's just that . . . well . . ."

He took her hand and squeezed it. "Don't try to explain anything, Paula. It's not my desire to ever put you on the spot. I want you to have fun when you're with me, not be miserable."

"I had fun."

One last squeeze and he dropped her hand. "Okay, I'll get you home now. Mind if I call you soon?"

"Can you wait a couple of days?"

She studied his profile and saw his jaw tighten before he gave a clipped nod. "Sure, if that's what you want, I can wait."

As soon as they turned the corner and her house was in view, Nick pointed to the car in front of it. "Are you expecting company?"

6

"Not that I know of. Why did you slow down?"

Nick sped up and pulled into the driveway behind the car. "Who do you know that drives a Lexus?"

Paula squinted. "The windows are so dark I can't make out who it is, but the hair is big so I'll venture a guess and say it's my mom." She held back the fact that her mother had always wanted a Lexus, but Paula managed to talk her out of it.

She heard Nick mumbling something, but she didn't stick around to hear what he said. She hopped out and walked straight over to the driver's side of the strange car.

Yep, it was her mom. As tempted as she was to yank open the door, she refrained. Instead, she folded her arms and stared at the silhouette until the window lowered.

"Hi, honey. Surprised?"

"Um . . . not really. What's wrong this time?"

"Why do you always have to be so negative?" Without waiting for an answer, her mother raised the window, got out of the car, and nodded toward the Town Car behind her. "Is that Nick?"

"Answer my question first. Why are you here?"

"Do I have to have a reason to visit my daughter . . . my only child?"

Paula worked hard to resist a good eye roll. "Come on in and I'll fix you something to eat. But first I have to get some stuff out of the car." She glanced over her shoulder then looked back at her mother. "Yes, by the way, that is Nick."

"Anything I need to know about?"

"No, nothing."

After Paula turned and walked toward Nick, he got out and helped her with the bags of food. "Need any help?" he whispered.

"Nah, I'll be fine. Last time she did this, all she needed was a little money to get something for Mack."

He squinted his eyes at the Lexus then looked back at her. "Doesn't look to me like she needs money."

"Nick."

He shook his head. "Sorry."

Paula saw Nick's jaw tighten. And she was glad he didn't tell her what else he was thinking. He didn't have to. She already knew. The only person Nick didn't seem to care for was her mother, who tried to charm him but failed because of the way she treated the one person who needed her most.

"Hey, Nick. You're looking good. Military life certainly agrees with you. Did you resign?"

Paula bristled at the flirty tone of her mother's voice. "Nick's on leave for a few weeks."

The bags Nick carried into the house weren't heavy, but his grunts made it sound like he was toting an elephant. "I'll just put these on the kitchen counter. It was nice seeing you, Mrs. . . . , uh . . ."

"Bonnie. How many times do I have to tell you to call me Bonnie?"

He forced a tight smile. "Nice to see you again, Bonnie." Then he glanced at Paula. "Call if you need me. I'm taking Mama to St. Nick's, but when I get out, I'll have my cell phone on."

After the front door closed behind him, Paula turned to face her mother. "Okay, Mom, what's up?"

Her mother fidgeted with her purse for a few seconds and shuffled toward the bags. "I thought you said you'd fix me something to eat. I'm starving. I drove straight here from Birmingham."

"Okay, sit down. I'll get it for you. Tea?"

"Yes, of course."

Paula valued the few moments of silence as she prepared a plate for her mother and put everything else in the refrigerator. She poured a couple glasses of tea and sat down at the table.

"This is delicious. Which one of Nick's aunts made this stuff?"

"All of them. Most of it's left over from his homecoming party."

"I don't care what you say, looks like the two of you are an item again."

"Don't assume anything, Mom. So why did you drive all the way down here without calling first?"

"Would you have told me not to come?"

Good point. "So are you gonna keep me guessing for a while, or—"

"Okay." Her mother put down her fork and leaned back in her chair. "Things aren't good for me right now."

So what else is new? Paula lifted her eyebrows but didn't say a word.

"Mack wants me to get a job."

"What's wrong with getting a job?"

"I've worked so hard all my life I deserve some time to . . . relax." She smiled at Paula. "Working full-time and raising a kid without a husband isn't easy, ya know?"

Paula wasn't about to remind her that she wasn't exactly Mom-of-the-Year. That would start a whole new discussion—one she didn't want to face again.

"What about the car?" Paula asked. "That thing wasn't cheap."

Her mother drummed her fingernails on the table. "I think I deserve a nice car."

"Okay, so the only problem you're having is that Mack wants you to get a job, and you don't want to?"

Her mother shrugged. "I guess things aren't going so well in other areas either."

"So do you need money?" That would be easy to take care of. Money was one thing Paula had enough of and some to spare.

"I always need money. Mack is such a tightwad. If I'd known—"

"Stop. I don't want to hear this."

Let the drama begin. Paula had been the sounding board for her mother ever since they left Alabama after the divorce.

"You're right. I shouldn't air my laundry to my daughter. You have your own life, which you obviously don't want me to be a part of."

She continued her rant about how Paula had made a success of herself and didn't want anything to do with the one who made her what she was. All her intentions were self-centered and narrow.

This went on for a good ten minutes until finally Paula held up her hands. "Mom, do you realize you've just told me what a horrible daughter I am?"

She got a blank stare.

"And if I'm such a horrible daughter, why did you come here?"

Her mother closed her eyes and checked out the way she always did when she didn't want to answer questions or face something distasteful. Everything she accused Paula of was exactly how Paula felt about her.

After not getting an answer, Paula stood up. "Are you finished eating?"

"If I wasn't before, I am now. You're awfully hard on me, Paula. I don't know what I did to deserve this."

"Mom, you know I'll be here for you if you really need me. But I can't solve every problem."

"I never asked you to."

"But you're here for a reason." Paula held her mother's gaze until she got a nod of confirmation. "Tell me what you need."

"A thousand dollars."

Paula's ears rang. "That's a lot of money."

"I know, but that's what I need." Her mother shrugged and looked down at the table before leveling Paula with a pitiful look. "If you don't have it—"

"Do you really need the money, or do you want it for something?"

"Um . . . I sort of need it, or I might have to turn the car back in."

Now Paula understood. "Do you have to have all of it right away?"

Her mother frowned as she glanced away. "I guess I can take half now and the other half next week. I'm two months behind on the payment."

"Does Mack know this?"

Her mother looked down at her hands and shook her head. When she glanced back up at Paula, all color had drained from her face. "I spent the money he gave me for the car payment."

"What did you spend it on?"

"I don't think it's any of your business, but since I have to beg for money, I'll tell you. I'm having some personal problems, and I've been seeing someone."

"A man?" Paula shrieked.

"Stop that nonsense, Paula. Yes, a man, but he's a shrink."

At least she knew she needed help. "Will you still be here next week?" Paula asked.

"No, of course not. I have to get back home. Mack doesn't even know I'm here."

Paula got up and crossed the room to get her checkbook. This wasn't the first time her mother had wanted money, but it had never been more than a couple hundred in the past, and it was always to catch up on some credit card payments she'd missed. She'd never even attempted to pay a dime of it back. When Paula tried to call her out on it, she sobbed about how much she'd sacrificed being a single mother—a situation forced on her. Maybe a shrink would help. At least he couldn't hurt. Her mother's willingness to get help made giving her money a little easier.

After Paula made out the check, she handed it to her mother. "I'll send the rest next week. I have to transfer some money from a savings account."

"At least you have a savings account." Her mother looked at the check, still frowning. "Oh, I need to give you the address to send the check to." She stuck the check in the corner of her handbag, pulled out a little slip of paper, and thrust it toward Paula.

"This is a P.O. box."

"Yes, I know. I just don't want Mack to know about this." She lifted her eyebrows. "If you ever talk to Mack, don't mention the shrink."

"First of all, I never talk to Mack. Second, don't you think you need to let your husband know these things?"

Her mother shrugged as she stood. "I used to tell your father everything, and look what happened."

Paula wasn't in the mood for one of her mother's rants about what an awful man her father was. She'd seen him a total of twice since he walked out on them nearly eighteen years ago, so all she had to go on was what she heard. And not a word of it had been good.

If she hadn't overheard her mother complaining about how difficult a child she was, she probably would have believed every rotten word about her father. But she didn't. Throughout her childhood, her goal was to keep her mother from falling into depression.

Without so much as a thank you, her mom walked toward the front door. "I'll look for the rest of the money in a few days, in case you're able to do something sooner."

Paula didn't budge from where she stood as she watched her mother leave. And it wasn't until she heard the sound of the car backing out of the driveway that she took a full breath and bowed her head.

⤣

If Nick hadn't promised to wait a couple of days before calling Paula, he would have called her first thing the next morning. He'd lain in bed all night staring at the ceiling fan, illuminated only by the sliver of light from the full moon creeping in between the shade and the windowsill.

He knew he still had it bad for Paula, but until he returned he hadn't realized just how intense the feelings were. The instant he spotted her mother, his armor of protectiveness for Paula emerged.

Stoic as ever, she pushed him away to face whatever problems her mother created. Bonnie Andrews—or whatever her last name was now—was the polar opposite of all the moms he'd ever known. Selfish, distant, and mean-spirited didn't come close to describing how he saw her.

Everyone else saw Paula as smart, witty, kindhearted, independent, and pretty, while he knew her as a woman who needed love but was too proud to ask for it—even from her own mother. He couldn't help smiling when he remembered how she'd finagled her position on the school paper in order to fit into the tight-knit community at Tarpon Springs High School. Other girls were trying out for cheerleading, dating jocks, hosting parties, and making friends with the movers and shakers. Paula never did anything the normal way, and that was exactly what attracted him in the first place. She even admitted that she applied for the newspaper job just to snag an interview with him. No one else would have come clean.

He'd always admired Paula because she was different. After high school, her honesty, integrity and beauty—both inner and outer—kept him close to home when other guys fled to the big cities. It's what kept him from joining the Air Force right after he graduated.

He'd held onto hope that eventually he and Paula would be together, but her mother told him she would probably never return to Tarpon Springs after college, so he followed his other dream and enlisted.

He should have known better than to listen to Bonnie Andrews. Nick kicked himself all over the place after he learned that Paula had not only returned to the area but established roots—something she'd never had before.

When his last opportunity came up to get out of the Air Force, he came home, only to discover Paula dating another man—Drew, the new associate pastor of their church. How could he compete with that?

Until he met Paula, he'd only gone to the Greek Orthodox church with his family. Paula had been the one to invite him to her church back when he was doing everything he could to hold her interest. Mama said she didn't mind him going to church with Paula as long as he went to church with his family too. He smiled at the memory of his first time at Paula's church and how he'd met the woman who brought Paula to church her first time—a next-door neighbor who noticed that the middle school girl spent the entire weekend home alone while her mother was who-knows-where.

Yeah, he should have gone up to the college and talked to Paula face-to-face. She'd told him to let her get through school without any distractions, but this was bigger than a distraction. Too bad he didn't realize just how much of a distraction it was at the time.

"Nick!" The voice echoed up the stairs, snapping him from his thoughts. "Are you up there?"

"Hey, Mama! Yes, I'm up here." He hopped back into bed and pulled the covers over himself.

"You still in bed?" He heard the thudding of her footsteps. "You might be on vacation from work, but that doesn't mean you can sleep all day." She appeared at his door smiling, defying her tone.

She flinched as he tossed back the sheet. "What's the matter, Mama? I'm dressed."

"Ya never know about those things." She entered the room. "So when are you coming to stay with us?"

"Whenever my time's up here."

"It's up. I just spoke to Ophelia and let her know I wanted my boy back." She sat down on the edge of his bed and stared at his face. "I miss you, Nick."

"I miss you too, Mama, but that straw thing you women do trumps anything the rest of us want."

"It's an old tradition we started before you were even born. If I'd known then . . ." She looked toward the window before turning back to face him. "So what's going on between you and Paula? She's such a sweet girl."

"I have no idea what's going on."

"Do you still love her?"

Nick didn't want to tell his mother before talking to Paula, but this was Mama. He nodded. "I don't think that's the kind of thing that just goes away."

"You should find a way to be together."

"You're forgetting one thing, though. We don't know if she still loves me."

"Oh, trust me, she does. How could she not? This is Nick Papadopoulos we're talking about."

Nick belted out a laugh as he sat up. "Thanks, Mama. You always did believe in me."

"That's because you've always been able to do anything you set your mind to."

"Most of the time."

"And you can this time too if you just talk to Paula and let her know how you feel."

"It's not that easy."

"And why not? Just because you're a man doesn't mean you can't communicate. Your father and I talk all the time."

She talked, and his father listened. It seemed to work for them, but that wouldn't work for him and Paula, who said what she thought but didn't say much about what she was really feeling.

"So when you gonna talk to her?"

"I don't know. You just sprang this on me, Mama."

She flipped her hand from the wrist as she stood back up. "Don't tell me you haven't been thinking about it. Don't forget, I know you better than you know yourself."

"That you do," Nick agreed. He went to the closet and pulled out a different shirt. "I'll get my stuff together and be at the house in about an hour, unless Aunt Ophelia has something for me to do around here."

"I'll have lunch ready when you get there."

After Mama left, he thought about what she'd said. Maybe she was right. And even if she wasn't, what would it hurt to have a heart-to-heart with Paula about where they stood?

He'd still have to wait a couple of days. Paula was adamant about keeping your word, and she'd had enough promises broken.

⌒≈⌒

Paula walked into Paula's Natural Soap and Candle Shop, flipping on the lights as she passed through. Rather than one large, intruding light overhead, she used softer lighting throughout the store to add to the ambience. Her regular customers often came in just to get away from the hustle and bustle of life. For them, she kept a pot of tea on the hot plate in the back room.

She'd just gotten the store ready for opening and signed on to her register when the bell tinkled at the door. "Hey, Steph."

"Back atcha. So what's going on between you and Nick?"

"Have you talked to him lately?"

Steph laughed. "Not since yesterday. But I heard his mother and mine had a powwow about him moving."

"Everyone wants a piece of Nick."

"Yep. Seems everyone does but you." She lifted an eyebrow. "Or do you?"

Paula's hand stilled over the counter as her breath caught in her throat. She didn't have anything to say, but the air was heavy with a question.

"That's a moot point, Steph. He's going back to his Army base in Texas and—"

"Air Force base."

Paula closed her eyes and shook her head. "Okay, Air Force base—what does it matter? He's leaving, and I'm still here."

"It doesn't have to stay that way."

"C'mon, Steph, not now, okay?"

Steph held her hands up in surrender and stepped back. "Okay, okay, I'm just sayin'."

"So are you working today?"

"Yeah, Mama has me scheduled at the bakery this afternoon, and Aunt Phoebe asked if I could play hostess tonight at Apollo's."

"I might stop by after work," Paula said. "What time will you be there?"

"That's what I came to talk to you about. Uncle Apollo said to come see if you wanted to have dinner with me there before I start my shift."

Paula knew she was up to something, but she couldn't turn down a meal at her favorite restaurant in Tarpon Springs. "Isn't it moussaka night?"

Steph tilted her head back and howled. "When it comes to food, you have the memory of an elephant."

"Yeah, and I'll have a body like one if I don't get a grip on my appetite."

"That's okay. Greek men like a little meat on their women's bones."

7

"Go unpack, Nick. And bring me your nicest pants and shirt so I can make sure they don't have wrinkles."

Nick grinned. "I'm a grown man, Mama. I can take care of my own clothes."

"Indulge me, son. I miss having my boy around."

"So why do I need to worry about wrinkles anyway? Am I going somewhere?"

"We're going to Apollo's." She glanced down and picked up a pillow that apparently had some invisible lint. As she picked at it, she chattered about how much everyone in the family missed him while he stood there staring at her. When she finally slowed down, he stepped closer and placed his hand on her shoulder.

"Mama, what's going on?"

She looked him in the eye for a split second then smiled. "The family sure could use you around here. If you don't want to go out on the sponge boats, you can help out in the stores. Your father and his brothers have to move stuff all the time, and it would be nice—"

"What's *really* going on?"

Her shoulders slumped, and she sighed. "Nick, just bring me what you're wearing tonight. I've already said too much."

His mother seemed to have shrunk since he'd last seen her. "Mama, have you had a vacation lately?"

"I can't get your father to go away. He's been so busy."

"But you can take some time off and just relax. Do things you miss, like . . ." He tried to remember what she used to do for fun, but he couldn't think of anything besides baking. What kind of vacation would that be for a bakery owner?

She placed her hand on his and patted it. "I'll be fine, my sweet boy. Now go get me those clothes."

It went against everything Nick had become to bring his clothes to Mama, but he did as he was told. He vowed to do something even better for her in return.

As he handed them to her, he gestured toward the living room. "I overheard you telling Papa you wanted some furniture moved. Just tell me where, and I'll take care of it."

"Your father said he'd do it."

Nick tucked his fingers beneath her chin and tilted her head up so she looked him in the eye. "Mama, I want to do it, and I won't take no for an answer."

Two hours and half a dozen different arrangements later, Nick brushed his hands together. "Looks good, Mama, but it's not that different from how you had it."

"I know. I'm so sorry to put you to all that trouble."

"It's fine. I'm here, and you wanted to see how it looked."

She studied the room a few seconds then pointed to one of the chairs. "How about if we move that chair over beside the sofa? Do you think it would cut into the traffic flow too much?"

He laughed. "We can move it and see. If you don't like it, I'll put it back."

After all the furniture was rearranged, she shook her head and clicked her tongue. "Now the pictures don't make sense. I'll ask your father to help me move those later."

"I'll do that too."

When Nick removed the pictures, they noticed the marks on the walls. "Let's put all the pictures in the closet. I'll get your father to paint after you leave."

"Mama, you know Papa's too busy to paint the house. I'll do it while I'm here."

"I don't want you to work the whole time you're here. You should be spending time with friends, having some fun. It's your vacation."

The only person Nick really wanted to spend time with had him on hold for a couple of days. "They're all working, and I don't mind painting. What color do you want?"

"I don't know." She took a step back and studied the walls. "All I thought about was moving the furniture. It didn't cross my mind to change the wall paint."

"Why don't we go to the paint store and pick something you like?"

"We can do that tomorrow."

"Why not now?"

"I have to go to the bakery."

"You told me Aunt Ophelia has Steph working there this afternoon."

"But—"

"I insist."

At that moment, Nick realized how much Paula was like Mama. He'd always heard that guys are attracted to girls with their mothers' traits. Both Paula and Mama were attached at the hip to their work.

Mama frowned. "Are you sure?"

"You were there earlier, Mama. Steph can handle whatever comes up."

Her eyes flickered around the room again, and she nodded. "Okay, but when we get back home, I want you to start getting ready for tonight."

Nick cut a glance around the room before settling his gaze on his mother. "Whatever you have up your sleeve for tonight must be a zinger."

She did an about-face and scampered toward the kitchen. "Let me get my purse, and we can go to the paint store."

Yep, she had big plans for him tonight, and Nick suspected somehow Paula might be part of them. He was okay with that, but he felt bad for Paula. She needed space—a concept his family didn't have a clue about.

"What's this for?" his mother asked as he handed her a sofa pillow on their way out the door.

"It'll help us pick a color to go with the furniture."

"My Nicholas is a smart man."

"You're the one who raised me." He winked at her then helped her into the car.

All the way to the store, she talked about which color she should paint the walls. "This one would look nice." She stabbed her finger at the pillow. "What do you think?"

He glanced at the color she indicated. "I think it would be perfect."

She held the pillow out and shook her head. "Nah, it's too dark. I don't like dark rooms."

They pulled into the parking lot and sat in the car for a few minutes, looking at all the colors on the pillow. "What color do you think we should paint?" she asked.

"Any color you want, Mama. And if you don't like the way it looks when we're done, we can do it over again until we get it like you want it."

"I don't want to do this twice. Let's go see what they got." Without another word, she got out of the car, clutching the pillow. He followed her inside.

"Ursa!" The paint store manager made a beeline toward them the instant they walked inside.

"Hi, George. We need some paint for the living room."

George gestured around the store. "We got plenty of paint. Take your pick."

She glanced around the store looking lost. Nick couldn't remember the last time the house walls were painted, so he suspected she was overwhelmed. "Mama, let's start over there."

It took her almost two hours to decide on a color, which was as close to what was already there as anything they'd seen. "If it works, why change it?" she said.

All the way home she chattered about food, the sponge business, and how he needed to look nice tonight, giving him very little opportunity to say a word. If he'd had any doubt she was up to something, it was gone now.

He carried the paint into the mudroom. His mother pointed to the corner. "Just put it there, Nick, and go get your clothes for me to press."

"We still have plenty of time before dinner. I can paint one wall."

"No."

"Okay, just thought I'd try."

He went to his room and emptied his suitcase on the bed. Before hanging anything in the closet, he selected a shirt and khaki pants to bring to Mama.

"Not that, Nick." She reminded him of his drill sergeant at boot camp when she folded her arms and shook her head. "I want you to look nice tonight."

"What's wrong with this?"

"It's not nice enough."

With nothing more than that to go on, Nick headed back to his room, tossed what he'd selected into the pile, and started digging some more. He did his best to think like Mama. What would she like? His gaze settled on a light blue shirt and some navy slacks. Yeah, she'd think that was nice enough.

"Much better," she said. "Now go start getting ready."

"I thought you said we needed to be there around six-thirty. It's not even five yet."

"It wouldn't hurt you to take a little extra time with your hair."

He reached up and raked his fingers through his close-cropped hair. "There's not much I can do with it."

Mama tilted her head and studied his face. She hadn't looked at him like that since before his first day at kindergarten.

"Okay, I'll go find something to do so you can finish whatever it is you're scheming."

"Nick!"

"I can see straight through you. I don't know what you're planning. All I know is there's something going on, and I'll find out in about an hour and a half."

⌘

By the time Mama brought him the crisply pressed shirt and razor-sharp creased pants, Nick had done everything he could think of in the grooming department. Mama gave him a once-over and smiled, nodding. "Very nice, Nicholas. Now get dressed. I don't wanna be late."

"Late for what?" Nick teased.

She rolled her eyes. "Don't be so suspicious." She walked away mumbling and clicking her tongue.

Nick got dressed and joined her in the living room a few minutes later. "So, am I presentable for whatever you have up your sleeve?"

She looked him over and nodded. "You look handsome as always."

"Is Papa coming home first?"

"No, he's meeting us there."

He crooked an arm. "Ready?"

Mama took his arm and nodded. "Let's go. I'm starving."

She fidgeted all the way to Apollo's, located at the base of the Tarpon Springs sponge docks—a block away from one of his dad's shops. When they got to a red light, Nick reached over and squeezed her tense hand.

"Wanna stop by and see Papa at work? We're a few minutes early."

"Nah, if he's still at work, he's busy. We'll just see him when he gets to Apollo's."

Nick parked the car behind the restaurant in the employee lot. "Wanna go in the backdoor or make an entrance?"

She frowned. "I'm not sure."

"Mama." Nick chuckled and grinned. "Since when have you not been sure about anything?"

"Let's go in the front door like civilized people."

Apollo stood at the host desk. "C'mon back and I'll get you seated."

Nick caught Apollo's conspiratorial wink at Mama. "I saw that."

"You didn't see nothin', Nick," Apollo roared. "You're imagining things." He belted out a laugh that echoed throughout the sparsely filled restaurant.

"My son is suspicious of everything," Mama said. "He doesn't even trust his own mother."

He patted her shoulder. "I do trust you, Mama. I trust that you're always doing things you think are best for me, which is why I know you're up to something."

"Have a seat and I'll let Stephanie know you're here."

"Oh, is Stephie coming too?" Nick said.

Apollo darted a nervous glance at Mama, then faked a smile. "She's here, but she's working."

"This just keeps getting more suspicious by the minute." He waited until Apollo left then turned to Mama. "So here we are at a table set for the whole Papadopoulos family. Who else besides Papa and Stephanie is coming?"

She tried to wave him off. "Oh, you know, the usual. Apollo called everyone and asked them to come for dinner. You remember how this family likes to show up when there's food."

"Mama. There's always food."

He caught his mother's nervous glance toward the door, so he turned to see who was coming. It was Apollo's wife, Aunt Phoebe, followed by his cousins Alexa and Charlene.

"Wow. This is a party."

"We're just having dinner."

Nick's family often got together for impromptu dinners, but this was obviously a planned event. They'd already had his homecoming party, and no one's birthday was on the calendar in his mother's kitchen.

Suddenly everyone got quiet.

He turned around to see what was going on behind him. First he saw Steph. Okay, no big deal. Then Steph stepped aside, and the big plan was revealed.

Paula walked toward the table, looking stunned. She smiled, but he knew it was a front. She was too polite to do anything else, but he imagined she wanted to bolt.

"Don't just sit there, Nick," Apollo urged. "Get the chair for your girl."

As Paula approached the table, he leaned over her and whispered, "Sorry about this. I knew something was up, but no one told me what."

"Hey, everyone's here! Opa!" Apollo held up his water glass, followed by the rest of the group.

"Opa!"

Nick offered an apologetic grin. "I hope you're okay with this. They mean well."

She shrugged. "I'm fine with it. I sort of figured it out as soon as we walked inside. Steph told me to meet her here before her shift, which isn't all that unusual since we've done that before." Paula looked at him with amusement. "But she was way more nervous than normal."

"What can I say? I have a conniving family."

❧

At least he had a family who cared. Paula lifted her water glass again to another chorus of "Opa!" and took a sip. She'd loved the Papadopoulos family from the first time she went home with Steph after school. Mrs. Papadopoulos had warm cookies waiting for them—something her own mother would never have thought to do, even if she didn't work.

Apollo personally served the family his moussaka special. Afterward, Paula turned down dessert, claiming she couldn't eat another bite.

"Why don't you two go for a walk?" Nick's mother suggested. "I'll catch a ride home with your father."

Nick held her chair then waited for Paula to lead the way out the door. As they walked down Dodecanese Boulevard, the sounds of the boats slapping against the docks blended with the music in the various shops. Good sounds. Sounds of home.

They crossed the street to get closer to the water. "Sometimes I miss this place so much I ache." Nick casually reached for her hand. "It feels like a million miles from my life now. I'm sorry about not giving you enough space. I guess I should have let someone know our agreement."

"That's okay. I understand."

He grinned down at her then gestured toward the boats. "I even miss those stinky old sponge and fishing boats."

"Your family misses you too, Nick."

He stopped and turned her around to face him, gently resting his forearms on her shoulders. "How about you? Do you miss me?"

She stood speechless as their gazes held. He pulled her closer, cupped her face in his hands, and looked her in the eye. She lifted her arms and wrapped them around his neck as he lowered his face to hers for a kiss. An earth-moving, tummy-fluttering, toe-curling kiss.

8

Nick gently broke off the kiss and gazed down at her. "My family means well."

"Yes, I know."

"Stephanie set you up, didn't she?"

"Uh huh."

"Sorry."

Paula playfully cuffed his arm. "Stop apologizing."

Nick suddenly turned serious. "This is crazy, Paula. I want to be with you, and from the way you kissed me back, I think you want to be with me too."

She looked down at her feet as she tried to make sense of her feelings. Impossible.

"Okay, so I do. But where does that get me after you leave? Where does it get either of us?"

"I don't know."

"See? It's not easy is it?"

"The older I get, the more I see how nothing is easy."

"If you weren't going back to Texas soon, everything would be different."

"Do you want me to stay?"

Paula lifted her arms and let them slap back down on her thighs. "So what if I do? You have to go back. I know enough about the Army to realize they don't let you decide to just quit on a whim."

A slow grin spread across his face.

"What's so funny?"

"You. I'm in the Air Force, Paula, not the Army. There's a difference."

"Sorry, but it doesn't matter which one you're in. Either one would expect you to come back."

He nodded. "You have a point."

"So if we continue on like this, with all this kissy-face stuff, we're pretty much setting ourselves up for heartbreak later."

"Well, maybe . . ." Nick took her hand and resumed walking. "It all depends on what we do with it."

"What can we do with it? You have to leave, and I have my business here."

"True, but either of those situations can change. My reenlistment is up soon. I don't have to stay in the Air Force if I decide I should be here."

"So are you thinking about it?"

He shrugged. "Maybe."

"I thought you loved your job."

"I do."

"Why in the world would you leave it if you love it?"

"There just might be something I love even more than my job."

Paula felt a smile coming on, but she wouldn't let it reach her lips. That would be dangerous, feeling the way she did.

"How much do you enjoy your soap and candle shop? Is it something you could ever give up?"

"Are you asking me to?"

"No," he said softly. "I'd never ask you to give up anything you wanted to do."

"I like the stability of owning my own store." She paused before adding, "And house. I never felt like I had any roots after Mom and I left Alabama."

"You were here the whole time, until college," he reminded her. "At least she didn't uproot you again."

"No, but there was always that threat—especially when Mom met someone new. She talked about marrying Mack long before she did, but I think she was afraid I'd run away if she did."

"Yeah, I remember. But you dug your heels in and didn't let anything stop you from getting what you wanted. I always admired that about you."

Paula admired everything about Nick. "I guess you can say we've always had a mutual admiration thing between us . . . but unfortunately that's not enough."

"You're right."

"I need to stay here where I have something solid, and you need to check out other places since you've always called Tarpon Springs home." Her insides hurt every time she thought about Nick's itchy feet. Ever since she first met him, he talked about leaving Tarpon Springs and getting away from the sponging and food business.

"The Air Force has been good for me."

They were getting close to her car, so she stopped and turned to face Nick. "I know it has. It's obvious that you love what you do, and I'm sure you're very good at it." And she couldn't think of anyone better to defend the country. "That's why we have to be very careful, or one of us will get hurt."

Too late for that. Nick was already in love with Paula—even more, now that he was older and more mature. He'd dated quite a few other women since Paula went off to college— none who could measure up to her.

But if she needed her space, he'd give it to her. "Want me to call you in a couple of days?"

She hesitated then gave a clipped nod before dropping his hand. "Sure, that would be fine. Let's just keep things light, okay?"

He couldn't make any promises. "I'll do my best."

When Paula didn't turn away, he started to reach for her but pulled back. He felt awkward, like he was back in high school staring at that smart, gorgeous girl who fearlessly marched right up to him and said she wanted an interview, and if he didn't grant her one, she'd have to talk to his coach.

No way would he be able to keep his feelings light for Paula Andrews. The depth of his love threatened to drown him at any moment.

She finally backed away. "That's all I can ask."

Nick stood and waited for Paula to pull out of the parking lot before he went in the backdoor of Apollo's. Everyone in the family, except Stephie, still sat at the table—laughing and talking. Nothing had changed with the family, but everything inside him felt as though it had shifted.

Mama grinned at him, and Papa winked. But Aunt Ophelia was the first to say something.

"Well, how did it go? Did you kiss her and promise your undying love?"

"Who put a stop payment on your reality check, Ophelia?" Aunt Phoebe said. She patted the chair beside her. "Come sit down, Nick, and tell us all about it. Did you and Paula have a chance to talk?"

He ignored her offer of a seat and remained standing. "Yes." After a glance around at all the eyes staring at him, he added, "And don't do this again—at least not in the next couple of days. I promised Paula I'd leave her alone until the day after tomorrow."

"No!" Aunt Ophelia placed her hands on her cheeks and shook her head. "You don't make that kind of promise when you only have a few weeks to get her to fall back in love with you."

"See, that's the thing," Nick said. "I can't get her to do anything she doesn't want to do. She loves Tarpon Springs. This is home to her."

"Don't forget, Nick, this is your home too."

"True," he agreed. "But not for now. I'm committed to my Air Force career, and that's not gonna change anytime soon."

Mama turned to Papa. "He's stubborn. Gets it from you."

"Just like Apollo," Aunt Phoebe added, shaking her head.

"All the Papadopoulos men are that way," agreed Ophelia, "and as much as we all hate to admit it, that's one of the things we love about them."

"So I'm going to spend the next couple of days painting for Mama. If anyone needs something done, let me know so I can put it on my list."

He turned to leave, but when Aunt Ophelia coughed, he stopped, one foot on the step up to the platform next to the kitchen. "I can fix that loose rail on your porch after I'm done at Mama and Papa's."

She smiled. "Good! I've been after Arthur to do that for months."

"Anyone else?" He looked around the table. When they all shook their heads, he waved. "I'll have my cell phone, so if you think of something, let me know. I'd like to stay as busy as possible. I'm sure you all understand."

As he headed for the door, he could hear Aunt Ophelia say, "What a sweet boy, wanting to help us while he's pining for Paula. I don't know what's gotten into that girl. She used to be so smart."

❧

"Are you insane?"

Paula glanced up to see Stephanie standing by the door of her shop. "Nice to see you too, Steph. What's got you all worked up?" She flipped her checkbook closed and stuck it beneath the counter.

"You." Steph crossed the room, joined Paula behind the counter, and got right in her face. "We went to a lot of trouble to help you and Nick out, and now he says you don't want to see him. This is your big chance, girl. What are you thinking?"

"I'm thinking that we need to take things slow."

Steph slapped her forehead and backed up. "It's been, what, fifteen years? How slow can you get?"

Paula took a deep breath then gradually let it out. She'd done such a good job of beating herself up last night, and she didn't need any help from Stephanie.

"I don't think it's something I can explain."

"You may be smarter than me, Paula, but I do understand some things—maybe even better than you. I know that when love strikes, you better grab it, or you'll be miserable for the rest of your life."

Paula tilted her head. "So are you speaking from experience?"

Stephanie tossed her hair over her shoulder and looked away. "Maybe, but that's beside the point. I'm sick of you acting like all you care about is this shop and your house. If you don't watch out, you'll wind up lonely and wishing you'd let your heart take over."

Paula rested her elbow on the counter and gathered her thoughts for a moment. "In case you don't remember, I was raised by a woman who followed her heart. And look what kind of trouble she got herself into."

"You are not your mother, Paula."

"No, and I don't intend to make the same mistakes she's made."

"So you're saying being in love with my cousin is a mistake?"

"I didn't say that. What I'm saying is I have to think with my head and not let my heart interfere with logic."

"You're gonna logic yourself right out of the market."

They glared at each other for a few seconds before they burst into laughter. Paula reached for Steph, who moved in for a hug.

"This is silly," Steph admitted. "I don't know what got into me."

"I do," Paula said softly. "You care."

"Yes, I sure do care—" Steph's voice sounded tight, and she abruptly stopped herself. She raised her hands and groaned. "See? I was about to start in on you again."

Paula laughed. "Seems I bring out the worst in people lately."

"Is that what happened? Did you bring out the worst in Nick?"

"Yes . . . no . . ." Paula shook her head and grinned sheepishly. "I don't know. All I know is that I'm not sure how to deal with Nick being here. I thought it would be easier, since so much time has passed and all."

"Time has passed, but your feelings haven't."

"Afraid so." Paula glanced around. "So what can I do for you today?"

"I'd like to say I'm here to buy candles, but that would be a lie."

"Yeah, I thought so."

"I guess I've done what I came to do." She tilted her head. "And I made a fool of myself. Sorry."

"Hey, don't worry about it. If a friend can't make a fool of herself and fuss at me, who can?"

"So what's the deal with making Nick wait before he talks to you again?"

Paula smiled and shook her head. "You're insufferable, ya know that, Steph?"

"Whatever that means. I want you to come to some stuff my family's doing, but if you don't want to see Nick, that'll be rough."

"Just give me another day, okay? I need a little breather after . . ." Paula didn't want to talk about the kiss, so she just added, "Whatever."

"Okay, so let me get this straight. After . . . *whatever* you'll be able to see him again, right?"

"Right." Paula laughed then reached beneath the counter and pulled out a candle. "I've been working on a new scent." She held it out toward Stephanie. "How does this smell?"

Steph took a sniff and nodded. "I like it. Reminds me of my mother's bakery."

"That's what I was thinking. It's got vanilla, cinnamon, and nutmeg."

"Are you keeping it off-white?"

"No, I'm thinking a smooth, creamy, caramel color would add some warmth to a room."

Steph touched her index finger to her thumb. "Perfect!" She lifted her shoulder bag and backed toward the door. "Call me when you're ready to do something, okay?"

Paula nodded. When Steph walked out the door, she pulled out her checkbook to finish balancing it. After she'd written her mother those checks, she was low on cash for a while. Fortunately, she was expecting payment for a shipment of candles she'd sent to her biggest account the week before. That would get her through a few months.

When she first opened the shop, most of her business came from tourist walk-in traffic. However, after a few happy customers went home and contacted her, she started a mail-order business, and soon after that her wholesale orders took off. Over the past couple of years the walk-in traffic flow had ebbed, but that was fine. It gave her a chance to work on candles and soap to ship.

The shop phone rang. "Paula's Natural Soap and Candles, may I help you?"

"Did you send the check yet?"

"Mom?"

"Yeah, it's me. Did you send it?"

Paula sighed. "Yes, Mom, I dropped it off at the post office yesterday morning."

"Good. It should be here tomorrow."

"Are you sure it's not more than just a missed car payment?"

"No, of course not. I just needed to get a few things, and Mack has cut me off."

"He has a point about the job thing."

"I already told you I shouldn't have to do that. Besides, no one wants to hire me."

"Have you looked? Maybe a part-time job would be good for you. Find something you like." A customer walked in, and

Paula smiled. "I have a customer. Want me to call you back later?"

"No, that's okay. I just wanted to make sure you didn't forget to send the check."

Paula hung up, smoothed the front of her skirt, and came around from behind the counter. "What can I help you with today?"

The woman thrust a business card toward her. "I own a chain of gift shops in New York, and I heard you do wholesale."

"Yes, in fact, that's become the majority of my business."

"I've been looking at your website, and your selection is quite impressive. Do you have any of the saltwater taffy soaps and candles here?"

"Sure." Paula led her to a corner that displayed all her personal blends. She picked up a saltwater taffy candle and handed it to the woman. "I'll leave you alone to check out the whole collection."

A half hour later, Paula was assured the biggest wholesale order since she'd opened the shop. She finished balancing her checkbook then put it away to work on lining up some people for production the following week, when she'd have the woman's order.

The sound of the door opening caught her attention. "Hey, Alexa," she said before she noticed the look on Alexa's face. "What's wrong?"

9

"I am so over it." Alexa rolled her eyes upward and groaned.

Paula had to stifle a smile at Alexa's typical drama. "So what are you over this time?"

"Mom and Aunt Ophelia." Her nostrils flared as she shook her head.

"What did they do?" Or more likely, what did Alexa do? But this wasn't the time to mention her history.

"I forgot to put cream inside the pastries, and they acted like it was the end of the world or something."

It just might be the end of the world for some people. Those cream-filled pastries were delicious.

"So they told me to take some time off and get my act together."

Paula lifted an eyebrow and studied Alexa. "Get your act together? Is there something I don't know about?"

"Not really." Alexa walked around the shop, picked up a few candles and soaps, sniffed them, and set them back down. "There's this guy . . ." Her voice trailed off, and she sighed.

"What guy?"

Alexa's face lit up. "Charlie Zimmerman. He delivers all the dairy." She nearly floated to the counter. "He is so nice."

"I can tell. Cute too, huh?"

Alexa's expression changed to surprise. "You know Charlie?"

"No, but based on how you're acting, he's your dream guy."

"I don't know about that, but I'd sure like to find out."

"So what's stopping you?"

"Every time he comes into the bakery, Mama gives me something else to do. It's like she doesn't want me anywhere near him."

"Does she know how you feel?"

"Of course not. You know how Mama is. She wants me to find some guy from Tarpon Springs—someone she knows."

"Someone Greek, right?"

Alexa shrugged. "I don't think that's a requirement, but it wouldn't hurt."

"I'm not Greek, but no one ever had a problem with me seeing Nick."

"That's because they've known you since you were a kid. Plus Nick's a guy. It's different for him."

"Have you tried talking to your mother?" Paula asked.

"I don't know what good that'll do."

"Give it a try. In the meantime, why don't you take a few days off and go have some fun?"

"I really need the money. That's another thing. Mama is trying to get me to move back in with her and Papa, but I like living on my own."

"I understand." Paula thought for a moment. "Hey, I have an idea. I just got a humongous order, and I could sure use some help around here."

Alexa's eyebrows shot up. "Really? I can help out here? I love working in your shop."

Paula laughed. "Of course you can help. In fact, you can start now if you want."

"If you can give me a couple of hours to go home and change out of these bakery clothes, I'd love to."

"Perfect. I'll finish up a few things here, and when you come back I can put you in charge of the sales floor while I start working to fill the wholesale order."

⌁

Nick stood outside his dad's sponge store and looked toward Paula's Natural Soap and Candle Shop. He'd been puttering around the house helping Mama until Papa called and asked him to make some deliveries. He needed to decide how to fill his time until Paula was ready to see him again.

Alexa came out of the shop, practically skipping. Obviously something good was going on, and he wanted to know about it.

"Hey, Alexa, wait up!"

She turned around and smiled. "Nick! Guess what!"

"No telling with you."

Her smile didn't fade. "I'm changing careers. Paula offered me a job selling soap and candles."

"What are they gonna do without you at the bakery?"

She shrugged. "They fired me, so that's their problem."

Nick knew his cousin well enough to see through the drama. He laughed. "It's about time Aunt Ophelia and your mom came to their senses."

Alexa waved him off as her lips formed a pout. "Actually, they just told me to take some time off for a few days, all because I made a stupid little mistake."

She was always making little mistakes, which was why she bounced from one of the family's businesses to another. They were willing to share the risk. The last time she "took time off" she dumped an entire load of sponges into the dumpster, saying she thought it was scrap after they were trimmed.

"When do you start working for Paula?"

Alexa's smile returned. "As soon as I get changed out of this hideous-looking outfit and into something cute."

"Then don't let me stop you." He snickered. "I'm sure Paula is as eager for you to come back as you are to work for her."

She folded her arms and rocked back on her heels. "You're not being sarcastic, are you, Nick?"

He stabbed a finger at his chest. "Who, me? Never!"

Alexa swatted at him. "Go on, get outta here. You're not supposed to be anywhere near Paula until tomorrow."

"Who told you that?"

"Word gets around. If you're done painting for Aunt Ursa, go talk to Mama or Aunt Phoebe. I think they wanted some work done in the bakery." With a teasing grin, she added, "That should keep you busy and your mind off Paula."

Nothing would keep his mind off Paula. She was all he'd thought about since he returned home.

After Alexa took off toward her car, Nick cast one more glance at Paula's shop before heading for the bakery. Aunt Phoebe stood behind the cash register, wringing her hands.

"Hey, Nick," she said. "This place is a mess."

He stopped by the door. "Alexa?"

"Yeah, how'd you know?" She didn't give him a chance to answer. "Never mind. What can I do for you?"

"I understand you have some work for me?"

Her frown instantly turned to a smile. "As a matter of fact, there's a little bit of handy work that needs to be done on the back of the house. It shouldn't take more than a couple of hours. I asked Apollo to do it for me, but between the restaurant and helping your dad get the sponges to the stores, he hasn't got a single extra minute."

"I don't mind. Just give me a list, and I'll take care of it right away."

She jotted some things down on the back of a cash register receipt and handed it to him. "If you'll hold on, I'll wrap up something delicious to take with you."

Nick watched as she dumped a whole tray of gorgeous-looking Greek pastries in a white paper sack. If he'd been a betting man, after what Alexa told him, he would wager his next paycheck that these didn't have the traditional custard filling.

Aunt Phoebe handed him the pastries. "If you have any questions about those"—she pointed to the bag—"just ask Alexa."

Bingo! He chuckled. "I'm sure they'll be fine."

"Better to eat them ourselves than have disappointed customers," she mumbled as he headed out the door with the to-do list in one hand and pastries in the other.

Once out of sight, he pulled a pastry out of the sack and bit into it. Hmm. No wonder Aunt Phoebe dumped the entire contents into the bag. He dropped the whole batch into the next public garbage can before rounding the corner to his car.

As Nick repaired a wall on the outbuilding that housed his aunt and uncle's lawn mower and other outdoor equipment, he thought about his approaching reenlistment deadline. Although he loved serving his country, Nick loved Paula more. All she had to do was snap her fingers and he'd move back home so fast everyone's head would spin. But she wouldn't do that. He'd known her long enough to realize she'd never ask him to give up his dream. Too bad their dreams collided.

Throughout high school, while most couples made out all the time, they talked and shared their deepest thoughts. Paula let him know how frustrating it was not to have roots—a place to call home. Getting to know Stephanie and being accepted by his family gave her the most stability she'd ever known. Her mother threatened to take her away from Tarpon Springs to manipulate Paula. Nick didn't think she would make good on the threats, but it sure scared Paula.

When it was Nick's turn to talk about how he'd never been interested in the sponge or food business, she always listened. He told her about playing soldier as a child. As he grew up, he and his friend Anthony Kourakis started talking about joining the Air Force. Paula encouraged him to follow his dream, but he didn't do it until her mother told him Paula didn't plan to come back to Tarpon Springs.

Instead of helping Paula find a way to go to college, Bonnie Andrews encouraged her daughter to meet a rich man to take care of her. That incensed Paula and made her more determined than ever to get an education. He should have known better than to listen to a champion manipulator, but the timing actually made sense.

When Bonnie told Nick that dozens of companies were wooing Paula, offering high-paying jobs after she graduated, he assumed she was telling the truth because he figured everyone else saw in Paula what he'd always seen. It wasn't until much later that he learned Paula's intention had always been to return to Pinellas County, Florida. She couldn't find a position that appealed to her, so she took some of the money she'd saved from her college job to open a shop. Uncle Apollo and Aunt Phoebe owned a tiny retail space that had been sitting vacant since they closed one of the gift shops, and they gave her a price break on the rent.

Last time he came up for reenlistment, he headed home, praying he and Paula would get back together, but when he saw her nestled into the crook of Drew's arm, a sick feeling settled over him. He'd never be able to live in the same town with Paula and another man.

"What did that wall do to you, Nick?"

He spun around and spotted Steph standing about ten feet away, smirking. "Hey, Steph. I'm just fixing a few things."

"Remind me not to get on your bad side." She took a couple of steps closer and lifted her hands in mock surrender. "Hold the hammer. I heard you were here, and I wanted to see how things were going between you and Paula."

"I'm still honoring her wishes to stay away for a couple of days." He took one more swing with the hammer then turned to face his cousin directly. "Any other girl and I wouldn't pay a bit of attention."

She snorted. "Any other girl and you wouldn't care."

"True." He dropped the hammer into the toolbox and pulled the crumpled list from his pocket. "Wanna help me paint the back porch?"

"Are you serious?"

Nick nodded. "C'mon, it'll be good for you."

Steph backed away. "I'm not very good at painting. You'll probably go faster if I don't help you."

"Don't pull an Alexa, Steph. You and I both know she sabotages her own work to get out of what she doesn't want to do."

"Yeah, and she's totally groovin' on working for Paula."

"I'm glad Paula's doing well enough to hire her then. Maybe it's time for more of the Papadopoulos family to branch out and see how other people live."

The instant Nick said that, he regretted it. He didn't want anyone in his family to think he wasn't grateful for everything, including the safety net of working for the family business if things went wrong.

"Nick." Steph clicked her tongue, just like Mama and his aunts.

"Okay, so do you wanna help me or not?"

Steph chewed on the side of her lip for a moment before she gave him a clipped nod. "Sure, just tell me what you want me to do."

He gave her a quick lesson on painting the trim before they got to work. At first they painted in silence, but after a few minutes she started chattering about keeping her schedule straight, Alexa working at Paula's shop, and how she'd like to work there too.

"Why don't you ask her?"

Steph paused and faced him. "Are you serious? You don't think that's taking advantage of her?"

"No. I think she'd actually like having you working with her."

"I think I'll do that then."

He laughed.

"What's so funny?"

"You." Nick pointed to his nose. "I sort of like that shade of yellow on you."

"I'll give you a matching one if you don't watch out."

As soon as her part of the painting was done, Steph handed him the paintbrush. "I'm done with this. It was fun, Nick. See ya." She turned and ran, not giving him a chance to thank her.

It took him another hour and a half to finish painting the porch. He'd just finished washing the brushes when he saw a late afternoon shadow come up from behind. This time when he turned around he saw Paula standing there.

"I thought you didn't want to see me for another day."

"I know. I talked to Steph."

Nick crinkled his forehead. "When did you see her?"

"About a half hour ago. She said she helped you do some painting, and I figured I'd stop by and see if I could help out."

"Nope. All done." He tapped the clean brushes on the side of the house and carried them to the table beside the outbuilding to dry. She followed him, but neither of them said a word until he wiped his hands on the towel and turned to face her.

She smiled. "Looks like I have good timing."

Nick folded his arms and widened his stance but never broke the gaze. "Maybe."

He could tell his look made her uncomfortable because she started shifting her weight from one foot to the other. It took every ounce of self-restraint not to laugh.

"So what are you doing now?" she finally asked.

"I'm heading back to the house to wash up."

"Would you like to come over . . . later tonight?"

He lifted a hand and rubbed his chin. "Why don't we stick to the original plan and talk tomorrow?"

Paula stood there and stared, speechless. "That's okay. We can end this distance thing early."

He shook his head. "Nope. You wanted a couple of days to think about things, and that's what I'm gonna give you. It's probably a good idea anyway. Both of us have a lot of thinking to do."

She opened her mouth, but nothing came out. Finally, she clamped her mouth shut and nodded. "If you're sure."

"Paula, you're a very smart woman—that's what I've always loved—um, liked about you. When you say you need time to think, it's best to give you that time."

"But . . ." Her eyebrows drew together, forming a crinkle above her nose. "I guess you're right. I just . . . well, I don't know why I thought—"

In all the years he'd known Paula, he'd only seen her speechless a couple of times before—once when she won an award for service to the school and the other time when he told her he loved her. This wasn't as good, though. He resisted the urge to wrap his arms around her and tell her he loved her more than ever.

"So I guess I should leave now, huh?"

Nick nodded. "I think that's probably a good idea, yeah."

"Okay." She waved good-bye, turned, and walked away.

"Paula!"

She shook her head and kept walking. "Come to the shop tomorrow. We'll talk then."

After she left, he stood there, stunned by his own actions. What had he just done? His time in Tarpon Springs was limited, and it certainly wasn't standing still.

10

Paula drove to her tiny house in Palm Harbor, about ten minutes from the sponge docks in Tarpon Springs. She wished she lived closer, but the places she could afford were a little farther south.

Her cell phone rang right as she pulled into her driveway. When she saw that it was her mother, her stomach lurched. "Lord, give me patience," she whispered as she flipped open the phone.

"Hey, honey."

"Hi, Mom. Did you get the money?"

"Yes, and I wondered if you could send me another couple hundred."

"Another couple hundred? What's going on?"

"I underestimated how much I'd need. Please, Paula, I really need this money."

Paula hadn't asked questions before, but she couldn't keep sending her mother money unless she knew why. "I don't have a lot of money floating around in my checking account. Why do you need so much?"

Her mother sniffled, the first indication that she might be crying. "It's Mack."

Alarms sounded in Paula's head. "Did he hurt you?"

"No . . . well, at least not physically anyway. It's just that . . . well—"

"Mom, you know I'll do whatever I can to help you, but unless you tell me what this is all about, I'm afraid I can't."

"Are you denying your own mother? I didn't realize I raised a selfish little—"

"Whoa. Stop. I've already given you a thousand dollars, so I wouldn't exactly call that being selfish. You know I'll help you. Do you need food?"

"Never mind. I can tell you don't really care about me."

Paula thought about it for a few seconds before she took a deep breath and slowly exhaled. "Okay, I'll send you a check for two hundred."

"Can you make that three hundred and send a money order?"

"Sure, I'll do that."

"Would it be too much to ask you to overnight it?"

"Why don't I just send it electronically and have it put in your account?"

"No. If you send it to my bank account, Mack will find out. I want you to send it to my post office box."

"Whatever."

"I'm glad you changed your mind. I'd hate to think my own daughter didn't care about me."

After Paula flipped her phone shut, she sat in her car staring at the front of her house. She'd been saving to do a few more things around the place, but now she'd have to postpone it.

Instead of going inside, she backed out of her driveway and drove straight to the bank for the money order. She managed to get the check in the mail with minutes to spare before the last pickup.

She went inside and looked around at her sparsely decorated living room. She had a sofa and one chair in the living room, blinds on the windows but no drapes to soften the lines. The only decorations she had were a few thrift store finds and discontinued candles from her shop.

The next morning when she arrived at the shop, she saw that Alexa had rearranged some of the display tables. It actually looked better now, but she wished Alexa had consulted her first. She'd have to talk to her about that later. Since they never discussed when Alexa would be back, she had no idea when she'd see her—until Alexa popped in a few minutes after opening.

"So how do you like what I did?" Alexa gestured around the room. "Now people can see everything at once."

"I like it, but in the future please ask me first."

Alexa's smile faded. "I didn't know . . ."

"Don't worry about it. I'm just talking about in the future."

The smile slowly crept back to Alexa's lips. "So you're saying there might be a future for me here?"

"All depends. Do you want to work here permanently, and if so, will your family be okay with it?" Before Alexa had a chance to answer, Paula deposited her purse in the back room then came back out.

"I don't know about permanently, but I'd like to work here as long as I can." She placed one of her bright red fingernails on her chin and thought for a moment. "I think my family will be happy with anything I do."

"That's fine," Paula said. "I can't pay much, but if I keep getting wholesale orders like my last one, I might be able to give you a raise."

Alexa tossed her long black hair over her shoulder. "I don't expect to get rich here, so do what you can. If I need money, I have Mama and Papa."

That was part of the problem, Paula thought, as Alexa put her handbag away. But she wouldn't dare say that. As loving as the Papadopoulos family was, they went overboard pampering their offspring. The guys got different treatment, but they never had to worry about someone being there for them, no matter what they did or where they went. Deep down, she understood why Nick felt the urge to leave, but she'd love to have had a smidge of what the Papadopoulos family provided.

The first customer came in, and Alexa offered her assistance. Paula observed long enough to know that Alexa enjoyed talking about aromatic candles and soaps. Paula rang up the customer, and Alexa bagged the items, talking nonstop about how they were always coming up with new fragrances.

After the woman left, Paula turned to Alexa. "You're good at this."

Alexa offered a shy smile. "Thanks. I like selling this stuff a whole lot more than baking and selling pastries. I always leave the bakery feeling so messy."

"Would you mind tending to the place alone while I run a few errands?"

Alexa gestured toward the door. "Go do what you need to do. I'll be just fine here."

Paula made it almost to her car when she heard her name. She turned around and saw Steph running toward her.

"What's up, Steph?"

"What did you say to Nick yesterday?"

Paula paused for a moment. She'd been so shocked by his dismissal she tried to put it out of her mind. "I just asked if he'd like to come over last night, and he reminded me that I didn't want to see him until today."

"And you left?"

"Of course. He wanted me to, and I'm not one to stick around when I'm not wanted."

Steph groaned. "I can't believe you didn't stand your ground, Paula. One of the things he likes about you is your self-confidence."

"This has nothing to do with self-confidence. It's more about wanting to do the right thing."

"Everyone but you and Nick knows the right thing is for you two to be together. Why do both of you have to be so stubborn?"

Paula laughed. Only Steph would have the nerve to say those things to her. "It's not about being stubborn."

Steph widened her stance and planted a fist on her hip. "Then what is it?"

"We don't want to make any mistakes."

Steph groaned. "If no one ever made mistakes, nothing would get done. You're the one who taught me to push forward to get what you want. If it weren't for you, I never would have moved out of my parents' house."

Paula smiled. "I hope you didn't tell your mom I had anything to do with that."

"You're skirting the issue."

"What issue?" Paula aimed her remote at her car and pushed the "unlock" button.

"You're good." Steph took a couple of steps toward her. "Nick and his parents came to dinner last night. When we asked him about you, he said the same thing you just told me—that he wasn't going to bother you until today."

"He hasn't bothered me yet, so maybe he won't even do that."

"One of you better start bothering the other because next time the rest of my family gets involved, you'll find out just how bothered you can be."

"Now that's interesting," Paula said. "But I don't think your family has to worry about Nick or me. We'll make the right decisions for us."

"Promise?" Steph said.

"Absolutely. But it might not be what you want."

Steph slapped her forehead. "Give me a break. Okay, I'll leave you alone about this—at least for now. But I can't promise the same for my mom or aunts." She turned to leave.

"Hey, Steph." When she turned around, Paula smiled. "Thanks for caring so much. It's nice to know I'm not all alone."

"Oh, trust me, as long as you have the Papadopoulos family around, you'll never be alone—even when you wanna be."

Paula laughed as she got in her car. She felt good about things as she ran her errands to get ready for the large order. On her way back to the shop, she stopped off at her house to grab a bite to eat.

She was about to leave when her phone rang. It was Nick.

"Mind if I come by for a few minutes? I won't be long."

"How long will it take you to get here? I was just about to leave."

"Not long at all. Open your front door."

⁓

"How's that for quick?" He grinned as she stood in the doorway, staring at him as though she didn't believe he was there.

"You're full of surprises, Nick. Come on in." She backed away and moved toward her kitchen. "Want something to drink?"

He got the feeling she was more interested in placing some distance between them than in being hospitable. "Sure, whatcha got?"

"Water, orange juice, milk . . . the usual."

"No root beer?"

She narrowed her eyes. "This is me you're talking to, Nick. The only sugar I like is in baklava."

"Yeah, Miss Healthy. I'll take some orange juice then."

She poured two glasses of orange juice, and they sat down at the table between the kitchen and the tiny living room. Her place was small but uncluttered—unlike all the houses in his family, where trinkets littered every available corner and surface. He liked Paula's minimalism.

"So what was so important that you had to come over right now?"

"You don't beat around the bush, do you?"

"Have I ever?" She leveled him with one of those looks she'd been giving him since they first met.

"Nope. I'd be shocked if you did. I just wanted to stop by and ask if you're busy tonight."

She looked down at the table then glanced back up at him. "I'm free tonight."

"Not anymore—that is, if you'd like to hang out with me. I thought we might take a drive down to Clearwater Beach and maybe grab a bite to eat."

With a nod, Paula said, "I'd like that."

"How about tomorrow? With Alexa working for you, can you spare a few hours to go shopping at Countryside Mall with me?"

She drained her juice and set the glass on the table before she met his gaze. "Let's take this one day at a time, okay? Ask me again tonight about tomorrow."

"Sorry, but I'm only here for six weeks, and one of those weeks is almost over. We've already wasted enough time."

Paula fidgeted with the corner of the napkin under her glass. "True. Okay, I can take a couple of hours to go shopping with you tomorrow. What are you looking for?"

He instinctively glanced at her left hand. When he looked up, he saw that she'd noticed. She quickly pulled her hand away and tucked it beneath the table.

"I understand you and Alexa have some sort of arrangement at the shop."

Paula lifted one shoulder and let it drop. "She needed a change of pace."

"I think Steph might be a little jealous."

She tilted her head and gave him a puzzled look. "Jealous? Why?"

"They're both tired of handling food. Can't say I blame them."

"Your mom and aunt would never forgive me if I hired Steph to work for me too, but I could certainly use the extra help."

"Want me to talk to them?"

"Um . . . no. I don't ever need someone else to do my job for me."

"Talking to my mom isn't exactly your job, Paula."

She laughed. "True. But, seriously, if Steph wants to work for me, she can come to me first and then talk to her mother."

Paula's independence had always intrigued him. When she wanted something done, she did it—never any of this manipulative shuffling to get what she wanted.

She stood up and reached for both glasses. "I really need to get back to work. In case no one told you, I just got the biggest wholesale order since I went into business, and it will make a huge difference to my bottom line." She grinned.

He got up and walked to the door. "Don't let me stop you. I'll pick you up at seven, okay?"

On the way to his car, he glanced over his shoulder and saw the blinds move, letting him know she was watching. He lifted a hand in a wave then took off for Apollo's where his dad and uncle asked him to meet them for a man-to-man talk, no doubt to give him some incentive to leave the Air Force and move back home. Only one thing would cut his military career short, and his family had nothing to do with it.

༨

Paula hurried and finished all her errands, only to arrive at the shop and find no one there. Her mind raced with questions, and she was tempted to call Steph to find out where Alexa was. Alexa had given her old cell phone to Charlene and gotten a new one—with a new number.

No matter how angry she was—and she was furious—Paula didn't call Steph. She decided not to get anyone else in the Papadopoulos family involved in whatever was happening.

She punched in the cash register numbers and made sure all the money was there. On top of the stack of twenties lay a handwritten note.

Mama slipped and fell in the bakery, so I left to take her to the emergency room. I asked Socrates next door to keep an eye on your shop. Alexa.

Paula sank against the counter as guilt washed over her. To think she'd thought the worst of Alexa.

The front door opened, and in walked Socrates, the man who owned the cigar shop next door. "Oh, it's just you. I saw someone come in here, but I had a customer. Did you get Alexa's note?"

"Yes," Paula said.

"Are you sticking around, or do I need to keep an eye on the place?"

"Let me call and see if anyone needs me."

Socrates pointed to his shop. "Come let me know, okay?"

She nodded as she punched Steph's number on speed dial. After Steph assured her everything was okay, and that she had plenty of family with her, Paula went next door. "I'm staying."

"Good." Socrates grinned. "I don't know a thing about candles, and if you were to ask my wife, she'd tell you I don't know much about soap either."

Paula laughed. "Thanks, Socrates. I'll let you know when I find out exactly how Alexa's mother is."

After he left, she tried Alexa's old cell phone, but no one, not even Charlene, answered. She thought about calling the bakery, but they were probably slammed, between customers and dealing with the accident. So she called Nick, who answered on the first ring.

"Did you hear about your aunt?"

"Yeah, I'm at the hospital right now."

"So how is she?"

"They just finished running some X-rays, and we'll know soon if anything's broken."

"I'll pray for her."

"Thanks. I better go. Mama needs me."

11

After Paula hung up, she reflected on how close the Papadopoulos family was. No matter what, when something happened they were there for each other. Like Alexa taking off to be at the hospital for her mother.

Paula's own mother could have used a lesson on family. The only time Paula ever heard from her was when she needed something.

The more she thought about her own lack of family, the more she ached. She swiped at a tear with the back of her hand.

People thought things came easy to Paula, and she let them believe it, when the reality was that everything was difficult for her. What came across as confidence was more of an act of self-preservation. She made good enough grades for a full college scholarship through dogged determination and the desire to be completely different from her mother rather than natural-born brilliance like her friends assumed.

Paula grabbed a tissue, dabbed at her eyes, and blew her nose. No point in shedding tears over something she couldn't control.

A few more customers walked through the door, and she made sales to all of them. However, the two phone-in whole-sale orders that afternoon totaled more than her last month's walk-in retail sales combined. She'd need to find at least a couple more salespeople to help her out now that she had such huge orders to fill. She also needed to find more people to hand-make the candles and soaps, which would involve weeks of training since she only used natural ingredients.

Since everyone was rallying around Alexa's mother, Paula assumed her date with Nick was off. He wouldn't leave his aunt's side as long as he thought he was needed. So Paula hung around the shop a few minutes after closing, not having a reason to rush home.

Finally, she locked up and left. As she pulled onto her street, her cell phone rang.

"Hey, I hope you don't mind, but I thought we might make it an earlier night, say around six-thirty?"

Her heart thudded. "You still want to go out?"

"Yeah, why wouldn't I?"

"Your aunt."

"Oh, she's fine. Just a little bruised. The doc said she needed to stop pushing herself so hard."

"She probably needs Alexa to come back to the bakery too, right?"

Nick laughed. "Actually, no. I think Aunt Phoebe is relieved to have Alexa somewhere besides the bakery."

Guilt mixed with relief washed over Paula. "Is there anything I can do?"

"You're helping out just by letting Alexa work for you and getting her out of the bakery. Don't tell anyone else, but Mama said that having Alexa there made everything twice as hard."

It was Paula's turn to laugh. "I'm happy to have her. She's an excellent salesperson."

"But a lousy baker. They had to dump everything she touched before she left, which was why Mama was so frantic."

"I'm just pulling into my driveway now, so give me a few minutes to change clothes and freshen up."

"Fifteen minutes enough?"

Paula swallowed hard. "Sure, that's fine."

Nick arrived ten minutes later.

"You're early," she said as she opened the door.

"But you're ready." He walked in. "I knew you wouldn't take long."

"I'm not doing a very good job of being the mysterious woman, am I?" She smiled and let out a nervous giggle.

"Oh, you're plenty mysterious. I always have to guess what's on your mind."

If he only knew. "So let's go."

He drove south on Alternate U.S. 19. As they left Palm Harbor and wound their way through the streets of Dunedin, Paula noticed Nick looking around like he'd never seen the place before.

"I forget how beautiful it is here." He pointed toward the St. Joseph's Sound past the stop sign near Bon Appetit.

"Remember when we went to your cousin Olivia's wedding reception there?"

He laughed. "How can I forget? It felt like we were walking through heaven."

"It was rather ethereal to have all white decorations and being suspended over the water with a three-way view of St. Joseph's Sound." Paula closed her eyes at the memory of her first kiss with Nick when they thought no one was looking.

They rode the rest of the way to Clearwater Beach in silence. After negotiating the roundabout, Nick found a parking spot not far from the beach.

"I feel like a teenager again," he said as he took Paula's hand. "Remember when we used to come here as kids?"

Oh yeah, she remembered. In fact, she and Drew had a date to walk on this same beach, but the memories of Nick were so intense she wound up with a headache and asked to go home early.

They took off their sandals and carried them as they strolled up the beach, dodging Frisbees and Nerf footballs. Nick tugged her over toward a volleyball game, and they stood to watch until finally he turned her to face him.

"The sun is about to set."

She smiled. Without another word, they turned to face the water and walked toward it, hand-in-hand. As the sun melted into the Gulf of Mexico, Paula felt that familiar twinge she always got when she and Nick watched the sunset together. It was like God had put on a show especially for them.

After the sun dipped beneath the water's edge, Nick let go of Paula's hand, inhaled deeply, and lifted his arms over his head. When they came down, one hand found its way to Paula's shoulder. Just like old times.

"Hungry?" he asked as he leaned over and dropped a kiss on top of her head.

"Sort of."

"Crabby Bill's or Frenchy's?"

"Crabby Bill's."

He grinned and tweaked her nose. "That's what I thought you'd say. Let's go."

Paula loved the rustic little restaurant where the service was good and the food delicious.

"So how does everything look?"

He turned and gazed into her eyes. "It's almost like time stood still. The strangest thing is I feel like this is where I belong."

"I'm sure your family would agree."

"I know." He reached over and fidgeted with the salt and pepper shakers before shoving them to the side and folding his hands. "But that doesn't take away from the fact that I love what I do now."

"That's important."

"I just might come back for good."

"Are you seriously thinking about it?"

He glanced down at the table then raised his gaze to hers as he nodded. "Yes. But I'll need to find some way to earn a living."

"You won't have to look far," she reminded him, her heart hammering at the thought of him coming home for good. "Your family owns a good portion of Dodecanese Boulevard."

"That's just it. You know I don't want to be a sponger or a baker."

She cleared her throat. "You could always sell or make soap and candles."

Nick tilted his head forward, looked at her from beneath his eyebrows, and grinned. "Don't tempt me."

"There's a poster about the Clearwater Jazz Festival," she said, pointing to the window. "They're still having it at Coachman Park."

"Wanna go?"

Paula stared at the poster for a few seconds then turned back to Nick. "Why are you doing this?"

His forehead crinkled as he frowned. "What do you mean?"

"It's like you want me to do all this stuff with you, and you're talking about living here again, but then you're leaving because you have to report back to work, and if the past is any indication, I won't hear from you again until you take another vacation."

He nodded then looked down at his hands before looking back into her eyes. "It's not fair to you, is it?"

"I didn't say that. I can handle myself. I just don't understand what you're doing or where you think this whole thing is going."

❦

Nick opened his mouth, but his voice stuck in his throat. How could he explain the turmoil he felt? Sticking around Tarpon Springs would make his family happy, and he'd love being with Paula, but one thing still bugged him. Would Paula feel obligated to go along with him simply because he'd made the career sacrifice? Some questions couldn't be answered in a simple conversation.

"I don't know." He couldn't get more honest than that.

She gave him one of her studious looks—like when she knew he was up to something and she wouldn't let him get away with trying to cover it. Yes, he was up to something, but he had no idea what to do about it.

"What are you thinking?" he asked.

"I'm thinking you're trying to play some kind of game, which isn't necessarily bad. I'd just like to know the rules so I don't lose miserably."

The one thing he loved most about Paula was her direct approach. But this time she was mistaken.

"No, I'm not playing a game, Paula." He wasn't sure if this was the time to tell her, or if he'd run her off. But he decided to go for it. "I'd like to see how things are between us now because I miss you like crazy, and I've been thinking about a more . . . permanent situation between us."

He heard her sudden intake of air. She put both hands in her lap and looked down at them for what seemed like eternity. When she looked back up at him, he saw the anguish in her eyes.

"Nick, I'm here to stay. You know about my past and how unstable everything was for me. I've never pretended to be anything I'm not."

"I know."

"And you know how Mom always threatened to move me."

"But she didn't," he reminded her.

"True, but that threat was always there. I need to know where I'm going to be. You, on the other hand, need some time away."

"Maybe that's changed." He cleared his throat. "Maybe I've changed."

She shook her head. "I don't think so."

He still couldn't read her well enough to make a decision. "It's hard to figure everything out, isn't it? Who knows where we'll wind up? I mean, besides God."

Silence fell between them until she reached across the table for his hand. "I guess in a way we all know where we're ultimately going to be, right?"

He nodded. "Yes, but I understand how you feel. It's interesting how I have the opposite problem from you—I crave adventure and the unknown. I get excited when I think about where my next assignment might be."

"I understand," she said. "You want what you've never had."

"Both of us do," he reminded her.

"Looks like we've found a way to get what we want, though, right?" She still clung to his hand as she gave him one of those crooked smiles he remembered being her reaction to irony.

"All except one thing." He turned her hand over and traced the back of her ring finger. "Do you think . . . I mean, if I didn't have to go back to the base . . . well, um . . ."

"What's going on, Nick? Why can't you just say what's on your mind?"

He interlocked their fingers and looked directly in her eyes. "Can you ever see us being together forever?"

Her gasp tugged at him, but she'd asked for it. "Isn't that a moot point?"

"No, Paula, it's not. I'm not saying you have to commit right this minute, but if everything fell into place, am I the man you'd want to spend the rest of your life with?"

His heart hammered as her eyelids fluttered. When she looked up and nodded, he felt like jumping right out of his skin.

"Yes, Nick, as difficult as this is to say, knowing you're heading back to your base soon, you are the only man I've ever even considered being with for the rest of my life."

Nick's mind raced with possibilities. "That's what I needed to know." He grinned at her and winked.

She continued smiling at him, but neither of them said a word. The waitress arrived a few minutes later with their food.

"That looks good," he said, pointing to her fish fillets.

"Want some?" Her voice was a little scratchy as she stabbed a piece and held it over his plate.

"Only if you'll take some of my shrimp."

"Deal."

In some ways nothing had changed, but everything was completely upside down now. Nick didn't want to ruin the magic of the earlier moment, so he didn't bring it up again. After they ate, they went straight to Nick's uncle's car. "I know you have a long day tomorrow, so I'll take you home. Alexa told me you've been pulling in some huge orders."

"I never expected what's happening."

"What did you expect?" He started the car and turned toward Palm Harbor.

"I dunno. I guess I saw myself selling soaps and candles to tourists and maybe some locals."

"That would be a hard way to make a living."

"I know that now. In fact, if some of these wholesale orders hadn't happened, I'd probably be looking for a job by now."

"God is amazing, isn't He?"

Paula nodded. "He sure is. After my first wholesale order, I thought it might be a fluke. Then I got a call from someone else who asked if I could send a catalog." She laughed. "You should have seen what Steph and I came up with."

"Steph helped you?" He lifted one eyebrow.

"Yes. If she hadn't, I have no idea what I would have done. That girl has a great eye for graphics. I can describe my candles and soaps all day long, but she knows how to make it look good on the page."

"That's an inherited talent," Nick said. "Her mother is the one who drew the menu for Apollo's. She saw Aunt Phoebe struggling with it, and Aunt Ophelia offered a hand."

"You have the best family, Nick. That's another blessing from God. He brought Steph and me together."

Nick wanted to remind her that He'd brought the two of them together as well, but after what she'd already said, it might sound like he was pressuring her, so he didn't.

"Have you ever thought about doing wholesale only?"

"No," she said as she slowly shook her head. "I don't ever want to lose touch with the retail customers. I love having people come in to let me know what they're looking for. I've learned that if one person likes something, there are probably hundreds—maybe even thousands—of others who would like the same thing."

"You're a good businesswoman, Paula." He stopped at a light and turned to face her. "I'm proud of you."

Her face turned a flaming shade of red. "Thanks, Nick. I'm proud of you too."

The second he stopped the car in her driveway, she opened the passenger door and stuck one leg out. "I can find my way to the door by myself."

"I know you can, but you didn't even give me a chance to act like a gentleman."

"You don't have to prove anything to me, Nick."

"I know. So what time will you be home tomorrow?"

"Why?" She stood by the door, leaning over so she could see him.

"The mall, remember?"

"Yeah, I remember. I was just testing you to see if you did."

He laughed. "Right. What time?"

"All depends on Alexa. Do you think she'll be free to work tomorrow?"

He pulled out his cell phone. "Give me about three seconds and I'll find out."

Paula sat back down in the car while he called his cousin. Alexa answered right away.

"Of course I'll work for her."

"Your mama doesn't mind if you leave her for a little while?"

She laughed. "She'll be glad to get rid of me. I'm driving her nuts."

Nick winked at Paula and nodded. "Good. Plan to close the shop."

"You and your woman got something planned?"

The expression on Paula's face let him know she'd heard. "Yes, Paula is going to the mall with me to help me pick out some stuff."

"Good, cuz when it comes to stuff, your taste is in your mouth."

Nick laughed. "Thanks, Alexa. Remind me to do you a favor sometime."

"You're welcome."

He clicked his phone off and stuck it back in his pocket. "She'll be there as long as you need her."

"Yes, I heard." She stood back up and waved then closed the car door.

Nick watched as she walked up the front porch and went inside. Once he'd turned the corner, he pulled his phone back out and punched in the number of his buddy back at the base.

"Hey, Nick. What's up?"

"Would you mind checking something for me?"

"Sure. Just a second." Brock covered the mouthpiece and mumbled something Nick couldn't hear. "Okay, so what do you need, buddy?"

"Can you find out the details on getting into base housing?"

"Why? Are you getting married or something?"

"You gonna interrogate me?"

Brock howled. "Is it that girl you used to talk about all the time?"

"Never mind. I should have known better than to ask you."

"Hey, man, don't be so touchy. I'll find out. What all do you want to know?"

They discussed what Nick was asking. After Nick got off the phone, he worked on a plan. There was no doubt in his mind that he and Paula were meant to be together, but now he had to find a way to persuade her. If it took leaving the Air Force before he was ready, so be it. However, with her wholesale business doing so well, she could work it from anywhere.

Now all he had to do was convince her of that.

12

So how was your date last night?" Alexa asked when Paula walked into the shop.

"Good. What are you doing here so early?"

"I wanted to make up for bugging out on you yesterday." Alexa held up a slip of paper. "Good thing I got here early because you got another big wholesale order."

"I never intended to go into the wholesale business, but now that's what's paying the bills." Paula glanced at the order and lifted her eyebrows. "Are you sure you got the numbers right?" *After all, being a night person and getting up this early . . .*

Alexa bobbed her head. "Positive. I asked the guy to repeat the numbers, just to make sure."

Paula crunched the numbers in the computer and looked back at Alexa. This order would pick up where the last one left off and leave her in the black for the next six months.

"God is amazing. He's watching us."

"Then let's give Him a good show. I have something you might be interested in." Alexa pulled a small vial from behind the counter and shoved it toward Paula. "Smell this."

Paula stepped toward her, leaned over, and sniffed. "Yum. What is that?"

"It's the special almond extract that Mama gets from Greece. I thought maybe you'd want to consider using it in one of your candles."

Alexa's thoughtfulness touched Paula. "I just might do that."

"You can name it Alexa's Almond Cookies." She replaced the vial. "I'm not saying you have to. It's just a thought."

Paula smiled. "And a wonderful thought at that. Do you think your mother would mind giving me the name of the source?"

"If you use my name, I'm pretty sure she will."

"I don't want to do anything to upset her," Paula said.

"I'll ask. But in the meantime, I need to get this back to the bakery. She doesn't know I took it."

"Why don't you do that now before we get busy?"

Alexa pulled the vial back out and scurried to the door. "Be right back."

By the time Alexa returned, Paula had taken another whole-sale order over the phone. She needed to train more people to make candles and soaps or she'd have to put some skids on the orders.

"Alexa, do you know anyone interested in producing some product for us? It needs to be someone with a kitchen big enough to handle a lot of candle and soap molds."

Alexa thought for a moment and nodded. "Some people at the Senior Center were looking for ways to make money, according to my mother's brother, who does some of their maintenance. I can ask them."

"Great idea. They have a big kitchen there too, don't they?"

"Yeah, for all those dinners they have."

"The only thing is I have to know they'd be committed to meeting deadlines."

"I don't think that'll be a problem, but I can ask."

The rest of the day was busy for Paula. Between an increased number of walk-in customers and charting out an action plan to fill all the wholesale orders, she lost track of time. When she glanced up at the clock, she blinked.

"It's closing time already."

"Oh, that's something else I wanted to talk to you about. I think you close your shop too early," Alexa said.

"You do, do you?" Paula planted her fist on her hip and looked at Alexa. "When do you think is a good closing time?"

"An hour later would be good."

"Do I hear any volunteers to work that extra hour?"

Alexa's lips twitched into a closed-mouth smile as she raised her hand. "That would be me."

"So are you proposing working here on a regular basis now?"

"If that's okay with you. I talked to Mama about it last night after she got home from the hospital, and she thought it was an excellent idea."

"Good. You're hired as a permanent employee. You can work afternoons until closing."

"Perfect. I never did like the early morning hours at the bakery, but that's when we did most of the baking."

"Since I'm a morning person, this will be perfect."

"What time do you want me here tomorrow?" Alexa asked as they prepared to leave for the day.

"Since you want to work late, why don't you come in after lunch?"

Alexa lifted her handbag and slung it over her shoulder. "I'll stop off at the Senior Center on my way here and talk to them."

As soon as Alexa left, Paula locked up and went to her car. Nick planned to pick her up as soon as she got home because he needed some help at the mall. She couldn't imagine why. He'd always had impeccable taste in clothes. Much better than hers.

Nick was parked at the curb in front of her house, waiting for her. He got out of his car and joined her on the porch. "Took you long enough to get home."

"Wanna come in?"

"Do you need to go in?"

She thought then shook her head. "Not really."

He gestured toward the car. "Then let's get going."

All the way to the mall, he seemed nervous. Each time he pulled up to a red light or stop sign, he looked at her with the oddest expression—as if puzzled. He was up to something. She would ask, but if he wanted to tell her, he would have already. And she was too tired to try to dig anything out of him.

When they arrived at Countryside Mall, he got out, opened her door, and cleared his throat. She took his hand and noticed that his palm felt damp. This was a first.

They started out in one of the larger department stores, where Nick wanted to look at household items. "I thought you lived in a barracks."

"I do, but that might change someday."

Her suspicion grew even stronger. "This isn't about anything specific, is it?"

"Paula," he began then shook his head. "I feel like such a klutz."

She laughed. "You are hilarious, Nick. And you're all mixed up. You're the graceful athlete. I'm the klutzy nerd."

"Well, if you wanna know the truth, I've always wanted to be the nerd. It seems like a whole lot more fun."

Paula cracked up. "I guess being the town golden boy must present a lot of problems . . . like stress and high expectations. The expectations have to be killer."

He didn't respond, so Paula stopped and tugged at him until he turned to face her.

"What's going on, Nick?"

His shoulders rose and fell as he inhaled a deep breath. He cupped her face in his hands. "Paula, I love you, and I'll do anything to keep from losing you again. I want us to be together forever."

Now she was speechless. When she tried to talk, her voice came out in a squeak.

He smiled. "And that's one of the things I love most about you. You're so confident, controlled, and unpretentious that when you're like this, I know it's not an act." He dropped his hands from her face and rubbed them across his shirt. "I've made you sound like a squeaky toy."

She cleared her throat. "It's not the first time."

"No, but in the eighteen years I've loved you, I can count the number of times on one hand."

"Okay," she said, trying to sound unfazed, "so now what?"

"Wanna go look at rings?"

Paula stared at him, dumbfounded. "What did you say?"

"All I said was—"

"I know what you said."

"Well?" He took both of her hands in his. "Do you?"

Paula allowed the shock to fade a few seconds before shaking her head. "I don't know if that's such a good idea."

"So you're saying you don't love me?"

"I'm not saying that."

The corners of his lips twitched. "I remember back a long time ago when you and I talked about eventually getting married. You didn't seem opposed to the idea then. And we talked about it again yesterday. Have you changed your mind in the last twenty-four hours?"

"C'mon, Nick, a long time has passed since we first talked about getting married, and our conversation last night was hypothetical. We're older now. We have responsibilities."

"Yes, and that's all the more reason for us to make our situation more permanent—either way."

"This isn't an ultimatum, is it?"

❧

Nick hated begging anyone to do anything, and that's exactly what this felt like to him. "No. Where did that come from?"

"The way you worded it . . . when you said either way."

"I didn't mean it like that."

"Why do I feel like we're always arguing now? It didn't used to be that way."

"You're only half right. We never used to argue, and we're not arguing now. I'm just trying to do something I should have done a long time ago."

She pulled her hands out of his. "So you're planning to get out of the Army and stay here?"

He couldn't help but laugh. "How can someone so perfect otherwise keep getting the Army and Air Force mixed up?"

"Just answer me, Nick. Are you getting out of the Air Force or not?"

Nick tightened his lips and slowly shook his head. "It's not that easy. I have to wait until it's time for reenlistment, and I can make a decision then."

"Okay, then, let's get this straight. You want to give me a ring before you go back, which has us in a long-distance relationship until you decide you're ready?"

That did sound pretty bad. "Now that you put it that way, I guess I can't ask you to do that."

"Oh, you can certainly ask, but I'd be a fool to go along with it."

"And you're certainly not a fool. If anything, I am for even considering getting engaged."

"No, Nick, you're not a fool." She reached up and placed her palm on his cheek. "You're a very sweet, romantic man who stole the heart of the nerdiest girl west of Tampa."

Nick laughed in spite of the ache in his chest. "A romantic man who loves the sweetest, prettiest girl in the entire universe. I guess I am a fool for that, huh?"

"No, not at all." She blinked then glanced around. "In case you haven't noticed, we've attracted a bit of attention."

He looked over his shoulder in time to see a couple quickly glance away. "Ask me if I care."

"Can we go someplace else and discuss this?"

"You want to talk about it some more?" A sliver of hope rose in his heart.

"Maybe that was a bad idea."

"No, it's a great idea." He pointed toward a bench about forty feet away. "How about we talk over there?"

"Um . . . Nick, do you realize that's right in front of a jewelry store?"

"So? If I can talk you into marrying me, we won't have to go far."

She gave him a gentle shove. "No wonder you get your way so much. You don't give up, do you?"

"Hey, watch it. I'm fragile."

"Right." She rolled her eyes but accepted his hand when he reached for hers.

They sat on the bench and watched a group of pierced, tattooed teenagers stroll by. One of the girls did a double-take and smiled at Nick. He recognized her—she was the daughter of one of his father's employees.

"Hi, Carmen," he said.

"Hi, Mr. Papadopoulos." Her hard-edged look softened. "I didn't know you were back."

"I'm just here on vacation. It's good to see you."

"C'mon, Carmen," one of the boys said. "Jimbo's mother's picking us up by Dillard's, and we're already late."

Carmen waved then turned back to her friends. Nick thought he heard some swear words, but he didn't want to assume anything. "I wonder if we ever came across like that."

"Nope." Paula shook her head. "You were the Tarpon Springs Sponger hero, and I was the scrawny little groupie running after you."

Nick cracked up. "I don't think so."

"Okay, so now where were we?"

"We were talking about getting engaged and riding off into the sunset."

"All the way to the . . . Air Force base, right?"

He grinned. "Yep. What's wrong with that?"

"You're stubborn as a mule, Nick. You already know how I feel about stability. It's the most important thing to me."

Even more important than him obviously. If he could, he'd turn in his resignation right then just to be with Paula. "You know, being married to me has some stability . . . at least it does in my book."

Paula nodded. "Good point."

"Tarpon Springs will always be home, no matter where we are."

"I wonder if part of what you're feeling is the absence-makes-the-heart-grow-fonder thing."

"Run that one by me again?"

"You know," she said. "I'm not there, so you think about how things used to be, and you fantasize about how we could go back to that and—"

"Whoa, wait a minute. I don't do that."

"Are you sure?"

"Positive. What I feel is very real. It's just that in the past the timing never seemed right. I thought maybe . . . well, perhaps . . ." He blew out a breath of exasperation. "Never mind. It was a bad idea, anyway." He stood and pulled her up. "Ready to go home?"

"Sure." She gave him a little resistance when he started walking toward the mall exit. "Since we're here, let's go take a look at those rings. Just for grins, okay?"

Nick could be with Paula for the rest of his life and still never figure her out. So he decided not to even try. "Fine."

"That one's pretty," she said, pointing to a small solitaire.

"You don't think it's too plain?" He thought about his mother's ring with the ornate scrollwork and diamond chips flanking the monster-size diamond in the middle. "How about that one over there?"

She lifted her eyebrows and made a funny face. "Not in this lifetime." She held out her hands. "Can you picture that honker on these stubby fingers? Whoo boy, that won't work for me."

Nick lifted her fingers to his lips and kissed them. "If we were to ever get engaged . . . and I'm not saying we will . . . how about a compromise and go for . . ." He glanced around at the array of rings on display until he settled on a teardrop solitaire flanked by rows of pavé-set diamond chips. "That one?"

An odd sort of serenity crept over her face as she studied the ring he pointed to. "That's very pretty, Nick."

"I know what would look good on you." He tugged her away from the store window. "But I wouldn't want to force you

to wear that ring since we're not getting engaged or anything
. . . at least not anytime soon." He smiled down at her.

He committed the ring to memory. Somehow, some way, he
would slip that ring on Paula's finger—no matter what he had
to do to put it there.

13

*Y*ou what?" Nick's mother couldn't hide the grin that played on her lips.

"I might not reenlist."

The smug look on her face belied her tone. "But I thought you loved military life."

"I do, but I love Paula more."

Mama put her hand on his shoulder. "I know you do, son, but before you take such a big leap, you better get a commitment from her."

"I'm working on that."

"Any other girl would be putty in your hands. You choose the one who stands up to you and makes you work for her affection."

"I know. Paula has a mind of her own."

"That's one of the things we all love about her. We never worried that she only cared about you for being a Papadopoulos."

Nick chuckled. "As if that carries any clout."

She tossed him an indignant glare. "In Tarpon Springs, it most certainly does."

"I reckon it does."

Mama couldn't hold back her smile anymore. "You reckon? Nick Papadopoulos! I don't think I've ever heard anyone but Paula use that expression."

"She's rubbing off on me, Mama."

"Good. That girl's smart and resourceful. Now what can we all do to help you out? I don't want you to have to do this on your own."

"Oh, trust me, you've all done quite enough."

Her smile faded, but she still held a glimmer in her eyes. "We like to help."

Nick hugged her. "I know you do, and I appreciate it."

"What do you have planned for the rest of your vacation?"

"Paula and I were talking about going to the Clearwater Jazz Festival. Any other suggestions?"

"That's a good start." She shook her head. "Can't think of anything else." Suddenly, her face lit up. "Maybe you can take her to Bern's Steak House in Tampa."

Nick nodded. "I wonder if she's ever been there. The one time I wanted to take her back in high school, she didn't want to go because it was too expensive."

"Oh, I'm sure she's probably been since then. We can ask Stephanie. She probably knows."

"I have a better idea, Mama. I'll ask Paula myself."

❧

Ever since the trip to the mall, Paula felt as though she were walking on air. She wished she didn't feel this way, but she was happy Nick still loved her. When she wasn't with him, however, she remembered his wanderlust and her need for staying put. She didn't want either of them to resent the other, and her business was doing better than she ever expected.

She'd worked hard to build something that was just now taking off.

She also knew she struggled to trust other people—even Nick. He'd never given her any reason not to trust him, but after what she'd seen with her parents, she realized that love could turn into something very bad and hurtful. It had been almost twenty years since her parents' divorce, and her mother still hadn't recovered—even after marrying Mack.

The one constant in Paula's life was her business. She'd poured all her money, time, and energy into growing it, and it paid off. Having Alexa working afternoons and nights freed her up to handle the wholesale orders and production, which was going quite smoothly. Alexa's idea for talking to the people at the Senior Center turned out to be pure genius. Paula agreed to pay the center's electric bill and pay wages to the people who did the work. The first batch turned out beautiful. It was good for everyone involved.

Paula was happy to see Nick, and she wanted to hang out with him while he was in town. But she resolved to maintain some emotional distance for self-preservation and sanity after he left. It would be difficult to resist his charms—particularly when he talked about building a life together—but the fact that he had limited time kept her from floating off on a cloud to Neverland. Mom hadn't taught her much, but she did show her how trusting in someone else could backfire.

Paula remembered her grandmother telling her that if an obstacle stood in the way and you couldn't move it yourself, leave it there and walk around it. She'd clung to that philosophy of independence most of her life. She certainly didn't get it from her mother, who never minded asking people for whatever she wanted but wasn't willing to get for herself. Paula suspected the main reason her mother married Mack was to be able to quit her job. She never kept her disdain for full-time work a secret. She'd worked one job after another and always found reasons to leave, sometimes for a miniscule raise but always blaming the former employer for not seeing her value. But, as Nick and his family reminded Paula, her mother did support her until she was on her own. As meager as it was, she always had a place to live and food on the table. She knew it wasn't easy for a single mom to support a child.

Alexa's first few nights of keeping the shop open later astounded Paula. She did almost as much business during the week as she did on weekends. Until now, she didn't realize how many local sales she was missing.

"Want me to open early on Sunday?" Alexa asked.

"No. I don't want you to miss church."

Alexa grinned. "You are the best boss I've ever had."

"Don't say that, Alexa. The only other bosses you've had were your family, and that's really not fair."

"Okay, so they treat me like a child, and you don't."

Paula thought about how much more adult Alexa acted around her than she did with her mother and aunts, but she didn't say that to Alexa. "I'm very happy with your work. You've been a great asset."

Tears sprang to Alexa's eyes, and she quickly turned away. Paula knew she was embarrassed by her emotions, so she walked to the other side of the shop. "How are these fat candles doing?"

Alexa dabbed at her eyes with a tissue before joining Paula. "They're starting to do well. I found a picture in a magazine of some movie stars' homes, and that's what they're all burning these days."

"Good thinking."

"Same with soaps. I read that some of the big stars are using aroma therapy in everything, including soaps, and they're going all-natural."

"It's a good thing you like reading all those magazines," Paula said. "You'll keep us up-to-date on the trends."

Alexa smiled and nodded silently then made her way back to the sales counter. Paula knew this was her way of regaining her comfort zone.

"Anything I need to know about before I take off?" Paula asked.

When Alexa didn't answer right away, Paula stared at her.

"I don't know if I should tell you this," Alexa began.

"Since you've said that much, you better tell me."

Alexa chewed her lip. "Mama and Aunt Ursa have been working on a plan to get you to marry Nick."

"What?" Paula hadn't intended it to come out in a shriek.

Alexa held up her hands defensively. "I know, I know. It's none of their business, but they've never let that stop them before."

"Does Nick know about this . . . this plan?"

"No, of course not. He'd never go for anything so devious or underhanded."

"Any idea what they're planning to do?"

"Not yet, but I'm keeping my ears open."

"You'll let me know, right?"

Alexa frowned. "Yes, but it feels sort of, well . . . I don't know . . ."

"Sneaky and underhanded?"

"Yeah."

Paula thought about her relationship with her own mother and how strained it was compared to the loving Papadopoulos family. She didn't want to create any friction between Alexa and her family.

"Then don't get involved. This is between Nick and me. Even if your mother and aunt try to make things happen, Nick and I are strong enough to do only what's right for us."

Once the words registered with Alexa, she smiled. "Thanks, Paula. You're an amazing person. Anyone else would have wanted me to act as a double agent."

Paula winked and lifted her finger to her lips. "Okay, motor-mouth, time to flip the switch to the off position."

She left the shop to the sound of Alexa's laughter. On the way to the Senior Center, she wondered what the Papadopoulos women had planned. By the time she arrived, she realized how blessed she was that they would go to so much trouble to bring her into the family. They'd always said she was like one of them, and now they were proving they meant it.

As she drove, she thought about what it would be like to be Nick's wife. A smile crept across her face as she realized her resolve was wearing down.

"Paula! I'm glad you're here. We were just arguing over some of these directions. You can settle it once and for all."

"Hey, Mildred, what's the problem?" Paula dropped her bag on the closest chair and joined the line of people making soaps.

"Alexa said we can use the same molds for candles as we use for the soap, and I said they have to be different."

Paula looked at the line of molds on the table. "Actually, you're both right. What you have here is fine. Some of the same molds are in duplicate because we don't want the ingredients from the candles and soaps to cross over."

Mildred, the self-appointed leader, looked at everyone else, and they all nodded their understanding. "Did everyone hear that?"

"Why don't we store the molds in separate cabinets?" Robert said. "That way we won't get 'em mixed up."

"If you have enough storage to do that, it's a great idea," Paula said. "How are you on essential oils? Do you need more of anything?"

Mildred held up the production order. "Looks like Alexa brought everything we need for this batch, but if you get more orders for those Alexa's Almond Cookies candles, we'll need a whole lot more of the almond oil."

Paula had to bite the insides of her cheeks to keep from smiling. "I'll talk to my source and see if I can get a rush order on it. I have a feeling it'll be a big seller."

"Oh, yes, I'm sure," Hazel agreed. "It has such a divine aroma. I'm going to be one of your first customers in the shop."

"You don't have to wait for it to be in the shop. As a perk you can each take your pick of the candles with every order."

Robert's eyebrows shot up. "You mean for free?"

Paula grinned at him. "It's not exactly free. Y'all are working hard on this."

"But you're paying us, so I just figured—"

"Hush, Robert," Hazel admonished. "We don't want her changing her mind."

"Don't worry, I won't change my mind."

Hazel smiled shyly. "Thank you."

Paula walked around and chatted with each person in the line. She was very happy with their work and the fact that she didn't have to worry about their integrity. This was working out better than anything Paula could have thought of herself.

When she finished talking to her crew, Paula went back to her car and jotted some notes about offering bonuses and gift baskets to all her new employees. Then she thought about Alexa and how much she'd contributed to the business. Paula could see that business might double in a year if it continued moving at this pace. It was beyond anything she'd ever imagined. If things kept going so well, she'd need to find more people to work at the shop and behind the scenes in administration.

Her cell phone rang. It was Steph.

"Hey, girl. I miss you."

"Yeah, me too." Steph's voice sounded tight. "I have a huge favor to ask."

"What kind of favor?"

"Before I ask, I need to tell you this wasn't my idea, and I'll understand if you say no."

"Just tell me, okay?"

"My aunt fired me from the bakery this afternoon, and when I showed up at Apollo's, he told me my services weren't needed anymore."

"You've got to be kidding."

"Oh, that's only half of it. When I went home and asked Mama if she had any idea what was going on, she said they thought I should work for someone outside the family for a while."

"Hmm. Any job prospects?"

"That's where the favor comes in. When I told Mama I had no idea where to start looking, she suggested talking to you. Apparently, Alexa has been telling everyone how successful your business is, and she thinks you might need some more help."

"Looks like today is my lucky day," Paula said.

She knew exactly what was going on, but that was fine. So be it if the Papadopoulos family was willing to sacrifice one of their own to get her and Nick together. She could handle that. In the meantime, she had the extra hands she needed to keep her business running smoothly. She wasn't sure exactly how their scheme was supposed to play out, but she'd definitely benefit.

"Your lucky day? Why's that?"

"Can you start tomorrow?"

Steph squealed. "Are you kidding me? I can start right now if you want me to."

"No, tomorrow is soon enough." Paula laughed. "Meet me at the shop at nine o'clock in the morning, and I'll give you a list of things to do."

"Nine?"

"Is that too early?" Paula asked.

"Oh, no, it'll be like sleeping in after getting up at four to go to the bakery."

"Trust me, in my business, there's hardly ever a reason to get up before daylight."

"This'll be a walk in the park," Steph said. "I never knew it would be so easy to find a job."

"It's normally not. You just happened to catch me at the right time."

"I promise I'll do a good job, Paula. You won't be sorry you hired me."

"I know you'll do a good job, Steph. You've filled in enough at the shop when Oria couldn't work that I know how good you are with customers."

She clicked off her phone and relaxed her shoulders. With that settled, she didn't have a thing to worry about—except a bunch of meddling but well-meaning Papadopoulos women . . . and obviously now the men too.

Until now Paula's business classes in college hadn't made much sense. However, with regular employees and a production crew, she could see the sense of what some of her professors talked about.

Her phone rang again, and this time it was Nick. "What time do you want me to pick you up tomorrow?"

"Tomorrow?" She couldn't remember making plans with Nick the last time she saw him. "Okay, I give. What's happening tomorrow?"

He groaned. "Don't tell me you forgot about the Clearwater Jazz Festival."

"Oh yeah, that."

"Don't get too excited."

"Sorry, Nick, it's just that—"

"Be careful you don't get so wrapped up in being a business tycoon you forget about the little people."

Paula laughed. "I'll try, but it's your job to keep me humble."

"I guess that works both ways, doesn't it?"

"Yep. You can definitely count on me to keep your ego out of the sky."

"Yes, I know that." Nick's somber tone made her laugh.

"I didn't mean to sound insulting."

"I know." Silence fell between them for a few seconds before he continued. "Okay, so do you still want to go to the festival or not?"

"I said I did, didn't I?"

"You make it sound like a chore. I don't want you to go just because you feel obligated."

Paula didn't feel that way at all. In fact, her pulse still raced from hearing Nick's voice.

"What time are we going?" she asked.

"How about I pick you up around ten tomorrow morning, and we can walk around the art show in downtown Clearwater first?"

"Um . . . how about later? I have to do a few things for the shop first."

She heard Nick's sigh of exasperation. "Since you're so busy, you tell me what time to pick you up."

"How about one o'clock?"

"Fine. I'll see you at one. Gotta run."

Paula slowly flipped her phone shut. This was one of those times she wished she had someone to talk to. Grandma had passed away a few years ago, Mom was useless unless she needed something, and Alexa and Steph had ulterior motives.

14

"What did you do with the money I already sent?" Paula couldn't believe her mother had the gall to ask for even more money.

"I don't think that's any of your business."

"Um . . . it sort of is my business. It's not like you're asking for spare change."

"If you don't have it, just say so."

Paula thought about the orders that kept rolling in and how much money she'd be making off them. Even after she paid her employees and production people, she'd still have more income in the next quarter than she had during the previous year—enough to replenish her savings and add more to her retirement fund.

"It's not about whether or not I have the money. I just want to know if there's something else you need more. This sounds like a problem way beyond money."

"Don't go lecturing me, Paula. I'm not a child."

Then stop acting like one, she wanted to say.

"So the question is do you care enough to help me out or not?"

Leave it to her mother to play the guilt card. "When do you need it?"

"Can you send it today?"

Paula thought for a moment. She expected the checks to start coming in about thirty days, but she did still have some savings that she could transfer to checking.

"How about I mail it tomorrow?"

After a few seconds of silence, her mother replied, "I guess that'll be okay. Just make sure you get to the post office before their pick-up time. I'll need it in my account by Tuesday."

"Mom, is this going to continue?"

"I'm not sure. Mack is really on my back about this job thing."

"Why don't you either find a job or talk to him about it?"

"He doesn't understand. You know how men are."

"Does he have any idea where this money is coming from?"

"Of course not. It's none of his business where I get my money."

Paula's frustration made her want to scream, but instead she closed her eyes, prayed for patience, and said she needed to go. Memories of her mother reminding her of how she felt smothered from the responsibilities of single parenting swamped her in guilt.

"Don't forget to mail the money first thing in the morning."

As soon as they got off the phone, Paula went online and made an electronic transfer of funds. Then she wrote the check and got it ready to mail. She placed it on the counter so she wouldn't forget to take it to the post office the next morning.

The phone ringing early Saturday jarred her from sleep. She lifted one eye and glanced at the clock on the nightstand. It was only six-thirty.

"Paula, we can't figure out your change of instructions on this last batch of soap." It was one of the production workers at the Senior Center.

"What y'all doing there so early?"

"We were all excited to get this done, so we met here at six. Did you want vanilla with Alexa's Almond Cookies, or do we leave it out?"

Paula sat up and rubbed her eyes. She couldn't remember the exact formula. "Give me a few minutes to get dressed, and I'll come over there and get you started."

"Okay. In the meantime we'll set up for the next scent."

She quickly washed her face, threw on some clothes, and ran out the door. When she got to the Senior Center, she was glad they had a fresh pot of coffee brewing and a platter of fruit and pastries.

As she sipped her coffee, she studied her notes. Mildred pointed to the differences between the soap and candle formulas.

"You have vanilla in one and not the other," she said.

"Yes, I see that. I must have made a mistake. Let me play with it for a few minutes before I decide."

A half hour later, Paula handed them the revised formulas. Mildred nodded as she took the paper.

"This is obviously a mix of science, art, and the sense of smell."

"Exactly," Paula agreed. "I'm glad you asked before you went forward."

The production people offered smiles filled with pride. "It's important to do a good job with this," one woman said. "You're the first person who has given us an opportunity to supplement our Social Security income, and we don't want to blow it."

"I'll have my cell phone with me all day, so don't hesitate to call again if you need more help," Paula said. "Thanks for the coffee."

Since she was already out, she went to the shop, where Alexa had a line waiting to be helped. Paula took a couple of the customers, and then Steph came in.

"I thought you and Nick were going to the Jazz Festival today," Steph said.

"We are, but not until one."

"It's already eleven, so why don't you go on home and get ready?"

Paula offered a lopsided grin. "What are you trying to tell me?"

"Don't sabotage your relationship with Nick, Paula." Steph took Paula by the arm and led her to the door. "The shop is in good hands. Alexa and I will take care of everything here. Go home and get ready for your date."

"Okay, okay." Paula did as she was told and went straight home. It wasn't until she'd showered and dressed that she remembered the check. The mail had already gone out.

She tried to call her mother's cell phone, but there was no answer. After a brief hesitation, she called her mother's home number. Mack answered.

"Hey there, Paula. Long time since I heard from you. How's business?"

"It couldn't be better. Is my mother there?"

"No, she's at work now. Want me to give her a message?"

"She got a job?"

"Yeah, she got one about two weeks ago. I thought she would have called and told you, but I reckon she was just too busy."

Paula hung up and stared at the phone. She didn't like how this was starting to look.

Nick arrived right on time. "I brought chairs and food from Mama."

"Baklava?"

He snickered. "Probably. She packed it, and I didn't ask questions."

"I don't think they allow people to bring their own food."

"We can eat it afterward. I thought we might head back to the beach after we leave the festival."

"Would you mind stopping by the post office? I have to get something in the mail right away."

"Sure. It's on the way to Clearwater."

⟡

Nick saw Paula's mother's name on the envelope as she pulled it out of her bag. He waited in the car while she ran inside. She returned looking flushed.

"How's your mother doing?"

"I'm not sure." Paula fidgeted with the edge of her handbag. "Something strange is going on with her, and I don't know what to think."

Strange was a mild word for Bonnie. "Wanna tell me about it, and maybe between the two of us we can figure it out?"

Paula pulled her lips between her teeth and shook her head. Nick concentrated on his driving and let her think about what she wanted to do. Finally, she spoke.

"She said Mack wants her to get a job, and she doesn't want to. Then she's been asking me for money."

Nick's insides tightened. "Your mother is asking for money? And are you giving it to her?" He grimaced as he realized why she needed to stop at the post office. "Was there money in that envelope?"

"Well . . . yes."

"Do you mind telling me what she needs money for? I thought Mack had a good job."

"That's what I can't figure out. The first time she said she needed it for her car payment because she'd fallen behind. This time she said she needed the money right away, and I was supposed to get it in today's mail, but I forgot. So I called. She didn't answer her cell phone, so I called her at home. Mack said she was at work."

"Okay, so she got a job. Maybe she won't need any more money."

"Mack said she's been working for a couple of weeks, but just yesterday she said she didn't want to get a job."

"Someone is obviously lying." And Nick knew who it was.

"Obviously," she agreed.

He lifted his hand, made a fist, and started to pound the steering wheel but stopped himself. He didn't need to let Paula see the anger he felt toward her parents. Her very selfish parents who were more blessed than they deserved.

When he stopped for a light, he glanced in her direction. She was staring out the side window, deep in thought. Instinctively, he reached out and touched her arm. She looked at him and smiled.

"Let's not talk about my mom, okay?"

Nick nodded. She was right. He didn't need to let someone else come between him and the woman he loved—the woman he had to convince to marry him in the almost four weeks he had left in Florida. But today he'd try to focus on the moment. She had enough emotional baggage weighing her down for the time being.

The festival was already well underway, and parking was nearly impossible to find anywhere near the event. "I don't mind walking," she said.

"Good thing because it doesn't look like we have a choice."

He dug the chairs out from the trunk. Without saying a word, she took one of the chairs. As they walked toward Coachman Park, he thought about what a great team they made.

The sound of saxophones filled the air, and the closer they got the more Nick felt at peace. He and Paula had been to this festival before—another gentle reminder that what they had was lasting.

On the way to the field Paula stopped by a couple of the art exhibits and admired the artists' work. Nick got some of their cards so he could contact them later, paying careful attention to what she said she liked.

"How about over there?" Paula pointed to the only spot of shaded grass available.

"Sure." They opened their chairs and plopped them down next to each other. Nick sat down and took a deep breath. "This is the life. Times like this I really miss it."

"Apparently not that much."

Nick looked at Paula. Her face didn't show even a hint of sarcasm. "Actually, I do miss it that much, but I figure I can always come back after I retire."

"That's a long time."

"Not as long as you might think. I've already been in almost eight years. I'll be able to retire in my early forties."

"Then what?" Paula's gaze settled on him.

❧

She wondered if he'd ever be happy living on the West Coast of Florida after moving around and seeing places he'd always dreamed about. "Do you ever really want to move back here?"

Nick stretched his long legs out in front of him and crossed them at the ankles. "All depends."

"On what?"

He took her hand. "Let's not go there." He squeezed her hand and warmed her heart with a sweet smile. "I'd like to leave all that for later."

"Yeah. Why don't we just enjoy the afternoon?"

"Great idea." He pointed to the new act taking the stage. "Aren't those local guys?"

"Those are the people who played at the St. Petersburg College Talent Show back when you were taking classes at the Tarpon campus."

"That's what I thought." He listened for a few seconds. "They look a lot older."

Paula burst out in laughter. "They are, and so are we. It's been . . . what, ten years or so?"

"Something like that."

They listened to the music until the bands changed again. "Want something to eat?" Nick asked as he stood. "I'm starving."

"Sure, I could use some food." She stood, but he pointed to the chair.

"You need to stay here and save the spot."

She sat back down. "Okay, I'd like a hamburger and whatever you have to drink."

Nick grinned. "French fries?"

"Of course."

"How about dessert?"

Paula thought it over then shook her head. "Better not. We'll be eating baklava later."

"I sure hope Mama remembered to pack some."

"If not, I'll forgive her," Paula teased.

"Look." Nick pointed to some people they knew back in high school. "I haven't seen them since I graduated."

"Sherrie used to be a regular customer at the shop, but lately she never buys anything, even though she still comes in to look. I think Patrick lost his job last year, and he's having a hard time finding a new one."

"That's rough. Patrick used to work for one of my uncles, remember?"

Paula nodded. "And he always showed up late."

"Does Sherrie work?"

"I don't know. In case you didn't notice, they have three little kids. Daycare is expensive."

"If Patrick is home anyway, why can't he watch the kids?"

"Good question." Paula watched as Sherrie hoisted one of the toddlers on her hip, took the hand of another, and glanced over her shoulder at Patrick, who stood there staring at the stage with his arms folded, apparently unfazed by their children.

"Looks like he's not all that excited about the kid thing."

Paula thought about how many people were in that situation. As she thought back to her own childhood, she remembered her dad spending quite a bit of time with her until the last couple of years her parents were together. He went from being an attentive father who came home every night and spent all his weekends with her to working late and playing golf on weekends. At least that was what he'd said. According to her mother, he wasn't playing golf.

They stayed at Coachman Park for another couple of hours until Nick stood. "Wanna take a drive down to south Clearwater Beach? I thought it might be nice and quiet around Sand Key."

Paula stood and folded her chair. "Sure, sounds good."

When they got to the beach, Nick opened the trunk. Paula reached for the tote, leaving the cooler for Nick. They stepped out of their shoes and walked over to a concrete ledge, where they put everything down.

Nick rummaged through the food and came up with a note. "I didn't see any baklava, but here's a note from Mama." He unfolded it, grinned, and handed it to Paula.

She read the carefully printed note. *Dear Nick and Paula, Here is a little bit of food in case you get hungry. Don't eat too much because a special meal will be waiting for you at Apollo's at 8:00. Love, Mama.*

15

Paula rocked back on her heels and stared at Nick, who grinned at her. "So what do you think?"

He shrugged. "Looks like Mama and the gang have something up their sleeves again."

"Should we have appetizers here and go see what they've cooked up?"

"It's up to you, Paula."

"We might as well play along."

Nick snickered. "I agree. If we don't, they'll up their game until we break."

"And since there are only two of us and . . . how many of them?"

"Dozens."

"Yeah." Paula thought about how determined the Papadopoulos family could be. "We don't stand a chance."

"What do you think they'll have?"

"Well . . . I like baklava, so I'm sure they'll have that."

Nick nodded. "And I bet the whole family will be there, since no one wants to be left out of the plan."

Paula lifted a finger. "You mean scheme."

"Call it whatever you want, it's still the same thing." He lifted the cooler. "Let's go closer to the water and spread the blanket. We can watch the sunset then head back to Tarpon Springs."

They nibbled on the assortment of mini appetizers and feta cheese. Nick lifted an entire jar of olives. "Here ya go. Mama knows how much you love Greek olives."

"Yeah, but not a whole jar!" She popped the lid, extracted a few, and handed it back to Nick. "Have some."

They chatted about military life, soap, candles, and everything else Paula could think of to avoid anything too personal, until Nick finally put his hand on her shoulder. "This is nice."

She sighed. "I know."

"Wouldn't it be fun to beat them at their own game?"

Paula tilted her head. "What do you mean?"

Nick shrugged, his gaze never leaving the water. "I don't know, like maybe tell them we're already engaged?"

She glanced at him then shook her head. "Getting engaged is too serious to turn it into a game."

"Yeah, you're right."

Nick tensed for a moment, but when she turned to look at him he relaxed, though he wouldn't look her in the eye. Instead, he kept his gaze toward the water. This time the silence was painful.

"Nick?"

He flashed a glance her way but didn't hold her eyes. "Wanna leave now?"

"No, I just wanted to know what you're thinking."

He shrugged but still didn't look at her. "Just the normal stuff."

Paula laughed. "Which is?"

After a couple of deep breaths, he slowly angled his face toward her. "I don't want you to feel like I'm pressuring you."

"I don't feel that way."

"Sometimes it seems like you do."

"I guess I just always feel so . . . I don't know . . . conflicted? It's like I want to be with you all the time, but to do that one of us will have to sacrifice everything we've ever wanted, and that might cause resentment later, and—"

Nick lifted a finger and gently pressed it to her lips. "Sshh. Let's not go there, okay? Not tonight, anyway. I want us to relax and enjoy each other where we are now."

It was just like Nick to know exactly what to say to make her feel better. Her heart melted at his thoughtfulness. "Okay," she whispered as she leaned her head on his shoulder.

"Look." Nick pointed toward the Gulf. The bottom of the sun had just touched the water, producing a postcard-like image. "This is my favorite part."

The bright orange sun slowly melted into the Gulf of Mexico, the reflection rippling and creating a breathtaking effect, as it seemed to spread and float in the water. The surrounding sky had an ombré effect, with the blues turning to green and eventually sliding into dark purples and pinks. As the sun made its final slip into the water, Paula sighed.

"What a beautiful sunset." Nick stood and reached for her hands to lift her to her feet. "We have some pretty sunsets in Texas but nothing like this."

They walked back to the car in silence. Paula thought about Nick's sensitivity toward her. She'd never loved him more than she did now.

"Wanna go to my parents' house, or should I bring you home first?"

"If we're going to be with your family for dinner, I need a shower and some fresh clothes."

Nick looked at her as he took the bag and put it in the trunk. She looked fabulous—even in shorts, a tank top, and sandals.

He pulled up in front of her house and tapped his watch. "Is an hour enough time?"

"If I take an hour, we'll be late."

"I'm sure a few minutes won't make that much difference. Why don't I pick you up in an hour?"

"No, that's okay. I can drive."

Nick didn't want her walking into Apollo's by herself. If what he suspected actually happened, she'd think he was in on whatever they had planned.

"I'll pick you up."

She remained standing by the car, holding onto the door as she thought about it. "Okay, fine. Can you get ready and be back here in forty-five minutes? That way we won't keep anyone waiting."

Nick swallowed hard. "Sure. All I have to do is jump in the shower and get dressed."

He waited until she went inside before driving to his parents' house, which was eerily quiet. As he walked through the rambling old house, he realized no one was home. His mother rarely remembered to bring her cell phone with her, so he called his dad's shop.

"Whatcha need, son?"

"Have you seen Mama?" Nick asked.

"She's at Apollo's with Ophelia and Phoebe. They're up to something."

"I bet I know what it is."

His father laughed. "I bet I do too. You might as well leave them to whatever they're doing. I learned a long time ago that when those three get together, there's no stopping them."

"I just don't want to upset Paula."

"Listen, son, your mother and aunts love that girl, and there's nothing they wouldn't do for her. If they're up to something, their intentions are good. I'm sure Paula's smart enough to realize that."

"I know." Nick shut his eyes and rubbed them. "Okay, I better run. I'm picking Paula up as soon as I get ready."

"Want me to have your mama call you if I see her?"

"Nah, there's no point. Like you said, she's gonna do what she's gonna do. I'll just deal with it later."

The sound of his father's laughter echoed as he clicked off his phone. He didn't waste any time showering and getting ready before hopping back into the monster-sized car to pick up his favorite girl.

She stood on the porch waiting for him, her golden-brown hair framing her sweet heart-shaped face. The face that had him mesmerized since he first saw her in the hallway at Tarpon Springs High School. The face he couldn't wait to kiss. The face he missed seeing for more years than he wanted to count.

As soon as she saw him, she held her skirt in place and hopped down off the porch. "I hope we're not keeping anyone waiting."

"Oh, I think they'll be just fine."

Steph greeted them at the door of Apollo's. She grinned at Paula and winked at Nick. "We have your table waiting for you. Follow me."

Paula cast a curious glance at Nick, but he didn't respond. Instead, he dutifully followed his cousin to the room they typically reserved for couples. His aunt teased his uncle and called it "the love nest."

"What's going on?" Paula asked as Steph stopped at a table for two in the dark, candlelit corner. "Where is everyone?"

"We thought the two of you might enjoy a little privacy." Steph placed the menus on the table. "Adonis will be here shortly to take your order."

Nick felt Paula's glare before he ventured a glance in her direction. Finally, he looked her in the eye. "I'm so sorry, Paula."

"What are you sorry about? I saw Steph wink at you. Why didn't you tell me it was just you and me?"

"I wasn't sure."

"Right." Paula lifted her water glass and took a sip. "Did you have any idea at all?"

Guilt flooded Nick. "I sort of suspected, but I wasn't sure."

"Then why didn't you say something? You knew I thought . . ." Her voice trailed off as she glanced around the room. "They're obviously determined."

"That they are." Nick placed his forearms on the table and leaned toward Paula. "Why don't we just enjoy the meal and the ambience? They went to an awful lot of trouble for us."

He'd no sooner gotten those words out when the violinist approached their table. Nick tried to give the musician a discreet sign to move on, but the man ignored him and stopped beside the table, playing "Love Is a Many Splendored Thing." Then he took a bow and walked away to play for someone else.

Prepared to apologize, Nick turned to look at Paula and found her stifling a giggle. He grinned. "What?"

"Now that takes the cake."

"The cake and a few other things. Look, Paula—"

She held up her hands and shook her head, still laughing. "You don't have to say anything. I know you didn't do that." She snorted. "That has Ophelia Papadopoulos's signature all over it."

"Yeah, it does, doesn't it?"

"And the table? This was Phoebe's idea."

Nick nodded his agreement. "Aunt Phoebe is the one who came up with the idea for 'the love nest.'"

As Paula broke up into another fit of giggles, Nick started to lose some of his humor. When she saw that he wasn't laughing, she stopped.

"What's the matter?"

"They wanted this to be perfect for us, Paula. Instead of laughing, you should be thankful they care enough about you to want everything to be . . ." Nick paused for a second, ". . . romantic."

She nodded, looking apologetic. "You're right. This is very sweet."

The waiter arrived to take their orders. Nick didn't look his mother's brother's only son in the eye.

After he left, Paula folded her hands on the table. "Would you like to say the blessing, or do you want me to?"

"I'll do it."

⁓❧

Paula was relieved. After losing control and laughing so hard, she felt terrible when Nick appeared offended. She bowed her head and listened to Nick's sincere prayer for thanksgiving. He expressed his gratitude not only for a perfect day but for a family who cared enough to go to so much trouble. After she whispered "amen," she opened her eyes to see Nick staring at her.

He tilted his head and lifted his eyebrows. "You were saying?"

Paula leaned back with her eyes cast downward, feeling worse by the second. When she dared look back up at Nick, he continued watching. Waiting.

"I'm sorry. I was out of line."

A slight smile played on his lips. "That's one of the things I love about you, Paula. You're not afraid to admit when you're mistaken." He glanced over his shoulder then turned back around. "However, I have to admit this is a little over the top—even for my family."

Paula wasn't about to continue with this line of conversation, or she'd dig herself deeper into a place where no apology would ever get her out. She lifted her water glass and winked at Nick. "Opa!"

Adonis brought their food—a delicious lamb stew that Nick's uncle was known for. Nick stared at his plate and inhaled deeply as though smelling it for the first time.

"Smells good, doesn't it?"

"You're not kidding."

"I have a feeling this is a combo meal."

Nick crinkled his forehead. "Combo meal?"

"Yeah, a combination of a romantic dinner for us and a lure to get you to stay in Tarpon Springs."

Nick lifted his fork and knife. "You're probably right."

Paula savored every last bite of her food. When Adonis returned for their dessert order, she told him she couldn't handle another bite. He looked panic-stricken.

"You don't want baklava? But—"

Nick took over. "Just order dessert to go, Paula. They made a special batch, exactly the way you like it—extra nuts."

Paula glanced up at Adonis, who had turned back to her. "You heard him. I'll take whatever he orders for me."

Adonis's head whipped back and forth between them.

"She'll take a dozen triangles of baklava to go," Nick said.

"Nick! I'll never be able to eat all that."

"Sure you will. Freeze it." After Adonis left, Nick stood up. "Wait here. I'm gonna go find my uncle and thank him for such a delicious meal."

Paula didn't have to wait long. Nick came back with not only his uncle, but Stephanie, Alexa, his mother, and the two aunts. "Did you have a nice dinner?" Steph's mom asked.

"Yes, it was delicious," Paula replied.

"How about . . . ?" Nick's mother gestured around the room.

Steph intervened. "I don't think she was talking about the food, Paula."

"Oh, um . . . yes, everything was wonderful."

"How about you, Nick?" his mother asked.

"Mama." Nick smiled at Paula before looking at his mother then scanning the rest of the crowd. "We appreciate everything you did for us, but in the future, why don't you at least warn us what you're up to?"

"Most people like surprises," his mother said, looking hurt.

Paula suddenly felt bad. "Surprises are wonderful. I enjoyed everything very much."

"Such a sweet girl," Aunt Phoebe said. "Don't let her get away again, Nick." She took a step away from the table. "C'mon, everyone, let's give them a little space. I'm sure they don't appreciate all of us hovering over their romantic dinner."

After they left, Nick turned to Paula, and the laughter that had been threatening to bubble up slipped out. "They are truly unique."

"Yep, my family is one of a kind." He stood back up and reached for her hand. "Let's get out of here before the violin guy comes back."

They walked along the sponge docks until Paula reminded Nick that it was getting late. Back at her house, she was glad when he walked her to her door but didn't ask to come in. It had been a long day, and she was exhausted.

"I had a nice time today, Paula."

"Yeah, me too."

He leaned over and dropped a kiss on her forehead. "Thank you for being such a great sport about everything."

"Is that what I am? A good sport?"

He snickered. With a wave and a hop off the porch, Nick was gone. She went inside and got ready for bed.

That night she fell asleep with a smile on her face and a familiar old floaty feeling she used to have after being with Nick. She slept until the sound of the phone jolted her awake.

"I need your help, Paula."

"Mom?" Paula sat up in bed and rubbed her eyes with her free hand. "What happened?"

"It's Mack. He's threatening me."

16

$\mathscr{P}$aula tossed back the covers and sat all the way up. "Are you in danger?"

Her mother sniffled. "No . . . well, yes, sort of."

"It'll take me all day to get there. Have you called the police?"

"Not that kind of danger, Paula. He's threatening to leave me."

Relief flooded Paula, quickly replaced by frustration. "What happened?"

"Well . . . he found out that I wasn't working, and he's even more furious about the private investigator I hired."

"Private investigator? I'm confused. Would you care to start at the beginning and explain?"

"It's so complicated, Paula. Why do men have to be so difficult?"

"Just tell me."

Her mother started at the beginning, when she told Mack she was bored. He suggested getting a job to stay busy and bring in some extra money. "He said he wanted to make sure we had enough money when we retired." She laughed between sniffles. "You'd think we were getting old or something."

"Why did you hire a private investigator?"

Her mother sighed. "Mack was away from home so much, and I remembered when your father did that he had a girlfriend."

"Is that why you needed the money all this time?" Paula's chest constricted. "You were taking money from me to have someone follow Mack?"

"You don't have to sound so shocked. I was trying to protect myself. You would have done the same thing if you'd been in my shoes."

No she wouldn't. Paula took a deep breath so she could move on and find out more. "So you told him you had a job?"

"Don't be so impatient. Let me tell my story." She went on to explain how she applied for a few jobs, but none of them would pay her enough to justify getting dressed up every day. "I had that kind of job for years, and after you grew up I swore I'd never do that to myself again."

"Why did he think you had a job?" Paula didn't have to ask, but she needed her mother to come out and tell her the truth.

"I didn't actually tell him I had a job . . ."

"But?"

"I sort of mentioned there was one I liked, and they liked me, and I got dressed the next day and left early, so he assumed . . ."

"And you didn't set him straight?"

"Paula, you should have seen him. I don't think I've ever seen Mack so happy—at least not since I accepted his proposal. He always loved me back in high school, but when we split up and I got pregnant . . . I don't know, I just sort of blew him off—"

"Whoa. Back up. You were pregnant in high school? With me?"

"Yes, with you."

"I thought you graduated and married Dad right away."

"I did . . . we did. Fortunately, I was only a couple of months along, so I was able to get through the rest of school without anyone else knowing." She sniffled again. "That was so long ago, and we were incredibly foolish. Back to Mack."

Paula listened to her mother drone on and on about how she'd deceived Mack, but her mind was still wrapped around the fact that her mother was pregnant with her before she got married, and that she'd taken money to have Mack tailed. Finally, she stopped yammering.

"Are you listening to me, Paula?"

"Yes, of course. What do you want me to do?" She held her breath, waiting for that all too frequent request for a check.

"I'm thinking about coming down there and staying with you."

Paula didn't want another complication in her life, but how could she turn down her mother? "When?"

"I'm not sure. I need to see how serious Mack is about what he said this morning."

"Would you like for me to talk to him?"

"About what?"

Paula thought for a few seconds. "Never mind. It's probably not such a good idea anyway."

"No, actually it might work out. Maybe you can tell him how hard I've worked all my life so you could go to college and have everything you needed. I don't think he realizes how many sacrifices I've had to make."

Paula bit her lip to keep from reminding her mother that she'd gone to school on full scholarship, and she'd worked hard to pay for everything else. "I have another idea. Why don't you find a part-time job that won't take up too much of your time and start trusting Mack? That way you'll still have a lot of time to yourself, and you'll appease Mack—at least a little." Unless it was too late. "How did you explain the private investigator?"

"It wasn't easy, but after he calmed down a little I reminded him of what your father did to me. I don't think he's completely over it, but he said he'd try if I did my part to make our marriage work. Then he started in on me about the job again."

"Mom, you might actually enjoy having your own money, and if it helps your marriage, it makes sense."

"Part-time jobs pay peanuts. You know that. I don't want to work at some minimum wage job where no one respects me."

Paula thought about all the minimum wage jobs she'd had when she needed them. "Maybe you can find something good."

"No, I don't want to do that." Paula heard the muffled sound of her mother covering the phone and muted voices. She came back on the phone. "I gotta run. I'll call you later."

After she hung up, Paula flopped back down on her bed. Just when she thought she had her life figured out, it flipped upside down again. First Nick and now her mother. And the issue with Nick was a walk in the park next to what she'd just learned about her mom.

Church wasn't for another couple of hours, but no way could she go back to sleep.

After coffee and a bowl of cereal, she showered and got ready for church. She was a little surprised Nick hadn't called to see if he could pick her up.

The first thing she did when she got to church was look around for the Town Car. Steph came running toward her as she was about to go into the Bible study room.

"Nick told me to give you this," Steph said as she thrust an envelope toward her. "He said to tell you he'll be here in time for church and to save him a seat. He went to early services at St. Nick's with the family, and now he's helping Aunt Ursa."

"Are you going to the Bible study?" Paula asked.

"No, Alexa and I agreed to work in the nursery so the babies' parents can go."

Paula nodded then went on inside. Drew approached her. "Where's your guy?"

"I don't know, but his cousin said he'd be here for church."

"Good."

Drew's fiancée Molly walked up from behind and placed her hand on his shoulder. "Ready to get started, hon?"

He took her hand and nodded. "See ya later, Paula."

Paula sat in the back by the door, while Drew and Molly went to the front of the room to lead the Bible study. Before it began, she unfolded the note and read the puzzling comments, which read like a travelogue. When the class ended, Paula darted out of the room before anyone else could ask her where Nick was.

She stood at the back of the church sanctuary scanning the rows. Nick wanted her to save him a seat, but she wasn't sure when he'd get there, so she found a spot on the side, about a third of the way from the back.

⌘

Nick got to the church barely on time. His mother had asked him to help her get some things out of the shed when they got home from St. Nick's, so when Steph stopped by on her way to church, he'd handed her a note to give Paula.

He made it through the double doors about three seconds before the music started. After a skimming glance around the room, he spotted Paula over on the side—not where they'd ever sat before. He slid into the empty space next to her.

"Hey," he said softly.

She held up his note. "What's this all about?"

"It's some information about where I live in Texas."

"Why?"

"We'll talk about it later." Nick pointed to the front of the church, where the pastor stood with his hands lifted to get everyone's attention.

Something was bugging Paula; Nick sensed it. Normally very calm in church, today she fidgeted—first with the corner of the service bulletin and then with the edge of her sleeve, something he knew she did when she was worried.

Nick felt Paula's presence throughout church. As they stood together, he had to resist the temptation to put his arm around her. And when they sat, he wanted to grab her hand and savor the softness of her skin. As she turned, he caught the fragrant scent of her hair and longed to bury his nose in it. But he didn't do any of that. He remained sitting there. Like a soldier. Without feelings.

Every so often Paula cut a glance his way. He smiled every time she did, but she never held the look long enough for him to have any idea what was going on between them.

After the last hymn, Paula seemed antsy to get out of there. "Whoa, Paula, what's going on? Did I do something wrong?"

She shook her head and glanced down. "I'm not feelin' so good."

"Are you sick?" He placed his hand on her shoulder and guided her off to the side so people could pass.

"I don't know, Nick. It's just . . ." She lifted her free hand and let it fall down to her side.

"What happened?"

When she finally looked at him, he saw that her eyes were bloodshot and her skin looked pale. "I got a call early this morning."

"Your mother?"

She nodded. "I'm so confused about everything."

"C'mon, let's go for a walk. You need to talk about this."

"I don't know, Nick. You have enough on your plate."

"Stop." Nick stepped in front of her and tipped her face up to his. "The only thing I want on my plate is you, Paula. If you're upset, I need to know what it's all about. I want to help you." He tweaked her nose. "I'm here for you."

He knew her well enough to know that when she tilted her head like that, she was thinking about what to do next. He held his breath until she nodded.

"Okay, let's go outside."

The church property sat on one of the natural beaches, so they put their things in their cars and headed down the shell-covered trail. "So what's going on with your mother?"

Paula recapped the early morning call from her mother. As she talked, anger welled inside him. Nick refrained from saying anything until Paula finished. She'd just said that her mother got pregnant before she finished high school, and Nick realized how this must have hit her.

"You never had any idea before?"

She shook her head. "I knew they got married young, but I thought they did that and *then* got pregnant. This was the first I'd ever heard that Mom and Dad had to get married."

"They didn't have to."

"I know, but back then wasn't like it is now."

"Well, at least they had you. There were options, even back then."

"True."

Nick thought for a moment. "Okay, so this is quite shocking to you since it was your parents. If you'd heard this about someone else, how would you have felt?"

She shrugged. "Not as upset."

"So your parents did what they thought was right. What's so bad about that?" He stopped and turned Paula around, taking both of her hands in his.

"I don't know." She blinked, but a tear fell anyway.

"They had you because the Lord had plans for you."

"But they didn't know that."

"It doesn't matter," Nick said. "What does matter is that you are your own person. You're a beautiful, kind, loving, successful businesswoman. You love the Lord."

Paula didn't say a word. She just listened.

"Don't forget that your mother is the one who first brought you to church here."

She nodded. "The only reason she did that was because the church ladies kept coming around, and she wanted to get them off her back."

"But she did it. She brought you here, and this is where you made friends and found your faith."

Paula grinned. "Now that you've shown me how ridiculous I'm being, I'm starting to get hungry."

Nick gave an answering smile. "Now that you're back to your old self, me too. Want some avgolemono soup?"

"Where?"

"Mama made it. She said to bring you home for lunch."

She paused only for a second. "Okay, sounds good. You know how much I love her avgolemono."

He laughed. "I remember when you refused to eat it because you didn't like chicken noodle soup."

"How was I supposed to know it would be so good?" She did an about-face. "Let's go now. I'm starving."

Nick walked Paula to her car then climbed into his uncle's car. He felt ridiculous driving around in such a humongous vehicle, but he couldn't very well say anything since it was free wheels while he was in town.

They reached his parents' house in fifteen minutes. His mother had left a note for them on the kitchen counter.

"Mama said she had to go help Phoebe and Ophelia, so we should just help ourselves." Nick pointed to the cupboard. "Would you mind getting a couple of bowls? I need to grab the butter and bread."

❧

Paula helped set the table, casting covert glances at Nick. Being with him felt cozy—at least for now. Funny how she vacillated between comfort and dizziness around him.

As they took their seats, Nick nodded toward her. "Your turn to say the blessing."

She thanked God for their food and for such a beautiful day. When she paused, Nick added a prayer for her mother. They opened their eyes and looked at each other.

"Thanks, Nick. You really put me in my place about Mom."

"I didn't mean to put you in your place. I just wanted to remind you that she loved you enough to have you. And she did work while you were growing up, so you never went hungry or anything."

"True, but there was always a threat of moving. I constantly felt like the earth was about to shift beneath me."

He put down his spoon and rested his arms on the table. Whoo boy, here it comes.

"That's just it, Paula. You *didn't* move. She stayed right here so you could finish school."

"I know, I know." Paula searched her brain for something else to talk about, but she didn't have to do that for long.

"Nick!" The shout came from the front door, followed by other voices.

"In the kitchen, Steph!" Nick hollered back. He winked at Paula. "Sounds like we're about to have a party."

Steph, Alexa, and Charlene appeared in the kitchen. "Aunt Ursa said she made soup." The three cousins converged on the kitchen and fixed themselves bowls of soup.

Paula loved times like this—when the Papadopoulos clan had their impromptu gatherings around the table. They never left her out or made her feel like she wasn't part of the family. Every now and then, she and Nick exchanged a glance, touching her heart even more.

"Sshh." Charlene held her hands up then glanced at Paula. "Is that your phone?"

Paula leaned back in time to hear it ring again. "Yeah, I didn't hear it."

"That's because Charlene is practically sitting on it, doofus," Alexa said, reaching for the bag in the chair her sister sat in. She handed it to Paula. "Here ya go."

The phone quit ringing, but Paula pulled it out and glanced at the missed call. It was the shop.

"Excuse me a minute." She scooted her chair back and got up. "I need to return this call."

17

*O*ria?" Paula said. "Did you need me for something?"

"Remember that kid who stole a bunch of soap last year? She's back."

"Does she know you're on to her?"

"Not yet."

"Find a way to keep her in the shop. I'll be right there." Paula went back to the kitchen to grab her handbag. "Sorry, folks. Gotta run. Emergency at the shop."

Nick's forehead crinkled. "Need any of us?"

Paula shook her head. "It's just some kid who thinks she's entitled to a free bath."

"Huh?" Nick's confused expression elicited laughter from everyone.

"She had a klepto last year," Steph explained. "A fifteen-year-old girl tried to take off with about two hundred dollars' worth of soap."

As Paula drove to the shop, she thought about how she'd deal with this kid. She didn't want to prosecute someone so young, and after dealing with her mother—the school bad girl when Paula went to Tarpon Springs High School—Paula knew she likely didn't have any support at home. If the "church ladies" hadn't persisted, that could have been Paula many years ago. Deep down she felt sorry for the girl, but she couldn't very well let her get away with stealing.

When Paula arrived, the girl was still in the store "looking" at merchandise, with Oria right beside her. "May I help you?" Paula asked.

The girl lifted a soap to her nose and shrugged. "Like I told this lady, I'm just looking." Her tone was gruff and rude.

Paula made a quick decision to confront the issue. "I remember you, Amanda, and so does my employee. You were told to stay out of my store."

"For a year," the girl said without looking up.

"That was only if you paid me back for what you took."

"I didn't take nothing."

"Amanda." Paula felt the frustration rise in her chest as she remembered the police officer ordering the girl to show the contents of her handbag. Amanda had dumped it on the floor and run out the door. The police officer caught up with her a block away.

Finally, Amanda turned, rolled her eyes, and walked toward the door. "I don't like being hassled."

The door opened and Nick walked in. Amanda nearly bumped into him.

Nick pointed to Amanda and gave Paula a questioning look. She nodded.

"Excuse me," he said as he closed the door before Amanda could get out. "I understand you have an issue to resolve here with my friend."

"Stop hassling me. I'm outta here."

"No, I don't think so." Nick leaned against the door and folded his arms as he stared down at Amanda, who shrank under his gaze. "So how's shopping?"

Amanda bobbed her head but didn't reply. Paula stood and watched, transfixed by the scene playing out before her.

"Any chance of letting me see what you got there?"

"I didn't buy anything."

Nick smiled. "I'm sure. How about what you didn't buy?"

"Nick." Paula took a step toward them to tell him they caught Amanda before she stole anything. He held up a hand to stop her. She paused.

Amanda shifted from one foot to the other and pulled her handbag close to her chest. "Dude, you're in so much trouble."

Nick extended his hand. "Just give it to me, Amanda."

He knew her name? Paula glanced over her shoulder at Oria, who shrugged.

Amanda slowly loosened her grip on her bag, reached inside, and pulled out a couple of soaps then threw them on the floor. "Satisfied?"

Nick looked up at Paula. "What would you like me to do now?"

Still stunned that the girl had managed to lift product with Oria on her tail, Paula opened her mouth but couldn't think of what to say.

Nick leaned down to look Amanda in the eye. "If I thought it would do any good, I'd call your mom, but you and I know she won't do anything. How would you like me to talk to your dad?"

"No. Don't do that. He'll kill me."

Nick chuckled. "I doubt that. Your dad's a decent guy. But he won't be happy about this."

Amanda turned and faced Paula with a pleading look. "Tell him not to talk to my dad."

"You need to do some work around here to cover what you tried to steal," Nick said. "If you do everything Ms. Andrews tells you to do for . . ." Nick glanced up at Paula. "How about three hours?" After Paula gave him another baffled look, he smiled and turned back to Amanda. "Nah, that's not enough. Four hours of sweeping, dusting, and whatever else Ms. Andrews says, we'll let you off the hook. But one more time and we're calling the cops."

Amanda's shoulders sagged. "Do I have to?"

"No, you don't have to, but if you don't, your dad will hear about this, and so will the police."

Amanda rolled her eyes. "Okay, what do you want me to do?"

Paula regained her voice. "Why don't you come back tomorrow and I'll have some stuff for you to do. In the meantime, I'd like to have a private word with Mr. Papadopoulos."

Amanda looked back at Nick, who nodded. Then she ran out of the store.

Paula approached Nick. "Okay, so what just happened? How do you know her name, and who is her dad?"

"Remember Sam Dunbar?"

"You've got to be kidding. Sam Dunbar with the pocket protector and geeky glasses?"

"That's the one."

"I didn't know he married—" She narrowed her eyes. "Wait a minute. You know whose daughter this is, right?"

Nick nodded. "Of course I do. Amanda is the product of a bad girl who was desperate after being jilted by one of the jocks she had a crush on."

Paula looked dazed. "I had no idea Amanda was Sam's daughter."

"Sam just happened to be in the way when Kate got dumped, and now he's been paying child support for fourteen years."

"But she's sixteen now."

"Yep. He didn't know about her at first."

Paula leaned against the counter. "How sad. Hey, wait a minute. How do you know all this? You never hung out with Sam Dunbar."

"You don't think your store is the first she stole from, do you? My dad's been dealing with her for years."

"No wonder she knew who you were."

"You probably thought it was just my infamous Papado-poulos charm."

Paula snickered. "Right. So now that you've made a deal with her, I'll have to supervise a kleptomaniac in my store where she can't keep her hands off the merchandise. What were you thinking, Nick?"

"I was thinking that over time she might actually learn something about values from a woman who pulled herself up from the trenches."

That made sense. But still . . .

Nick shot Oria a glance then looked back at Paula. "I doubt she'll try to steal anything as long as she's busy, but if she does let me know and I'll deal with it."

"If she steals anything else from me, I'll deal with it," Paula said. "I'm perfectly capable of taking care of myself."

"Yeah." Nick turned and walked back to the door, mumbling something that sounded like "And what a shame."

Paula ignored the comment. "Don't forget to tell your mama how much I enjoyed her soup," she called after him.

He just lifted a hand and waved as the door closed behind him.

"I don't know about you, but I'm not looking forward to having that brat in the store," Oria said.

"I'm not exactly thrilled about it either, but I do understand why Nick did that."

"He should have talked to you first."

If he had, she would have said no, but Paula wasn't mad about it. "We'll be fine, Oria. I'll try to get her to work off her time as quickly as possible, and you'll never have to deal with her."

"Thanks. I don't know what I'd do if I had to keep an eye on her every single second while I'm here." Oria lifted a magazine from the counter and flipped a few pages. "I didn't see my name on the schedule next week. Do you need me?"

"Only on Sunday, unless you need more hours," Paula replied.

"No, that's fine. I have just enough hours for what I want." She continued turning pages in the magazine.

"Do you need the hours this afternoon? If not, I'll take over."

"I was sort of counting on it."

"Okay, fine. Since you'll be here, I'd like to go home for a little while."

"Yeah, go get some rest," Oria said. "I'll call if there's a problem."

Paula had been so busy she hadn't found time to do laundry or leaf through her supply catalogs. After dumping a load in the washing machine, she grabbed a handful of catalogs and plopped them on the kitchen table. She poured herself a glass of sweet tea and sat down.

The entire afternoon was quiet. No phone calls or unexpected visitors. This was the first day like that since Nick came home.

❧

Nick stopped back by Paula's shop on his way to the car, but Oria said she'd left and gone home. He mentioned stopping by to see her, but Oria told him Paula was exhausted and needed some rest. So he refrained.

He had a plan when he'd ordered Amanda to do time for her crime. However, the more he thought about it, the worse he felt for not discussing it with Paula first. It was her shop, not his. He had no right stepping in and taking over like that. He just had a feeling that Amanda was a smart girl who needed a break . . . and someone who cared enough to steer her in the right direction. That person certainly wasn't her mother, who had one of the worst reputations in school. And he doubted her dad would do anything but threaten to get custody of her, which neither of them wanted.

Nick took a walk toward town, where Sam's small accounting firm had an office. He wasn't surprised when he glanced inside and saw a light on.

The door was locked, so he knocked. Sam came toward the glass door and unlocked it. "Hey, Nick, when did you get back?"

"A couple weeks ago. So how's business?"

"Couldn't be better." Sam gestured toward the pile of papers on the counter. "That's what pays the bills. How long you in town?"

Nick chatted with Sam long enough to learn he hadn't spent much time outside his office over the past year. That was all he needed to know.

"Gotta run, Sam. I saw your light on and figured I'd stop by and say hi."

"Tell your dad I'll set aside some time for him next week. He's due to send in his quarterly taxes, and I want to look it over before it goes out."

"I'll tell him."

Nick went back to his car then headed home to his parents' house. He hoped no one would be there, but his mother greeted him at the door, wiping her hands on a towel. "Why aren't you out with Paula?"

"She had some things to do." He took a couple of steps toward his room.

"What's this I hear about Amanda stealing from her shop? Did you call the police?"

He stopped and turned to face his mother. "No, Mama, I think Amanda needs something the police can't give her."

His mother's face softened, and she smiled. "You have always been attracted to hurting people. I hope you know what you're doing. I'd hate to see Paula get hurt by that girl."

"Don't worry. Paula can take care of herself. But I'll make sure nothing happens as long as I'm here."

"Are you gonna tell her parents?"

"I went by Sam's, and he was so busy I don't think he'd hear a word of it, even if I told him." He cleared his throat and glanced down at the floor. "And I'd rather not talk to Kate."

"Can't say I blame you, son. That girl has always wanted you. If she even thinks you're interested, there's no stopping her."

That was exactly why Nick had never wanted to talk to Kate about Amanda. In fact, he knew he was taking a chance simply being nice to the girl. He counted on Amanda not telling her mother about seeing him, due to the circumstances.

"Oh, Mama, I have a question."

"What's that?"

"Since when did Papa start having Sam do his taxes?"

"Since Sam offered to do them instead of having Amanda put in juvie."

"So Sam knows about Amanda?"

"Of course he does."

Nick shook his head. "This is one crazy place."

She grinned. "Yes, and we love it, Nick. So do you. You just haven't figured it out yet."

Nick waited until Tuesday to stop by Paula's shop. "Have you heard from Amanda yet?"

Paula shook her head. "Nope, not yet."

"If she doesn't contact you by tomorrow, let me know."

"Nick, I'm really not sure this is such a good idea. I'm not equipped to deal with a girl with her problems."

"Oh, but I think you are. All you have to do is hold her accountable for what she did and show her what grace is. That should come natural to you."

She smiled. "Thanks for the compliment, but this is something I don't have experience with."

"I wasn't saying it to compliment you, Paula. It's a fact. That's what attracted me to you when we first met."

Paula picked up a piece of paper and pretended to fan herself. "And all this time I thought it was my dazzling good looks and Southern charm."

"Well, that too." He grinned.

"Okay, I'll do what I can—that is, if she comes by."

"So do you want to do something with me Friday night?"

Paula tilted her head and gave him a mock coy smile. "Why Friday? Why not tomorrow?"

"No reason. Wanna go out tomorrow?"

"Why, Nick, sugah, I was thinking you might want to stop over at my place for a bite of dinnah. I can cook up somethin' real good."

He laughed and shook his head. "Are you serving grits?"

"If that's what your little heart desires."

"Okay, Paula, this is over the top, even for you."

She gasped. "I can't believe you actually came right out and said that. Where are your manners, mistah?"

Nick edged toward the door. "What time do you want me at your place?"

"Seven would be good." She batted her eyelashes and waved the paper a couple more times before putting it down.

"Are you serious about cooking, or should I bring something?"

Paula laughed. "I reckon I can handle one little measly meal."

"Yeah, I reckon you can." He left the shop laughing. "Is Alexa working today?"

"She's coming in late because she has a dental appointment."

A little after three o'clock, the bell on the front door jingled. Paula came out of the back room to greet her customer. It was Amanda. "Hi, I see you decided to grace us with your presence."

"Us?" Amanda glanced around. "Who else is here?"

Paula rolled her eyes. "Are you here to work?"

"No, I'm here to rob you blind." She bobbed her head and let out a throaty growl. "Just tell me what you want me to do so I can get it over with."

"C'mon to the back room. I have a broom and dustpan with your name on it."

"Seriously? With my name on it?"

"No, Amanda, that's just an expression." This girl really did need some attention. When Paula got to the back room, she glanced over her shoulder to make sure Amanda was with her. She picked up the broom and dustpan and handed them to Amanda. "Start at the front and work your way to the back."

Amanda took the broom. "Just put the dustpan over there, and I'll get it when I need it."

Paula knew this was a power play, but since it didn't matter she did what Amanda asked. A customer came in, and Paula waited on her. Every so often she glanced at Amanda out the corner of her eye and saw that the girl was listening to every word she said. Another customer came in, keeping Paula busy for another ten minutes.

Finally, after the last customer left, Amanda stopped sweeping and stared at her. "What?" Paula asked, realizing too late the word came out more harshly than she intended. "Did you need something?"

"Why did you open this shop?"

"I wanted my own business, and there wasn't a soap and candle shop already here."

"There are a lot of things not here. Why soap and candles?"

Paula explained how she'd seen all-natural candles in a store in Atlanta and that it made sense to be more earth friendly. What surprised Paula was how attentive Amanda was. "As for the soaps, that seemed like a natural thing to add to the mix."

Amanda nodded. "I like your stuff."

That was obvious, but Paula didn't want to talk about what Amanda had tried to steal. "Have you ever thought about what you want to do when you're older?"

18

Sometimes." Amanda held the broom at an angle. "I've thought about a lot of different things."

"Anything you'd like to tell me about?"

Paula expected Amanda to blow her off, but she didn't. "I might like to do something with old people."

That was something Paula never would have guessed. "Like what?"

"There's this lady who got my grandma her apartment, and she helps my grandma with all her doctor appointments. I think I might like to do what she does."

"So you want to help older people?" Paula thought that sounded like a very grown-up aspiration. "Do you know anything about how she got her job?"

Amanda shook her head. "I asked my grandma what that lady's job was, and she said she was a social worker."

"Did you know you have to go to college for that?"

The girl shifted her broom and cast her gaze downward. "Yeah, so I guess I better come up with something else, 'cause I'll never get into college."

"And why not?" Paula took a step closer.

"My grades are terrible, my mother doesn't have the money, my dad doesn't want anything to do with me, and who would want me anyway?"

"What grade are you in now, Amanda?"

"I'm a junior."

Paula studied her. She certainly didn't seem like the same person who'd tried to steal from her a couple of days ago. There was something different. Something vulnerable about her.

"It's not too late to turn the grades around," Paula said. "As for the money, there are scholarships and grants for people who really want to go to college."

Amanda snorted. "As if I'd ever get one of those."

"Seriously, you might if you really want it. You have to work for it, though." Paula walked back to the counter. "But maybe you don't want it enough to do what it takes."

"Yeah, maybe not." Amanda started sweeping again. Paula thought the conversation was over, until Amanda stopped sweeping abruptly. "You really think I can do it? I mean the college thing?"

"Yes, I do. But it won't be easy. You'll have to spend a lot of time with your nose in a book."

Amanda rolled her eyes. "I hate history."

"Wanna know a secret?"

"Yeah."

"So did I. And I had to work really hard to get a B in it. It seemed like no matter how hard I studied, I couldn't make an A. There was this one teacher . . ." Paula tapped her finger on her chin. "Can't remember her name, but she didn't like me at all. I tried hard to get everything right with her, but no matter what I did, I felt like she had it out for me."

"I have a teacher like that." Amanda had stopped sweeping again. "Ms. Nelson."

Paula widened her eyes. "That's the same lady. She must be, like, a hundred years old by now."

Amanda smiled. "At least. She makes us read a whole chapter in one night. It's so boring."

"I'll tell you another secret, Amanda. After I graduated from college, I went back to visit some of my old teachers."

"You went to see Ms. Nelson?"

"Not intentionally, but my favorite teacher just happened to be in the classroom next to hers. She heard me, so she came to say hi. She said she was glad I'd made something of myself because I was always one of her favorite students."

Amanda snickered. "Why didn't she ever give you an A?"

Paula shrugged. "I guess because I didn't earn one. But she knew how hard I tried."

"You should have gotten an A just for that."

"So how bad are your grades?"

Amanda thought for a minute. "Um . . . mostly Bs and Cs. One D."

"The D is in Ms. Nelson's class, right?"

Amanda nodded and cracked a smile. "Of course."

A customer came in, so Paula told Amanda to finish sweeping and they'd talk later. As Paula helped the woman find the scent she wanted, she noticed that Amanda seemed to be listening to the conversation again. After the customer paid, Paula dug out a form to start working on her next order.

"Do you think I might be able to get a C in Ms. Nelson's class?"

Paula looked up. "Probably. No guarantee, but I might be able to help you."

Amanda lifted her eyebrows. "How?"

"Why don't you bring your history book with you tomorrow, and I'll show you a few things."

"We're having a test on Friday."

"Perfect timing then." Paula smiled. "I bet we can study for that too."

Alexa came in at five. "Sorry, but I had to wait at the dentist's office. Someone came in with a dental emergency."

"That's fine, but I need to run. Nick's coming over for dinner."

Alexa grinned. "Yes, I know. Have fun."

On the way home, Paula picked up some food for dinner. Nick would eat anything she put in front of him, but since his family worked in the restaurant business, he had access to the best Greek food in town. So she figured she'd fix him something different. Something her mother used to cook—baked chicken and macaroni and cheese. Couldn't mess that up if she tried.

Nick arrived a few minutes before time to pull the food from the oven. "Mmm. Smells good." He followed her into the kitchen. "I heard Amanda came by today. So how'd it go?"

"Good to know the grapevine in Tarpon Springs is still alive and buzzing." She put on her oven mitt and paused. "You were right about Amanda. She's not as bad as I thought."

"So what did you have her do?"

"She swept."

"Is that all?" He stood at the door, filling the space with his arms folded and his feet shoulder-width apart. Paula nearly gulped as she glanced away. His attractiveness overwhelmed her at times.

"Is that all?" she repeated. "What do you want me to do to that girl?"

"Make sure she repays you for the trouble she caused." He tilted his head toward her. "And let her see how much better her life will be if she stays on the straight and narrow."

"You're such a do-gooder, Nick."

"Are you still mad at me about her?"

"I wasn't mad, just annoyed." She pulled the chicken out of the oven and checked to see if it was done before sticking it back in. "Ten more minutes."

"Well?"

Paula pulled off the oven mitt and plopped it on the counter. "I understand now why you did that. Amanda needs some guidance, but who am I to give it? I don't have experience with kids."

"You're perfect. But it's not just guidance she needs."

"Yeah, she needs hope."

"And the Lord," he reminded her.

"Well, that goes without saying."

"Is she coming back?"

Paula nodded. "And she's bringing her history book. You'll never guess who her teacher is."

"Nelson."

"How did you know?"

"The way you said it. Plus I knew she was still teaching."

"Get a load of this, Nick. I'm going to try to help her bring her grade up in Ms. Nelson's class."

"Don't you wish someone had done that for you?"

"Actually, someone did. Remember? You spent countless hours helping me remember stuff for my tests."

Nick made a face. "Yes, I do remember."

"I guess it's my turn to pay it forward."

Nick closed the distance between them, and Paula thought he was going to put his arms around her. He stopped a few feet away and opened the oven door. "I think it's done now. I'm starving."

The next morning Paula got to the shop early. Alexa was scheduled to stay until closing, but since Amanda was coming after school, Paula told her she'd be back.

"You don't have to come back," Alexa said. "I can supervise her."

"I promised I'd help her with history."

Alexa propped her elbows on the counter. "So you're helping her now, huh?"

"Yeah, the poor girl is struggling with Ms. Nelson."

"Poor girl is right. I had Nelson, and she's enough to make anyone want to drop out of school."

"I figure if I can help her get a decent grade in history, she'll feel like she can do anything."

"Isn't that the truth!"

"So I thought I'd run some errands, grab something to eat at home, and come back to take over."

"I'll stick around and take care of the store so you can concentrate on Amanda."

"Thanks." Paula grabbed her handbag. "I'll need all the concentration I can get."

The people at the Senior Center were just finishing up a covered dish lunch when she arrived. Mildred motioned for Paula to follow her to the kitchen. She pointed to a row of ceramic molds. "What do you think about having a manger scene in soap and candles?"

"It's a little late for that," Paula replied.

"I was thinking for next year."

The expression on Mildred's face melted Paula's heart. She didn't have the heart to say she wasn't interested. "I'll ask the man who makes my molds if he can come up with something."

Mildred smiled. "I thought you'd like it. We're working on the saltwater taffy candles this afternoon. Can you afford to hire one more person?"

Paula nodded. "I have an idea. Why don't I give you a budget and put you in charge of production? You can bring in as many people as you need for each project."

Mildred's eyes lit up. "I'll be a supervisor?"

"Yes. We'll have to discuss some of the legal issues of paying people by the project, but I think it'll work."

"That'll be wonderful. I always wanted to be the boss."

Paula laughed. "Now you get to do just that."

With that out of the way, Paula ran home and ate a late lunch. She got back to the shop a few minutes before Amanda came walking in, looking dejected.

"What happened?" Paula asked.

"I told Ms. Nelson I was going to study for the test, and my goal was to get at least a B."

"So what's the problem?"

Amanda rolled her eyes and sighed. "She told me I'd get a B when pigs fly."

Fury raged through Paula as she remembered how mean-spirited Ms. Nelson could be. "Tell you what, Amanda. With enough of a push, pigs can fly just fine. We're gonna get you so studied up, Ms. Nelson will see pigs flying all over that classroom."

Amanda burst into laughter. "That would be hilarious. Too bad we can't make a real pig fly."

"Maybe not, but we'll show her that no one talks to Amanda Katsaros like that and gets away with it." She took some of the books off Amanda's stack and led the way to the back room, where she'd set up a folding chair next to her desk. "Let's get all your other assignments done so we can concentrate on history."

Paula spent a half hour teaching Amanda some tricks and tips on grammar and math. "Nothing is as complicated as we try to make it," she said.

Amanda looked dazed. "This is awesome. I always wondered how the smart kids remembered all this stuff."

"Now you know. If there's not a trick, make one up. That's what I always did." She stuck Amanda's math homework back in the folder and pulled out her English. "This is where you're gonna soar. English is fun when you really get into it."

"You're kidding, right?"

"Nope, I'm serious as a heart attack."

Amanda giggled. "You are so funny." Suddenly her smile faded. "I can't believe you're doing all this for me, after what happened. My mom says you must have some sort of interior motive."

"You mean ulterior motive?"

Amanda nodded. "Yeah, that."

Paula tapped a pencil on the edge of the desk. "You know, your mom is right. I do have an ulterior motive. If your grades improve, and you make something of yourself, you won't have to steal from people like me."

"It still seems weird."

Paula smiled and wiggled her eyebrows. "I've never been accused of being normal."

Amanda laughed again.

"But I have to be honest with you about something. It was Nick's idea for you to come in here and do work for me."

"I know. I was here, remember?"

"Yeah, if he hadn't set this up, we wouldn't be here right now making you all smart and studious." Paula pulled opened the English book. "What page are you on?"

Paula was surprised at how little Amanda understood about the parts of a sentence. But after a half hour of tutoring, Amanda caught on.

"Good job. Now for the dreaded history. Let's see what we can do for you with that."

Amanda groaned and Paula made a face, pretending to gag herself with her finger. They heard a sound by the door and glanced up to see Nick standing there, leaning against the doorframe.

"Looks like the two of you are having way too much fun to be studying." He pulled away from the door, walked over to them, and looked over Amanda's shoulder. "History, huh? I hear you have Ms. Nelson."

"Yeah, and she hates me," Amanda said.

"She hates everyone," Nick said. "But there are people like that everywhere you go, so consider that part of your lesson."

Amanda looked at Paula. "You don't have to deal with people like that, do you?"

"Some of my customers can be rather difficult."

Nick offered a mock salute. "I gotta run. I just wanted to see how the two of you were doing. Call me later, okay?"

Paula nodded and waved as he left. Once he was gone, she caught Amanda staring at her with a curious expression. "Did you have a question?"

"Is Nick your boyfriend?"

19

$\mathcal{P}$aula pondered the question before looking at Amanda. "It's complicated."

Amanda leaned back, folded her arms, and smirked. "Wait a minute. You just said nothing's that complicated."

"I sure did, didn't I?"

"So it's a simple yes-no question. Either you're together, or you're not."

"We used to be . . . boyfriend and girlfriend, but, well . . ." Paula shrugged. "I went away to college, and he joined the Arm—er, Air Force."

"But he's here now, and you're all done with college." Amanda never dropped her gaze. "So what's stopping you?"

"I have my business, and he's leaving in a few weeks."

"People have to work," Amanda reminded her. "And they find ways to hang out if that's what they really want. Are you not into him anymore?"

Paula was very *into* him. Way more into him than ever. "I don't know, Amanda. Let's get back to your history so you can pass this test."

Amanda snorted. "You've got it bad." She reached for her book and held it up. "So how are we gonna get all this stuff in here?" She slapped the side of her head.

"We're gonna make a game out of it."

"A game, huh? This I gotta see. Okay, so tell me how we're supposed to play this game."

With only a few interruptions from Alexa, Paula managed to teach Amanda more history in two hours than her teacher had since the beginning of the school year. "You caught on fast, girl," Paula said with pride.

"I guess I never really thought any of this stuff was real until you explained it."

All Paula did was compare some of the historical events with Amanda's favorite TV shows. "It's very real."

Amanda picked up a pencil and tapped her chin. "When I think about all this and how people like Nick are willing to go out there and make sure I'm safe . . ." She shook her head. "I don't know, it's just so strange that no one ever talks about it."

"People do talk about it."

"Maybe grownups, but no one at school ever does."

"Maybe you can start a trend." Paula organized Amanda's schoolwork and handed it to her to stuff into her bag. "Now I have to help Alexa close up shop. Are you coming back tomorrow?"

"Nah, I think I'll go home after school and study on my own."

They stood, and Paula placed her hand on Amanda's shoulder. "You're a very smart girl, Amanda. Don't let anyone else tell you otherwise."

"What am I supposed to do when they try?"

"Nothing. They're just tryin' to get your goat."

"My what?"

"They just wanna get you all riled up. Don't let them do that. Hold your head high and know they're the idiots for sayin' stuff."

"First you have pigs flying, and now you have goats." Amanda snickered. "You are too funny."

"And you are very smart," Paula said with a grin.

Amanda stared down at her feet for a few seconds before reaching over and hooking Paula in her arm. As Paula hugged her, something strange fluttered inside her.

Amanda abruptly pulled away and grabbed her books. "Gotta go now." She took off, leaving Paula standing there wondering what all the strange feelings were floating around in her chest.

The bell on the front door jingled, signaling Amanda's departure. Paula went out to see how Alexa was faring. "How's business?"

Alexa lifted an order form. "You just got another wholesale order from the West Coast."

"As in California?"

Alexa nodded. "Apparently one of the big suppliers out there can't keep up with the natural candle and soap orders, so they're having to scramble to find a new vendor. Apparently, they heard some good things about us from another outlet."

"Amazing." Paula glanced at the order. "Are you serious?" The numbers were more than double her last big order.

"Positive. In fact, as always, I had her repeat the numbers just to make sure, then I read them back to her. She said they have shops in LA, San Francisco, and San Diego."

"This is insane," Paula said as she read the order. "I'm gonna have to hire even more people."

Alexa grinned. "I thought you might, so I called Mildred and she said everyone wants more hours, and there's already a waiting list of more people who want to work."

"How did I ever manage without you?"

"I don't know. I'm wondering the same thing." Alexa laughed.

"Seriously, girlfriend, you're amazing."

"Someone needs to tell my mother and Aunt Ophelia that."

"Maybe you're not cut out for the baking business. I think you're a natural here, though."

The bell on the door jingled again, and Steph came walking in, a grin covering half her face. "I heard about your order, Paula. That is terrific!"

Paula gestured toward Alexa. "She gets the credit for taking this order." Then she frowned. "How do you know already? I just found out myself."

"I was at the Senior Center when Alexa called Mildred. They're over there celebrating."

"Celebrating?"

"Are you kidding?" Steph said. "You've just given all those people a chance to do some of the things they couldn't afford to do until you hired them."

"Alexa's idea." Paula turned to Alexa. "You are absolutely incredible. Until you spoke up about the Senior Center folks working for me, there was no chance of growing my business much bigger than it was. But now . . ." She lifted her hands. "The sky's the limit."

Steph winked at Alexa. "Good job, cousin." She tilted her head as a pensive look washed over her face. "Now I need a job."

"I could use you a whole lot more here," Paula said.

"That's what I was hoping you'd say." She gave a thumbs-up. "Think you can manage another ten hours a week?"

Paula laughed. "At least that much with all this production we have going on. I appreciate being able to use the Senior

Center, but I have a feeling that won't last forever, since it's supposed to be for the community."

"I can try to find a place if that would help."

"That would be great, Steph. With Alexa handling wholesale orders and you being my facilities person, there's no way we can fail."

~❧~

The next morning Nick's mother greeted him with a cup of coffee and a scowl.

He looked up. "Did I do something wrong?"

"You need to be more aggressive with Paula."

"Huh?" He rubbed his neck with one hand and cleared his throat as he stirred his coffee with the other hand. "What brought that on?"

"She's too busy being a businesswoman because you're not spending enough time with her."

"What's wrong with her being a businesswoman? You are."

"I know, but if her business keeps going like it is, she'll never be able to quit."

"Mama." He shook his head and took a sip of his coffee. "I would never ask her to quit. She loves her soap and candle shop."

"Apparently you haven't heard the latest. She just got another big wholesale order, so she's having Steph scout out new locations for a factory."

"I'd like to think of that as a good thing."

His mother made her clucking noise then mumbled a few words in Greek. "Nick, you're not getting any younger. If you want Paula to marry you, it's time for you to make your move before it's too late." She scowled again. "And I'm not just talking about window shopping for rings at the mall."

Nick lifted his eyebrows. She had spies everywhere. "Who said anything about marriage?"

"Oh, come on, Nick, I wasn't born yesterday. I know the look of love when I see it."

He put down his coffee, glanced at the headlines in the *St. Petersburg Times*, then turned back to her. "So tell me more about what I should do."

She held up one finger. "For starters, you should do everything you can to sweep her off her feet. Then you need to let her know how you feel, deep down." She made a fist and tapped her chest. "Then you need to promise to be a good husband."

Nick managed not to laugh. "Is that what Papa did?"

"Well . . . not exactly, but you don't want to do what he did."

"What exactly did he do?"

Mama frowned. "You don't wanna know. It doesn't matter anyway. Paula is different. She's a modern woman who needs a man to show how he feels."

Nick understood exactly what his mother was saying. His father had never been a man of words. In fact, he couldn't remember his dad ever coming out and telling his mother he loved her. But everyone, including Mama, knew he loved her with his entire being.

"So after I do all this, what if she isn't ready to commit to a lifetime with me?"

Her lips twisted as she thought it over. "I don't know."

"There are some big obstacles here, ya know."

"Of course I know that, Nick. But she won't say yes if you don't ask."

"I have a better idea. Why don't I try to spend more time with her while I'm here, and then I'll invite her to visit me on the base." He already planned to do this, but he wanted Mama to think she'd helped him come up with the idea.

"She won't go."

"And why not?" Nick asked.

"Paula loves her shop too much. I don't think you'll ever get her to leave unless there's incentive."

"Oh, I think I might be able to now that she has Alexa and Steph to help her run the place."

His mother pursed her lips then smiled. "Maybe so. I guess it's worth trying."

Oh yeah, it was definitely worth trying. He changed the subject while he ate the eggs and toast she put in front of him. After he helped her clean the kitchen, he got ready for his day of wooing Paula.

The first place he went was her shop. Alexa greeted him and told him Paula wasn't due in until afternoon. "I think she's still at home, so why don't you try her there?"

He went to Paula's house next, but she wasn't there either. Instead of running all over creation, he pulled out his cell phone and tried calling her, but she didn't answer. He decided to try one more place—the beach beside the church.

Nick recognized her silhouette from a distance as he turned onto the road leading to Crystal Beach. Watching her, his heart thudded as he remembered all the times they'd sat together on that very same bench, talking about their hopes and dreams for the future. Funny how neither of them actually came out and talked about marriage, but he always assumed it would happen someday. But if he didn't act soon, it might not.

He pulled into the shell-covered parking spot near the bench. Her body stilled, letting him know she was aware of someone behind her, but she didn't turn around—even after he started walking toward her.

"Paula," he said softly.

She lowered her head then slowly turned to face him. He couldn't read her.

"Is everything okay?" Nick stopped and waited for a sign that it was okay to get closer.

Paula nodded. "Couldn't be better." But she didn't smile or invite him closer.

"Mind if I join you?"

"That's fine." She turned back and faced the water. "So much has happened lately, I needed a little time to regroup."

"Oh, okay." A sense of relief flooded him. "I hear you just got another big wholesale order."

"Yeah. I didn't expect it."

"It sounds good, though. Business is thriving."

"For now, anyway."

"You sound worried." He sat down on the other end of the bench, not sure of how much space she needed.

"I don't know how long this will last. It's a lot harder than I thought it would be. If I expand too fast, it might implode, but if I don't expand at all I'll never know how successful it might be."

"So you're basically expecting the other shoe to drop." Nick should have realized this. After all, Paula had experienced one disappointment after another from the moment he'd first met her. When something good happened, something bad always followed.

"Yeah, I guess."

"Well, maybe things have changed, and it'll only get better."

The downward slope of her shoulders said she didn't believe that would ever happen. Since he knew it was futile to try to convince her otherwise, he decided to change the subject.

"So how's our little friend Amanda doing?"

Light flickered in Paula's eyes as she turned to him. "That girl is very smart. I spent some time helping her study for

English, math, and history, and she managed to catch on very quickly."

Nick nodded. "She did seem smart." Then he snickered. "But more than that, she was a smart aleck."

"Oh, she's definitely a smart aleck. I'd hate to get into a battle of words with that one."

"For the first time, you might have met your match," Nick said.

Paula frowned. "What's that supposed to mean?"

"It means that you're better with words than anyone else I've ever known."

"Until now," Paula said with a hint of a smile. "Now we have Amanda."

He scooted closer to Paula, and when she didn't say anything he closed the distance. She leaned into him and sighed.

His cell phone rang, and Paula pulled away. When he looked at the number, his heart thudded. "It's your shop."

"You better answer it then. I left my phone in the car."

As soon as he flipped open his phone, Alexa didn't bother waiting for him to say anything. "Is Paula there?"

"She's right here. Why?"

"I need to talk to her now."

Nick handed the phone to Paula. "Alexa wants to talk to you."

"What's going on, Alexa?"

"Amanda's here."

Paula glanced at her watch. "She's supposed to be in school."

"I know. You really need to get over here right now. It's serious."

"I'll be right there."

Paula jumped up. "There's an emergency with Amanda."

"I'll follow you," Nick said as he headed for his car. As soon as they were on the main road, Nick called the shop. Alexa told him she couldn't talk at the moment because someone very important needed her help. He knew that meant Amanda was standing there next to her. "Don't let her leave until we get there."

"Oh, trust me, that won't happen."

Paula pulled into the lot behind the shop then took off running without waiting for him. By the time Nick made it inside her store, Amanda was in Paula's arms, sobbing.

"I promise, I didn't do it," she kept saying.

Nick frowned and looked at Alexa, who motioned for him to follow her into the back room. Once there, she whispered, "She made an A on the history test, and Ms. Nelson accused her of cheating. She's been suspended from school."

20

"Where's her mother?" Nick asked.

"She went to the school, signed the papers, then kicked her out of the house."

Nick rubbed the back of his neck. He had no idea what to do to help this girl.

"Nick!" The sound of Paula's voice snapped him out of his thoughts.

Alexa nodded toward the front of the store. "You better go see what Paula wants."

As soon as Paula saw him, she shook her head. "Someone has to talk to the people at the school. That old . . . Ms. Nelson has no right to accuse anyone of cheating, just because they did well on a test."

Amanda's shoulders shook as she continued sobbing. "I should have known better than to get all smart and everything."

"You didn't just get smart, Amanda, honey. You've always been smart. It's just that some people are too blind to see past their noses." Paula put her arm around her and rubbed her back. "We're gonna help you through this." She glanced up at Nick. "Aren't we?"

He had no idea what he could do, but he nodded. "Yes, absolutely."

Paula glanced back and forth between him and Amanda a few times before she finally settled her gaze on him. "Why don't I stay here with Amanda, and you try to talk to her mother?"

Nick wasn't sure how wise that was. Kate Katsaros had been trying to get with him since high school, and until now he never had a reason to say more than a few words to her. But he couldn't very well let Amanda or Paula down.

"Okay, but don't expect a miracle."

Amanda sniffled and rested her head on Paula's shoulder. Nick felt an unfamiliar tug at his heart. He placed his hands on both of their shoulders and bowed his head. Paula lowered her head, but Amanda simply stared at him.

"Lord, we pray for mercy on those who have falsely accused Amanda of cheating. Guide us as we try to resolve this . . . situation. I pray that my words to Amanda's mother Kate are uplifting and pleasing to you, Father. I also pray that every-thing will be okay at the school. We pray this in the name of Jesus. Amen."

When Nick looked up and saw the twinkle in Paula's eye, he felt another flutter in his chest. Amanda's eyes were round and curious. He suspected she'd never heard such an intimate prayer before, and he vowed he'd do whatever he could to change that.

"Okay, I'll go find Kate. Any idea where your mother might be, Amanda?"

She nodded. "I think she's taking the rest of the day off, so she's probably at home." She gave him the address.

Dread washed over Nick as he thought about going to Kate's house alone. But he couldn't very well back out now.

He left Paula and Amanda at the shop and drove to the edge of town, where rows of smaller houses lined the street. A glance at the address confirmed what he suspected. The house with the peeling paint and overgrown lawn belonged to Kate Katsaros. The shiny red sports car in the driveway confirmed that she was home.

He parked behind her, got out, and took a deep breath. Might as well get this over with. He trudged up to the front door and knocked. A few seconds later Kate flung it open.

A slow grin spread across her face. "So what brings you to the ghetto, Nick?"

His jaw tightened. "I'd like to talk to you about Amanda."

Her smile tightened into a scowl. "My daughter is none of your business."

"Your daughter is hurting right now, and she needs someone to listen to her."

"You know what she did, right?" Kate tilted her head and planted a fist on her outthrust hip. "That girl had the audacity to cheat on a test and get caught. How stupid is that?"

"She didn't cheat." Nick felt the tremor of fury, so he took a step back. How could a mother accuse her own daughter of something so awful without giving her the benefit of listening?

"How do you know? Were you there?"

"Not at the school, but I did see her studying hard for the test."

Kate narrowed her eyes and glared at Nick. "You've been with my daughter lately?"

"Calm down, Kate. There's some stuff I need to tell you, and it's gonna take a while." He nodded toward the door. "Mind if I come in?"

She hesitated a second before taking a step back. "Okay, but I'm not sure how much talking you'll have to do to convince me my daughter didn't cheat. I know her a whole lot better than you do."

The inside of her house was much nicer than the outside—the opposite of the woman herself. Plush furniture and lots of pillows made the living room very cozy. Very intimate. And very romantic. "Can we sit at a table?" he asked.

Kate laughed. "Yes, of course."

Once they sat down, Nick told Kate about Paula catching Amanda shoplifting. She slammed her fists on the table as she stood.

"Why didn't someone come to me then?"

Nick inhaled deeply and pointed to her chair. "Sit back down, Kate. I think she wanted to get caught."

"That girl is sending me to an early grave. I've told her to stop stealing, but does she listen to me?"

"Amanda needs you to listen to her, Kate. When was the last time the two of you sat down and had a calm mother-daughter conversation?"

"It's impossible to be calm with a cheating thief."

Nick thought about how Jesus dealt with the thief on the cross. He wanted to share his faith with Kate, but if he started that right now it would seem like he was preaching at her. Better to let Kate see Christianity in action.

"I've seen firsthand how well Amanda responds to attention. Paula has been tutoring her in several subjects, and she's doing much better in school. In fact, that's the problem. Ms. Nelson assumed she cheated because she actually studied and made a good grade on the test."

Nick paused to let Kate process the information. Her jaw clenched, but she nodded. "Go on. Tell me everything I don't know about my daughter."

He explained how Amanda had been working off her crime when Paula agreed to help her with her schoolwork.

"Why would Paula do that? Most people call the cops."

Nick shrugged. "Paula's different."

"You can say that again." Kate rolled her eyes. "I never understood what you saw in that girl."

Anger flared in Nick, but he tamped it down. "I'm not here to discuss my feelings for Paula. This is about Amanda."

"Mind if I have a cigarette?" She reached for the pack on the edge of the table.

"I'd rather you didn't."

Kate gave him an odd look. "No one has ever said that to me before."

"What's the deal with Amanda not being able to come home?"

She shoved the pack of cigarettes away and folded her arms. "I told her if she was so smart, she could make it on her own." Kate shook her head. "But she knew I didn't mean it. I say stuff like that all the time. When she gets all high and mighty, I tell her to go out there and find a way to take care of herself."

"So you're saying you didn't kick her out?"

"Not really. I might have said something to that effect, but she knows I didn't mean it. I just needed some time to cool off."

Nick stood up, placed his hands on the back of the chair, and leaned forward. "Sometimes you have to accept the word of those you love."

"That girl has lied to me since she said her first words. Why should I start believing her now?"

"Kate, have you ever taken Amanda to church?"

"You sound like my mother."

Nick's frustration swelled, and he couldn't deal with her anymore. "Okay, I see that you're not listening to anything I'm saying. If you want to see Amanda and listen to her, you'll probably be able to find her at Paula's shop or my parents' house, where I'm taking her if you don't come and get her."

Kate didn't respond. As she sat there staring down at the table, Nick left and headed to his parents' house. He figured he should give his mother a heads-up that they might need to get another room ready for a guest.

"You know I don't like to interfere in another family's business, Nick," his mother said as she took off toward the guest room, defying her own words. She opened the door and started stripping the bed. "I have to wash these sheets since no one's slept here in months." As she bundled up the sheets, she mumbled about how Cletus would be furious with her for letting a thief sleep in their house. "I can't very well let a young girl sleep on the streets, though, can I?"

"Mama, you're wonderful," Nick said. He planted a kiss on her cheek. "I gotta go tell Paula now. I hope we can get this thing resolved. Kate really needs to put her own personal issues aside and find a way to relate to her daughter."

When he arrived back at Paula's shop, Alexa was there alone. "Paula and Amanda went to the high school."

"Why?"

"Paula called the principal and told him she'd been helping Amanda study. Ms. Nelson denied that anyone could catch up so quickly, so Paula challenged her. The principal agreed to let Amanda take another test on the same material in a room alone."

Nick wondered how Amanda felt about that. "I sure hope it works out."

"Yeah, me too. Amanda threatened to throw the test, since no one ever believes her anyway." Alexa snickered. "Paula lit into her so hard Amanda didn't know what happened. I have a feeling Amanda won't get a word in edgewise all the way to the school."

"I think I'll go see my dad and come back in an hour or so. Call me if they get back before that."

Alexa nodded. "This is gonna be a very interesting day."

⸙

Paula felt like she'd been talking to a wall. Amanda kept saying she would throw the test, in spite of the fact that this was the best way to vindicate herself. When they got to the school, Paula turned to her and said, "If you throw this test, Amanda, you're not as smart as I thought you were. Wouldn't it be better to show everyone how mean-spirited Ms. Nelson really is and how she accuses people without knowing what she's talking about?"

Amanda just looked at her without responding. They walked into the school together in silence. Ms. Nelson waited in the principal's office wearing one of her vintage smirks and a suit to match.

Forty-five minutes later, Amanda walked out of the tiny room behind the principal's office grinning. When Ms. Nelson and the principal took off with the test to grade it, Amanda gave a thumbs-up. Paula sighed with relief.

It didn't take more than fifteen minutes for Ms. Nelson to grade the test, but she didn't come back to the office, where Paula and Amanda waited. Instead, the principal handed Amanda the paper with a huge, red "100%" written across the top.

"Good job, Amanda," he said. "I apologize for what happened. You've obviously studied very hard for this test, and I made a big mistake." He looked down then back up at her. "I'd like for you to come back to class tomorrow."

Amanda opened her mouth, but Paula put her hand on Amanda's arm and shook her head. "Not so fast. I want you to move her out of Ms. Nelson's class."

"But—"

"You don't really think she'll be able to go back into that . . . Ms. Nelson's class and actually learn anything, do you?"

The principal steepled his fingers and nodded his head. "You're right. I'll see what I can do." He smiled at Amanda. "Come in here first thing in the morning, and I'll have a new schedule for you. I'll try to keep as many of your classes intact as possible, unless there's something else you want me to change."

Amanda's eyes flickered for a second before she shook her head. "That's the only change I want."

"Good. Would you like for me to call your mother?" he asked.

Once again Paula spoke up. "Yes, why don't you call her now and let her know we're on our way to her house?"

As they walked to the car, Paula chuckled. "You had me scared there for a while, girl."

"Why?"

"All that talk about throwing the test."

"I was just talking smack. When you said I could show how awful Ms. Nelson really was, there was no way I could throw the test." She paused when they got to the car. "Paula?"

Paula paused with her hand on the door. "Yes?"

"Thank you for doing all this."

"You're welcome, but you don't think you're getting away without paying me back, do you?"

Amanda grinned as she slid into the front seat of Paula's car. "I've swept your floors and studied my brains out. What more do you want from me?"

"A promise that you'll never steal again—from anyone—and for you to go to church with me."

Amanda scowled. "I don't know about the church thing."

"So you're scared of church, huh?" Paula challenged.

"I'm not scared of anything."

"Then what's your problem?"

Amanda looked down at her clasped hands then met Paula's gaze with the most vulnerable look Paula had ever seen on her. "I've never been to church before. What will I have to do?"

Paula reached for Amanda's hands and squeezed them. "Nothing hard. Just sit next to me and do what I do."

"Are they gonna call on me and ask questions and stuff?"

"No, it's nothing like that. What we do at our church is sing worship songs, read Scripture, and listen to a message about how much God loves us."

"That's not what Mom said. She told me they try to make people feel bad for having fun."

Paula wasn't about to tell Amanda how bad her mother was. "Maybe we should invite your mother to go with us."

Amanda tilted her head back and laughed. "Now that's the funniest joke I've ever heard."

"I'm serious."

"As a heart attack?"

Paula looked over at Amanda and winked. "At least. Maybe more."

When they got to Amanda's house, her mother wasn't home. Paula was disappointed, but she didn't want to show it.

"Wanna go back to the shop now?"

Amanda looked out her window and shrugged, but she didn't say anything. Paula had a pretty good idea of how she felt, and she ached for the girl.

When her phone rang, she pulled it out of her handbag. It was Nick.

"Hey. I'm at my parents' house with Amanda's mom."

Paula felt sick to her stomach, but she didn't want Amanda to know, so she took a deep breath before talking to Nick. "I have Amanda. Want us to come there?"

"That's what I was hoping for."

"We're headed there now." Paula flipped her phone shut and turned the car toward Spring Bayou. "Amanda, honey, I want to warn you. We're going to Nick's parents' house."

"So?" Amanda still faced the window.

"Your mother is there with Nick."

Amanda's head snapped around so fast it startled Paula. "What?" she shrieked. "What is she doing there?"

"Don't ask me. Nick just told me she was there, and he wants us to come over."

"I don't want to go to Nick's parents' house."

Paula pulled over again and put the car in park. "Amanda, I know how much you're hurting right now, but you need to take the high road in this relationship with your mother."

"What are you talking about?" Amanda slumped down in the seat as if she could make herself invisible. "My mother hates me."

"She doesn't hate you." Paula pondered what to say then decided to just speak her mind. "I used to think my own mother hated me too, but Nick reminded me that she worked hard to make sure I had a roof over my head and food on the table."

"At least she didn't kick you out."

"No, you're right, she didn't. But *she* ran away a few times."

Amanda turned to face her head-on. "Your mother ran away? Are you serious?"

Paula smiled through the pain she'd dredged up. "Yep. When my mother hit her boiling point, she took off—sometimes for days." Paula forced herself to continue in spite of the sick feeling in her stomach. "When she got back, she acted like she'd never left. I learned to pretend . . . and to take care of myself."

"That's crazy." Amanda frowned. "So what did you do?"

Paula lifted her hands. "I did what any self-respecting teenager would do. I ate cookies for supper and stayed up late on school nights."

Amanda rolled her eyes. "Did she always come back?"

"Yep. And she never even mentioned leaving. It was strange, but I eventually accepted this about her. In fact, if we went more than a couple of months without her taking off, I wondered if I'd done something wrong."

"Your life was crazier than mine is."

"You can say that again." Paula turned back to her steering wheel and put the car in drive. "So let's go see what's going on with your mom and try to make some sense of all this."

"Is that possible?"

Paula hesitated for a moment then shook her head. "Probably not, but we can at least give it a try."

21

Kate was having coffee with Ursa Papadopoulos, laughing and chatting. As soon as she looked up and saw Paula and Amanda, her smile turned to a scowl.

"What are you doing here?" she asked, focusing her attention on Paula. "I thought I was just going to see my daughter."

Nick stepped in the door behind Paula and Amanda, and when Paula didn't say anything, he spoke up. "I asked Paula to come in with Amanda. She's been beside your daughter through all this, and I didn't want anyone to forget that."

Kate smoothed the side of her very tight jeans and flipped her hand. "Whatever." Her gaze moved to her daughter, and her lips quivered into a smile. "So you really are smart, huh? Who would've figured?" She extended her hand to her daughter. "You must have gotten your brains from your father."

Amanda tensed, and Paula wanted to reach out and hold her. But she didn't. This was something Amanda needed to deal with—to confront head-on.

Nick stood behind Kate and gestured toward the door. Paula nodded and followed him. He turned and looked over his shoulder. "Coming, Mama?"

She wiped her hands on a dishrag and frowned. "But—"

"Mama, I really need to show you something. Now." The tone of Nick's voice was commanding. His game voice.

Once they were out of the kitchen, Nick's mother shook her head. "I'm not sure it's such a good idea leaving those two alone. Kate is a very bitter woman, and Amanda is such an innocent girl."

"Not so innocent, Mama," Nick reminded her. "Don't forget she stole from Papa and Uncle Arthur . . . and Paula."

"She's just a child."

Paula studied her. What she wouldn't give for a mother like her.

Nick placed his hand on his mother's shoulder and looked her in the eye. "In two years, she'll be a legal adult, and dealing with her demons now might keep her from paying a much bigger price for her actions."

His mother looked at Paula, who nodded her agreement. "I suppose you're right, Son. It's just so hard for me to see something like what's going on in there. You don't think Kate would hurt Amanda, do you?"

"She's already hurt her, Mrs. Papadopoulos," Paula said. "In the worst kind of way."

The older woman pulled her lips between her teeth as her eyes glistened with tears. "I wish there was something I could do."

"Let's see how things work out. Kate did tell Amanda to leave. She says she talks like that all the time but doesn't mean it."

"That's terrible."

"I don't think it's the worst thing in the world," Nick said. "Sometimes people need a break to appreciate the ones they care about."

Seizing the opportunity, Nick's mother smiled and nodded. "I have the bed in the guest room ready. You and Paula can go to her house and help her pack."

Paula was still hung up on Nick's last sentence. Her break from Nick had lasted years.

Nick chuckled. "Mama doesn't miss a beat, does she?"

"You better believe I don't. With kids like you and your brother, I had to stay on top of things."

"And you were very good at it." Nick paused before turning to Paula. "I wonder if Papa would be interested in hiring Amanda to work part-time."

"I don't think so," his mother said. "He's trying to cut back."

"I can probably give her a few hours if she really wants a job," Paula said. "Not many, though, and someone else will have to be there when she works."

Nick nodded. "That's fine. I just thought it would be a good idea for her to have something to look forward to after school, since her mother isn't home."

"Want me to ask her?"

"Let me talk to Kate first," Nick said. "I want her to be okay with it before we bring it up to Amanda."

Mrs. Papadopoulos decided to check on Kate and Amanda. "They might need some food."

Nick suppressed a grin, but Paula couldn't hold back a laugh.

Nick gestured toward the kitchen. "Then you better go find out before they starve to death."

His mother swatted at him with the dishtowel she'd been twisting then headed toward the kitchen. When they heard her clicking her tongue, Paula cast a puzzled glance in Nick's direction.

He smiled. "That's a happy sound. C'mon, let's go see what's going on."

In the kitchen, Paula saw Kate and Amanda smiling at each other. A strange mix of relief and anger flooded her. She was happy to see Amanda smiling, but she knew it was temporary. Kate was too needy to always put Amanda first, so the next time a problem came up, Amanda would have farther to fall.

"Looks like everything is fine now," Nick said.

Kate beamed. "I'm so proud of my daughter. She really is smart."

Nick shifted his weight from one foot to the other. "Hey, Kate, can we talk for a minute?"

Kate pointed her thumb toward herself and lifted her over-arched eyebrows. "You wanna talk to me?"

He nodded. "Privately."

Paula saw Kate's smirk as she stood up and followed Nick out the door, prissing the whole way. When she looked at Amanda, she saw that the girl was studying her.

"You know my mother thinks Nick is cute," Amanda said.

"A lot of people think Nick's cute," Paula replied, trying hard to keep the sarcasm from her voice.

"Just wanted to make sure you knew that."

"Thanks."

"Any idea what he's talking to her about?"

Paula shrugged. "Maybe, but I don't want to say until they come back."

Nick and Kate were gone for about fifteen minutes, but it seemed a lot longer. Amanda lit up when her mother returned.

"Hey, Amanda, how would you like to earn your own money?" Kate asked.

Amanda looked puzzled. Paula glanced over at Kate and Nick, who both nodded.

"I need someone to help out a few hours a week at the shop, and I wondered if you'd be interested."

Amanda's eyebrows shot up. "You want me to work for you? But—" She looked at her mother then cast her gaze downward.

"Are you gonna take this job or not?" her mother said. "In this economy, I don't see how you can turn something like this down. A good job is hard to find." She forced a shaky grin at Paula then turned back to her daughter with an equally forced stern look. "If you earn your own money, you can buy whatever you want without having to come to me for a handout."

When Amanda looked back up, tears were streaming down her cheeks. Paula wanted to comfort her, but she held back. It was her mother's job.

"Why are you being such a crybaby?" Kate asked. Paula noticed the corners of her mouth twitching into a smile, but she managed to keep it under control. She lifted her hands in mock surrender. "If you don't wanna work, just say so."

"But I do."

Kate rolled her eyes, laughing. "Teenagers." She glanced at Paula. "Are you sure you want to deal with this?"

At that moment, Paula had never been more sure of anything in her life. "Positive. We'll start out with just a couple of afternoons a week, after school. If you like the job, maybe we can give you some Saturday hours."

Amanda's tears quickly dried up, and she broke into a wide grin. "I'm gonna have a job. A real live job."

"Better get used to it," her mother said. "It's something you're gonna have to do for the rest of your life."

Paula cleared her throat. "One thing I'll have to insist on, though, is that you keep your grades up." Since Kate didn't mention it, she figured someone needed to. "You can come right after school and do your homework in the back room before your shift. I'll set up a desk and lamp."

All eyes were on Paula, but she focused on Amanda. "I want to be there when you work your first few shifts. After you get the hang of it, I'll probably have Alexa be your direct supervisor."

They remained in the kitchen chatting for another half hour until Kate looked at her watch. "I better get home. Bill might call."

"Who's Bill?" Nick's mother asked.

"My boss." Kate grinned. "We've been flirting since I started working for him, and he finally got the nerve to ask me out."

"Do you think that's such a good idea?" Mrs. Papadopoulos asked. "What if things go bad? Won't it be hard to work for him?"

Kate shrugged. "There are other jobs." She cackled. "Maybe Paula will think about hiring me."

Not in a million years. Paula smiled and remained silent. Out of the corner of her eye, she saw Nick's lips twitching in amusement.

After Kate and Amanda left, Mrs. Papadopoulos moped around the kitchen, preparing supper. Paula cast a puzzled glance toward Nick.

"What's wrong, Mama?"

"I was looking forward to having a house guest. I miss having young people staying here."

"Michael needs to visit more often with his kids," Nick said.

"That's what I tell him. You'd think St. Petersburg was on the other side of the world, as much as I see him."

"You know how the restaurant business is, Mama. Being the manager of his father-in-law's seafood place is a seven-day-a-week job."

"I know, I know," she said as she closed the oven door. "Maybe I can pull your father away from his sponges for a day so we can go see him."

"That's a great idea," Nick agreed. "When was the last time you and Papa took a drive?"

She shook her head. "It's been a long time."

Paula stood up to leave. "I guess I better get going too."

"Why don't you have supper with us?"

"I have to go to the Senior Center and check on some things, but thanks anyway."

"I'll walk you to your car." Nick placed his hand on the small of Paula's back. "I'll be back in a few minutes to help you set the table, Mama."

◈

Nick had never loved Paula more than he did at that moment. She was always kind to everyone, but it was obvious her heart had grown even bigger.

"Thank you for what you did. Because of you, Amanda has hope."

"No," she corrected him. "Because of God, Amanda has hope." She looked at him with soulful eyes. "Nick, you know what I went through at her age. Without Christ, no telling where I would have wound up."

"Ya know, it's amazing how your mother was the one who brought you to church that first time—and she never went back."

"It was totally a God thing that kept me going."

"Just like when you and I met. Without you, I don't think I'd lean on the Lord like I do."

"Don't give me credit for that, Nick."

"See? That's what I'm talking about."

Paula laughed. "We need to keep praying for Amanda and Kate. I don't think their problem has disappeared as easily as it seems."

"Oh, I'm sure." He rested his arm on her open car door. "Are you working tomorrow?"

She snickered. "What do you think? Alexa has singlehandedly made sure I'll be working my tail off for the rest of my life."

"And you're lovin' it."

"Absolutely. The shop is my dream." She glanced down at the ground then back up at him. "Just like the Air Force is yours."

Nick watched her for a few seconds before tucking his fingers beneath her chin and lifting her face to his. "Paula, I don't know if this is a good time to say it, but I don't care anymore. I love you, and I want to do whatever it takes to be with you."

He felt himself go numb as silence fell between them. Finally, she swallowed and pulled away. "Nick, this isn't a good time to talk about us."

"When is it a good time?"

Her shoulders sagged. "You're going back to Texas soon, so I'm not really sure it's ever a good time."

"I won't accept that. There's still something between us, and you know it as well as I do. We're too old to act like teenagers."

She pulled her lip between her teeth as she met his gaze. Then she lifted her keys and jangled them. "I really need to go now. Why don't you call me and we can get together next weekend or something?"

Nick felt helpless when it came to Paula. On the football field, he'd been in control. With other women practically throwing themselves at him, he knew he could call the shots. But with Paula, the earth constantly shifted beneath him.

"I have a better idea. Why don't we make plans now?" Nick paused then added, "I'll pick you up Saturday around six o'clock, and we'll drive over to Tampa. Wanna go to Bern's Steakhouse?"

She smiled. "Now you're pulling out the big guns."

"I'll do anything it takes, Paula. I just want you back in my life."

"Okay, six o'clock is good, but we don't have to go to Bern's."

"I'll take you wherever you wanna go. Just name the place."

"Bye, Nick. See you Saturday." Without another word, Paula got in her car and pulled away from the curb. He stood there and stared at the street, long after she'd gone.

When he went back inside, his mother clicked her tongue again. "You've lost your touch, Nick. I thought you might convince her to stay for supper."

"My charm never worked all that well with Paula."

"Oh, but I disagree. She was the one who picked you, remember?"

He nodded. "But her technique was different. More intelligent."

"That girl is very smart," Mama agreed. "Don't let her get away."

"We have a date Saturday night. I plan to pull out all the stops."

"Good boy." She pointed toward the cabinet. "Get some water glasses and put them on the table. Your father called and said he's on his way home."

The next morning Paula hopped out of bed before the alarm went off. The night before, Mildred had shown her the schedule for production. The woman was organized to a fault.

"I don't want anyone working too many hours," Paula reminded her. "The job is repetitive, and I don't want folks burning out."

Mildred laughed. "Trust me, burning out on candle making isn't gonna happen here."

Paula grinned. "You're doing a great job."

"What's this I hear about you hiring a high school kid to work at your store? Do you think she'll be able to do the job?"

Word sure did travel fast. "I need another pair of hands in the shop for just a few hours a week."

"I could've done that."

Obviously, Mildred didn't know the full details about what had transpired. "But I need you here."

Mildred placed her hands on her hips and nodded. "Yeah, you're right. Without my organization, this whole operation would fall apart."

"I wanted to talk to you about the new locations we're considering."

Paula spent an hour discussing what they needed to make the candles and soaps. At first Mildred balked at moving from the Senior Center, but Paula said she'd continue donating money for their cause. That seemed to satisfy her.

On her way to the shop, Paula's mind raced with all the changes. She'd never envisioned having more wholesale business than retail. Having retail customers was fun and interesting, but the wholesale orders paid the bills and enabled her to help other people.

When she arrived at the shop, she made her way from the back to the front. A few minutes after she unlocked the front door, the bell jingled and she glanced up.

"Hi, Paula." Kate walked toward her as though on a mission. "You and I need to clear the air."

22

Paula braced herself for a tongue-lashing. She'd never forget the time Kate lit into her back in high school, letting her know she was playing out of her league with Nick.

She plastered on a smile. "What's up, Kate?"

"My daughter. Something has come over her, and I want to know what you did."

"What I did?"

Kate bobbed her head. "Yeah. What have you done to her?"

Paula's shoulders tightened. What happened to the happy woman she'd talked to yesterday? Was this a threat? She couldn't tell. "Um, I've just been helping her study."

"After we got home, I told her to come clean. She gave me the details about when she got busted trying to swipe some stuff from your shop." Kate glanced around the store then turned back to face Paula.

"I thought we cleared this up yesterday," Paula said.

"Yeah, but you and I both know that was all for show. For Nick and his mother. Now it's just me and you. Why didn't you call the cops when you caught Amanda? You had every right."

Paula stared at Kate in disbelief. This was a conversation she never expected to have. "As far as I know, she didn't get away with anything. She came clean and didn't try to deny what she'd done."

A look of pride flickered across Kate's face. "My daughter might be a thief, but at least she's honest."

"And smart too," Paula reminded her.

"That's what I wanted to discuss with you. Why are you doing all this for Amanda? What do you want from her?"

Paula glanced down at the counter as she pondered what to say. She couldn't very well mention that Amanda reminded her of herself when she was younger. Kate never tried to hide the fact that she always thought Paula was a loser. Finally, she looked Kate in the eye.

"I saw something special in Amanda. There's a spark of intelligence that let me know she had something going on. I think she might have wanted to get caught because she's smart enough to have gotten away with a few candles and soaps."

Kate bobbed her head. "Yeah, her father was always pretty smart, and I'm not stupid. I guess she comes by that from both sides."

"Thank you for agreeing to let her work for me."

Kate snorted. "You've always been a little weird like that. I'll probably never understand why you would want a thief working in your store."

"I don't think, deep down, that she's a thief."

"Either you're being naïve, or you see something no one else can. Her father and I have beaten ourselves up over what to do about that girl. He wanted to send her away to a camp for bad girls, and he certainly has the money to do that, but I didn't want her to be around other kids who could teach her more bad stuff."

Paula could imagine Sam Dunbar wanting to get rid of his daughter. After all, everyone but Paula knew she was his daughter, and if she continued getting into trouble, it might hurt business. Suddenly, an idea flickered through her mind. This might be a good time . . .

"How would you feel about Amanda going to church with me sometime?"

"Church? Get real. You're kidding, right?" She flapped her hand. "If those church people find out she's my daughter, they'll probably toss her to the street."

"No, they'd never do that."

"So you think church is the answer, huh?" Kate chewed on her bottom lip. "I doubt Amanda will agree to go to church with you or anyone."

"That's one of the things I told Amanda I wanted her to do to make up for trying to take stuff."

"I don't know." Kate flipped her hair over her shoulder. "We've never been all that churchy."

Paula smiled. "Being churchy isn't required. Besides, there are some nice kids who go there."

"If they're the ones from school, they won't have anything to do with her."

"Maybe not. A few of the kids go to Tarpon Springs High School, but since it's in Crystal Beach, most are from Palm Harbor University High School. I think she'll make friends."

Kate frowned as she thought about it. "I don't know. You're asking an awful lot."

"You don't have to make a decision right now. The offer will always be open."

"Okay . . . thanks." Kate walked around the store, picked up a candle and sniffed it, then put it back down. She glanced over her shoulder at Paula with a curious expression.

"How would you like to go to church with me?" Paula blurted.

"Now I know you've lost your mind. Are you insane?"

Paula shrugged. "Maybe."

"Why would you want to be seen with me? Won't your church friends get upset, knowing you brought the town bad girl to a holy place?"

"It's not like that at all." Paula came around from behind the counter. "Besides, most people there don't know you."

Kate flicked her wrist again and grunted. "I'll never understand any of that church stuff. Besides, God will probably faint if I show up in church."

"Oh, I think God will be happy to see you there."

"Why would you ask me to go, Paula? Are you trying to set me up for something? I mean, I wasn't exactly your best friend in school."

"We've been out of school a long time, Kate. I'm over it."

Kate snickered. "Yeah, I guess you are." She turned over a candle, studied the price tag, then put it back down.

Paula decided to give Kate some time to think rather than try to persuade her to go. "It's up to you, Kate. I'd love to have you be my guest at church, but I don't want to force it on you."

"Tell you what," Kate said. "I'll drop Amanda off at your house on Sunday morning, and she can tell me about it later."

"Okay, that's fine," Paula said. At least now Kate trusted her with Amanda. "Now I have a question for you."

Kate looked leery. "What?"

Paula pulled one of her new candles out from behind the counter. "I've been working on some new scents, and I'm still undecided about this one."

"Let me take a whiff." Kate lifted the candle to her nose, closed her eyes, and inhaled. Paula held her breath until Kate opened her eyes and smiled. "It smells delicious. What is it?"

"It's a blend of lemon and vanilla. I wasn't sure if it was the right balance."

"I think it's perfect. When will you have it for sale?"

"Not for a few months."

The disappointment on Kate's face touched Paula.

"Too bad." She tried to hand the candle back to Paula.

"Keep it. I made a batch of them in different molds, so I have more."

Kate lifted her eyebrows. "Are you sure?" She dropped the candle into her bag. "How much do you want?"

"It's a gift."

"Nothing's free. What do you want from me?"

Paula understood exactly where Kate was coming from, and she didn't want to step on her pride. "I just appreciate your opinion. Consider it payment for that."

Kate hesitated before nodding. "Okay, thanks." She glanced at her watch. "I guess I better run. I'm supposed to be picking up some doughnuts for the office."

After Kate left, Paula rehashed their interaction. Something had changed between them, and she was relieved.

A while later Nick stopped by with lunch. "Uncle Apollo wanted me to bring you this."

Paula opened the bag. "Yum. Spanakopita."

"So I hear Kate paid you a visit this morning."

She laughed. "Nothing gets by you, does it?"

"Not if it happens on the sponge docks. Is everything okay?"

Paula nodded. "She was checking me out to make sure my intentions were good for her daughter."

"That takes a lot of nerve after what happened."

"I don't know. I think I would have done the same thing if I'd been in her shoes. In spite of the way she behaves, she loves Amanda."

Nick tilted his head and narrowed his eyes. "She loves her so much she told her to get lost."

"Yeah, that does seem rather drastic," Paula admitted. "They have somewhat of a tumultuous relationship, don't they?"

"Oh yeah."

"I bet there's other stuff we don't know about—at least not yet. Amanda still has some mighty rough edges."

"You're probably right. I'm sure you'll get it out of Amanda eventually. You're good at doing that."

"Grandma used to say guilt was the biggest torture, and it would eventually get people to talk," Paula said.

"Your grandma was smart."

"Yes, she was very smart." So smart she'd managed to keep her daughter from leaving her husband as long as she was alive. Less than a year after they buried Grandma, Paula came home from school one day and discovered her stuff packed in a car. Her mother informed her they were moving to Florida—without Dad.

"So how did your visit with Kate go?"

Paula shrugged. "I think okay. She's dropping Amanda off at my place on Sunday before church."

Nick lifted one eyebrow. "So you're taking Amanda to church? Are you sure you wanna do this?"

She looked him in the eye. "Yeah, why not?"

⟞⟍

Nick knew exactly what was going on. Paula saw herself in Amanda, and she wanted to do the same thing for the girl that someone had done for her. Only with Paula, it happened at a much younger age—at a more malleable time of her life.

"Want me to pick both of you up?"

"No, I think it would be better for me to take Amanda, just the two of us. Besides, I'm kind of hoping Kate might decide to join us."

"You're kidding, right?"

"Nope. I asked her if she'd like to go."

Nick chuckled. "And what did she say?"

"She seemed to think I'd lost my mind."

Nick was inclined to agree with Kate, but he'd also known Paula long enough to understand what she was doing. "I guess miracles do happen."

"Yes, and you're looking at one."

Maybe so, but in his eyes she was more of an angel who came into his life when he needed her. Before Paula, Nick felt like he could have whatever he wanted, but nothing made him happy. Once they started seeing each other, he didn't want as much, and everything made him happy. That hadn't changed as long as he was with her.

"So do you want me to get there early and save seats for you and Amanda?"

Paula looked around her shop then turned to face him. "That would be nice."

"Would you like to hang out afterward?"

She laughed as she tucked a strand of hair behind her ear. "Let's just play that by ear, okay?"

"Okay." It was obviously time for him to leave. He backed toward the door. "See you on Sunday."

Paula smiled and nodded. "Since Amanda hasn't been there before, maybe you should pick a spot somewhere toward the back. I don't want to make her nervous by sitting too close to the front."

Over the next few days Nick tried to put Paula out of his mind, but that was impossible. The harder he tried, the more her image popped up in his head. He loved her now more than ever, and he knew nothing else in the world mattered more to him than being with her for the rest of their lives. The problem was he only had a couple of weeks left in Tarpon Springs before he had to return to his base in Texas.

True to his word, he saved a seat for Paula and Amanda. He remembered to sit near the back of the church—but not the very back. He kept glancing over his shoulder, waiting for Paula and Amanda. When he spotted Paula leading the way toward him, his heart did a double thump. And when he saw Amanda and Kate right behind her, he almost fell off the seat.

"Hi, Nick," Kate said as she squeezed into the pew. "I bet you're surprised to see me here."

He didn't want to lie, so he just smiled and said, "Hi. I'm glad you could come."

They were lined up in the pew—Nick, Amanda, Paula, and Kate. From a stranger's perspective, they probably looked like a group of happy friends. However, Nick remained stunned as he noticed Paula guiding both Amanda and Kate through the service. He tried to help with Amanda, but Paula was so quick he didn't have to do anything but smile.

After church, Kate shook her head. "I never realized church was like this before. Thank you for talking me into coming. The music was actually very nice."

"You were ready for this," Paula told her, then turned to Amanda. "So what do you think?"

"Can I come back next week?"

"Yes, of course," Paula replied. "Nothing would make me happier than for both of you to continue coming to church."

Nick had no doubt that she meant every word of it. He was about to ask Paula to come to his mother's house for lunch, but she announced that she wanted to treat Amanda and Kate to lunch at the Lucky Dill Deli in Palm Harbor.

"Would you like to join us?" she asked.

He thought for a moment before shaking his head. "Mama is expecting me. Besides, I'm sure the three of you wanna talk girl-talk, and that's just not my thing."

Paula gave him a curious look. He winked and smiled.

"See you tomorrow?" she asked.

"Sure. I'll stop by the shop in the morning. Maybe we can make plans for later in the week."

Paula waved as he left. Before he exited the church, he glanced over his shoulder and saw Paula introducing Kate to some other women. Amanda was a few feet away talking to a couple of kids her age. Yes, Paula was a miracle worker, he thought as he drove home.

Nick had no idea how to do it, but he had to act fast or he'd lose out on Paula. His mother noticed him picking at his food.

"Girl trouble?" she asked.

"Not really." He stabbed some of the lamb then slowly chewed it as she continued staring at him. Finally, he put down his fork and looked her in the eye. "Actually, I need some advice."

She looked pleased as she pulled out a chair and sat down. "It's about time. What can I help you with?"

He opened up to his mother about his confusion over what to do about Paula. She listened and nodded. It had been a long time since he'd poured out his feelings to her, and it felt good.

When he finished talking, her eyes glistened with tears as she reached for his hand. "You can't rush this, Nick."

"Rush it? But I thought you . . . well, I've loved her for years."

"Yes, I know, but you haven't been together for so long. Why don't you do things differently this time after you leave?

Before you leave, tell her you're not giving up. Then send letters, call her, and visit more often."

He nodded. "I can do that."

"Give her time to gather her thoughts and know you mean business."

Nick laughed. "I absolutely do mean business."

She finally stood up and started clearing the table. Nick helped load the dishwasher. "If you don't have anything else for me to do around the house, I guess I can go help Aunt Phoebe with some more of the stuff she said Uncle Apollo's been too busy to do."

No matter how hard he tried, Nick couldn't stop thinking about how to convince Paula they should be together. Phone calls and letters seemed too easy. The next morning, he forced himself to wait until she had a chance to open the shop before he went to see her.

"How'd it go yesterday?" he asked.

"Amazing. Kate was totally open about everything, and Amanda loved church. She recognized a couple of the kids from school, and one of the boys actually came up and talked to her after you left."

"Amanda's a cute girl."

Paula nodded. "She has a fun personality too, once she lets down her guard."

They discussed the changes in Kate and Amanda for a few minutes before Nick managed to turn the conversation to the two of them. "I only have a little time left here, and I'd like to spend as much of it as possible with you. You need to understand that I plan to show you how much I care about you, Paula." He glanced down then looked back into her eyes. "I don't want another of my days here in Florida to go by without seeing you at least once."

Silence fell between them. His heart felt like it would jump out of his mouth. She finally nodded. "I'd like that."

Nothing was concrete besides the fact that they'd see each other every day before he went back to Texas. At least he had that.

⁕

A piece of Paula's heart went out the door with Nick. To her dismay, she loved him now more than ever, but she needed to remember that he was about to disappear again. She might not have been able to turn him down, but she could guard her heart in the time he had left in Tarpon Springs. Enough people had let her down before, and she couldn't expect anything to change.

23

*P*aula pulled out her favorite dress then changed her mind. Nick had said he wanted to take her to Bern's, but she didn't want to go to such a romantic place right before Nick left. She'd suggest Crabby Bill's instead.

She pulled on some jeans, a tank top, and over-shirt then stepped into a pair of espadrilles. She tucked her hair behind her ears and put on her standard makeup—a dusting of powder, a touch of blush, some mascara, and tinted lip balm. After a close look in the mirror, she decided to add a little more color to her lips. Then she was ready to go.

Nick showed up on the dot as always. "Been waiting long?" He looked her up and down and grinned. "I guess we're going casual tonight, huh?"

"I guess."

"Care to clue me in? Tonight I want everything to be all about you."

Paula leaned away from him and shook her head. "Okay, what's up, Nick? What's going on? Are you planning to blind-side me again with talk of marriage?"

"Maybe."

"You know how I feel. It's pointless to talk about something you can't follow through with."

A forced goofy expression washed over his face. "Are you saying you don't trust me?"

She sensed that she might have hurt his feelings, and he was trying to cover it up, so she playfully put a finger on her chin and gave him a goofy look right back. "That's open for discussion."

"Seriously, where would you like to go?"

"I'll give you a clue. They have the best baked oysters in the world."

"Crabby Bill's, huh?"

"Hey, you're good."

"You need to give me a harder clue next time. I'd sort of hoped to impress you more. You sure you want to go there?"

"Why wouldn't I be impressed by Crabby Bill's?" She gave him a teasing look.

"No reason. They do have good food."

Nick held the passenger door open for her then slid behind the wheel of the Town Car.

"I remember the first time we ever went out to dinner you took me to Crabby Bill's in Clearwater."

A slight grin played on his lips. "And I remember your reaction to baked oysters." He mimicked her "eww" sound and laughed.

"How was I supposed to know how good they are?"

"Good point. I suppose you needed someone to teach you about the finer things in life."

Paula thought about that for a few seconds and nodded. "Yes, you did teach me about a lot of the finer things in life."

"I didn't mean that like it sounded."

"I know, but you really did teach me a lot, Nick. My mother never had the money or the time to take me out to eat. In fact, she didn't even believe in cooking dinner every night. She said it got old very fast."

"That always baffled me," he said. "At my house, I could set the clock by dinnertime."

"Our backgrounds are so different I'm amazed we ever got together."

Nick put both hands back on the steering wheel. "I think that might have been some of the attraction—our differences, that is. I used to watch you and be amazed at the way you processed information. You saw things I never even noticed."

"And you were always so rock-solid steady. I'd never met anyone like you before."

He laughed. "I guess you and I were the heads of each other's fan clubs."

"I think you might have been the only member of mine. Everyone used to wonder what you saw in me."

"That's crazy. My family thought I was dating way out of my league, and they were thrilled about it. I think Mama was happy you came along and saved me from the Kates of the world."

"Speaking of Kate, did you know she's been in to talk to the pastor?"

"I'm not surprised, since you're involved."

Paula frowned. "What's that supposed to mean?"

"You have a way of getting people to see the important things in life. So do you know what they talked about?"

"According to Amanda, mostly her. The pastor convinced Kate that Amanda would get so much more out of church if the two of them went together."

"I agree," Nick said. "What does Kate think about it?"

Paula shrugged. "As far as I know, she's agreed to do it. She really loves her daughter."

"Why would she kick Amanda out of the house if she loves her so much?"

"Oh, that's another thing. I finally got Amanda to talk about it, and that was only half the story. Apparently, Kate was being truthful when she told us Amanda knew she wasn't really getting kicked out. They argue a lot, and when Kate gets really mad at her, she tells her if she's so smart, she can just leave and go take care of herself. This time, Amanda said she was gonna do it, and Kate pointed to the door."

"I can't imagine a mother telling her child to do that, even if she doesn't mean it."

"Maybe you can't," Paula said, "but I can."

"I don't remember your mom telling you to leave."

Paula leaned her head back and scrunched her face. "She's the one who always left, remember? My mom ran away from home more than any teenager I ever knew."

Nick nodded.

"Anyway, they had a fight, Amanda called her mom's bluff, and she hightailed it to my shop to tell on her mother, knowing she'd get some extra attention."

"So it was just harsh words spoken in the heat of an argument." Nick shook his head. "I should have figured that. You do realize Amanda manipulated you, right?"

"Yes, of course. I might be a bleeding heart, but I'm not blind. I recognize the need for attention when I see it."

He changed the subject. "So I'm glad my cousins are working out so well. Alexa seems to be in her element."

"Alexa is definitely in her element. She can run that place without me there. I have complete and total trust in her. She and Steph both have been lifesavers."

Nick smiled. "I'm glad, because according to the family rumor mill, Alexa's goal in life is to take your business international, and she's been working on some ideas."

"She does have some great ideas." International, huh? Paula had never dreamed that big, but it sure sounded good.

They were seated right away at Crabby Bill's. "Looks like we beat the crowd," Paula said. "Last time I drove by, there was a line out the door."

As soon as the server took their order, Nick propped his forearms on the table and leaned forward. "We need to talk about where we're going."

"Where *we're* going? You mean where *you're* going. I'm not going anywhere," Paula reminded him.

"I'm talking about with this relationship."

She shrugged. "I think the fact that you're leaving soon and I'm staying here makes that a moot point."

Nick smiled and leaned back. "Not necessarily."

"Long-distance relationships are hard," Paula said. "And I don't think that's such a good idea anyway."

"I don't want to keep talking about the same old thing."

"Then why do you keep bringing it up?"

"I think we can work through the problem, Paula. Where we live is just a place. You and I belong together. I think you know that as well as I do."

Paula couldn't deny she often thought that. She lowered her gaze and lifted her shoulders in a half-shrug.

"What if I decided not to reenlist when the time comes? I can come back to Tarpon Springs for good."

She looked up and met his gaze. "Would you be happy, though? Seriously, Nick, as much as you love the Air Force? We've already talked about that enough."

"At least you got it right this time," he said.

"What are you talking about?"

"Air Force. You used to say Army."

"Whatever. I don't think you'd be happy stuck in Tarpon Springs, working for your dad, no matter how many compromises we make."

Nick held her gaze for several seconds before he slowly nodded. "Paula, if I can have you, I'll always be happy, no matter where I am or what I'm doing."

The thought of Nick staying more than appealed to her, but she couldn't hold him back from his dreams. "No, I don't think that's such a good idea. You don't need to pin all your happiness on me. That's too much pressure for both of us, and you'd wind up resenting me and Tarpon Springs."

"Are you willing to at least give us another try, or do you just want to end it all right now?"

"Whoa." Paula fidgeted with the corner of her napkin. "You don't beat around the bush, do you?"

"I think we're past all that."

"True."

"Then answer me. Are we over for good, or do you think there's any hope for us?"

Paula wasn't about to lie, even if it meant baring her feelings to the one person who could still hurt her. Since he'd laid his feelings on the line, she looked him in the eye and blurted, "I never quit caring about you, Nick."

The corner of his lip twitched, but he didn't smile. "Does this mean what I hope it means—that one of these days we just might . . . well, you know . . ."

She propped her elbows on the table, folded her hands, and rested her chin on her hands. "If you're asking if we might wind up living happily ever after, it doesn't look possible, but . . ." She looked into his eyes. "I guess we can still see each other when you come to town."

"How about coming to see me in Texas?"

"That might be more difficult. I have a shop to run, remember?"

"Yes, and you have some key employees who can take over in your absence. You even said Alexa can run the place without you."

Paula pointed a finger at Nick. "You're right. I did say that."

"I might consider coming for a short visit," she said softly.

"That's all I needed to hear." Nick's grin widened, and her resolve all but melted away.

❧

Paula was always smart, but Nick saw right through her tactic of steering the conversation back to his family, the shop— anything but their relationship or her feelings. Even though they started with the same old argument, she gave him a little more hope each time they were together. And he understood. After growing up the way she did, she was used to feeling abandoned. She wasn't about to put herself in that position again, which was why she didn't want to leave her business in someone else's hands and put her life completely in his.

Every now and then he caught Paula watching him, but when he looked her in the eye, she would glance away. She'd once told him that he was the only person who had a clue what she was thinking.

After dinner they drove to Crystal Beach and walked on the path that ran between the water and the church. They talked a little, but when silence fell between them, Nick felt the strongest connection.

They were almost at the end of the path when Nick stopped, turned Paula toward him, and pulled her close to his chest. He felt a slight bit of resistance, but she relaxed as he wrapped his arms around her. This felt right. Paula had always fit him so well, and that hadn't changed.

When she sighed, he knew it was a sign to release his grip, but he didn't let go completely. She leaned back and looked up at him, a silly grin on her face.

"What?"

She snickered. "Ya know there's a fine line between hugging and holding on so tight the other person can't escape."

He lifted an eyebrow with a challenging gaze. "Are you trying to escape?"

"Maybe."

"Want me to let go?"

She scrunched her face and shook her head. "Nah, I didn't say that."

"So are you saying you like hugging me?"

She bobbed her head. "If I tell you, where's the mystery?"

"Oh, trust me, Paula, with you there's always plenty of mystery."

"C'mon," she said as she pulled away, still holding onto one of his hands. "Let's head on back. I'm done with this walk."

He wanted to think that was all she was done with. As he held the car door, she stood on her tiptoes and gave him a quick kiss.

He grinned down at her. "What was that all about?"

"You just look so kissable I couldn't resist."

"Now that's something I need to practice."

"Don't. You'll lose some of the charm."

He tweaked her nose. After he closed the door and got into the driver's seat, he turned to her. "Where to now?"

"How about some ice cream at Strachan's?"

"Your wish is my command."

He got back on Alternate 19 and headed south. A few minutes later, he pulled into the parking lot and found a spot by one of the wooden cows.

"I miss stuff like this," he said.

"I can imagine." She hopped out of the car and waited for him to walk up to the tiny ice-cream shop. After she told him what she wanted, she glanced out the window. "Why don't I go save us a seat at a picnic bench outside?"

The girl behind the counter smiled. "You and your wife make such a cute couple."

Nick opened his mouth to set her straight, but the only thing that came out was, "Thanks."

"What would you like?"

He ordered two double ice-cream sundaes with everything. Paula hopped up to open the door for him then rubbed her hands together. "That looks yummy!" She grabbed her sundae, put it on the picnic table, and glanced at his. "Copycat."

"I know. I didn't want to get something different because you always make yours look so good."

Nick knew Paula was doing everything she could to keep things light, and he suspected this would continue for the duration of his time in Florida. As she chattered with her cute, funny quips, he knew he would never stop trying to prove that he was what she needed.

Suddenly, mid-sentence, she stopped. "You haven't been listening to a word I said, have you?"

"I'm hanging on every word."

"No, you're not. What did I just say about this caramel sauce?"

Nick thought before saying, "You said you like it."

"See? I knew you weren't listening. I didn't say anything about the caramel sauce."

He put down his spoon, lifted his hands, and laughed. "Busted."

"At least you still fess up."

"But only after I'm caught." He lifted his spoon. "You have to admit this is excellent caramel sauce."

"The best." She licked the back of her spoon before refilling it with ice cream.

"Mama asked if we could stop by later. She said she has a present for you."

"A present?"

"She made another batch of baklava."

"If I keep eating all that baklava your mother sends home with me, I'm gonna get fat."

Nick looked back and forth between her nearly empty ice-cream bowl and her. "I don't think you have anything to worry about."

She shoved her bowl away. "Okay, in that case, I'm done messing around with ice cream. Let's go to your parents' house for some serious baklava."

When they arrived at his parents' house, Nick's dad was outside whacking at some shrubs. "Need some help, Papa?"

"Nah, I'm just about done. Your mama's been after me to trim the yard, so I left the store early."

"I would've done it if she'd asked," Nick said. "It's late. Why don't you let me take care of this tomorrow?"

His dad stopped, smiled at Paula, then looked at Nick. "Sometimes wives want their husbands to do things just to show their love. I think this is one of those things. Your mama never was one for flowers, but she's crazy about me when I do yard work." He lifted the clippers and took a few whacks before pausing again. "It helps to keep the romance alive."

"Interesting," Nick said before lowering his voice to a whisper only Paula could hear. "But a little strange."

"Not really," Paula whispered back. "That's called love language."

"Love language?"

She nodded. "There's a book about it."

"So this is a book you like?"

Paula shrugged. "I guess. The pastor mentioned it during a sermon, so I got it. I read it one day when business was slow. It's pretty interesting, if you like that sort of thing."

Nick made a mental note to buy that book. He needed every advantage he could get.

24

The clerk handed Nick the bag. "I hope you enjoy the book. I had my husband read it, and it's made a huge difference in our marriage."

Nick tucked the bag under his arm. "Thanks. That's good to know."

He left the bookstore and headed back to his parents' house, hoping to get to his room without having to stop and chat with his mother. He wanted to start reading right away, just in case the book had some sage advice he needed to take before he left.

He'd nearly made it to his room when he heard his mother's voice. "Nick, I've been looking all over for you."

He turned to face her. "Did you need me to do something?"

"That woman Kate has been calling."

Nick groaned inwardly. He wasn't in the mood to fend off advances of a delusional woman.

"You need to call her back. I think it has something to do with Amanda."

He nodded. "Okay, Mama. I'll call her in a few minutes."

"Whatcha got there?" She pointed to the bag.

"Oh, I just bought a book. I figured it would be good for some of my alone time." He held his breath, hoping she wouldn't ask specific questions about it.

"Good idea. I'm glad you like to read. You'll never be bored as long as you have a book."

As she turned to leave, he felt his muscles relax. That was a close call.

He wanted to start reading his new book, but instead he found Kate's number and called her. To his surprise, she didn't offer even a hint of flirtation. Instead, she got right to the point.

"Amanda's been so difficult since she became a teenager. I just wanted to thank you for everything, Nick."

"Paula's the one you should thank."

"Yeah, I know. I figure what's been happening is payback for how I was when I was Amanda's age."

"Amanda's fine," Nick said.

"Now I'd like to pay you and Paula back for being so helpful."

"You don't have to—"

"I know, but I want to," Kate said. "It's nothing, though— just a helpful hint on relationships. Don't let her get away. You and Paula were meant to be together."

"Uh . . ." Nick was speechless. He didn't expect something like this.

"Oh, and Sam and I have been talking. Ya know, he's a decent guy. Back in high school, I managed to lure him to the wild side for a night, but I never dreamed he'd ever be interested in me later."

"So what are you saying, Kate?"

Her eyes seemed to twinkle. "Each time we get together to talk about Amanda, we wind up talking about us. I think we might just have something special."

Nick tried to hide his surprise. "That's awesome. Good for you."

"You and Paula deserve to be happy, Nick, so don't ever give up on each other."

"Thanks for the advice, Kate. Have a good day."

After he hung up, he thought about Kate's words. At first he didn't think she'd changed, but now he realized that she had matured.

He pulled his book out of the bag, flopped over on his old bed, and started reading. No wonder Paula liked it. There was quite a bit of wisdom in the pages. By the time he finished reading he knew exactly what he needed to do.

Nick freshened up and went to the kitchen to let his mother know he'd be back late. "I'm going to spend some time with Paula before I leave."

"I thought you were giving her some space."

"Changed my mind. I'd rather see if there's anything I can do to help her around the shop."

Mama smiled and tweaked his cheek. "Smart boy. Let her know what she'll be missing if she doesn't take you back."

Shaking his head, he snorted. "Can't pull anything over on you, can I?"

"As Paula would say, not in this lifetime."

Paula glanced up at the sound of the bell on the door in time to see Nick walking toward her, apparently on a mission. "Hey."

"You look nice today," he said as he pulled a bouquet of flowers out from behind his back. "I brought you something."

Paula smiled and took the flowers. "How nice. Thank you."

"Is there anything I can do around here to help out?"

She cast a curious glance at him. "What do you mean?"

He followed her to the back room, where she grabbed a tall glass and filled it with water at the sink. "Anything need fixing? Do you need some extra hands?"

She turned around and shook her head, the curious expression still on her face. "No, everything is just fine. Why?"

He took a couple of tentative steps toward her and reached for her free hand. "I want my last few days in Tarpon Springs to be special."

Paula stood transfixed, not knowing what to do or how to react. Nick was always attentive, but something seemed different. "Okay. Maybe we can do something tonight after I check on some things at the Senior Center."

"Want me to go with you?"

"Nick, what is going on? Why are you acting like this?" She pulled her hand away from his, turned, and walked toward the front. He followed. She placed the flowers on the counter then spun around to face him. "Who are you and what have you done with Nick Papadopoulos?"

He folded his arms and set his jaw as he stared at her, looking like he wanted to say something but wasn't sure how to say it.

"Just tell me," she urged.

Nick lifted his hands in surrender. "Okay, so I went out and bought that love languages book you told me about."

She grinned. "And you read part of it, right?"

He nodded. "Yeah. I tried to figure out which one was yours, and I can see a little bit of all of them, so I thought I'd try everything."

Paula tried to hold back the laughter, but she couldn't. He looked hurt. "I'm sorry. If you'd asked, I could have told you."

"But I thought—" He rolled his eyes and grinned. "I want to make you happy, Paula."

"Quality time is my love language."

"I sort of thought so, but I wasn't sure."

"So you decided to tell me I look nice, give me a gift, offer your services, and touch me to cover all the bases."

"Yeah, pretty much."

"I have to admit I'm flattered you'd go to all that trouble for me."

"You know I think you're worth it, Paula."

They stood there looking at each other for a while until he closed the distance between them. He didn't utter a word as he lifted her fingertips to his lips and dropped a kiss on each one. She glanced down at the floor to gather her thoughts. Through a hammering heart and swirling emotions, she slowly looked up at him.

"Please don't try too hard, Nick."

"I don't want to risk not having you in my life, Paula. You mean everything to me. All you have to do is say the word and I'll give up the Air Force when it comes time to reenlist."

"Stop. I've been thinking about visiting you, and I can't very well do that if you get out of the Air Force."

His eyebrows shot up. "Are you serious?"

She nodded. "But I don't know when yet."

"That's fine. I'm just glad you've been thinking about it. We'll make it work, Paula. I'll—"

She held up a finger to stop him. "One thing at a time."

The warmth of his satisfied smile filled the room. Paula remembered her first physical attraction to Nick, and she had to stifle a gasp. She'd never be immune to this man.

"I promised Papa I'd deliver something to his buddy in Tampa tonight. Wanna go with me?"

Paula was tempted to turn him down, but she stopped herself and nodded. "Yes, that would be nice. Where in Tampa?"

"Hyde Park. We can grab a bite to eat in Channelside afterward."

"Sounds good."

"What time can I pick you up?"

After they made arrangements, Nick left the shop, and the tiny space was instantly devoid of energy. Paula closed her eyes, remembering some of the old times they had together. No matter what she'd been through with her mother, as soon as she was with Nick, all was right in her world.

She spent more time on the phone with large wholesale orders than with retail walk-ins. When Alexa arrived, she took over the phone orders.

"We might want to have a separate division for wholesale orders," she said after getting off the phone with a West Coast customer. "Sometimes it's difficult to handle walk-ins when I'm talking to a long-distance client."

"I've already got the Web guy working on the online order form, so it should get a little easier," Paula said. "Tell me your thoughts on phone orders."

Alexa explained a plan that sounded like a good one. She'd obviously put quite a bit of thought into it.

"Would you like to head this up permanently?" Paula asked. "Since it was your idea, I figured it would make sense to put you in charge of it."

Alexa beamed. "I'd love to."

"Ya know, I've been thinking about all you've done for this business, and I believe it's time to give you a raise."

"You don't have to do that. I like working here."

"That doesn't mean you shouldn't get paid for bringing in more business. Without you, Alexa, we wouldn't have half the orders on the books."

Tears sprang to Alexa's eyes. "And without you, I'd be a loser. I never caught on to the whole baking thing, but I love what you have here."

Paula nodded. "You're definitely in your element. I'm going to get with Charlene and see what we can do."

Alexa grinned. "It's funny how my sister is your accountant. I always thought she was the successful one in the family, and I was just along for the ride."

"Well, in my book . . ."—Paula planted her fist firmly on her hip—". . . you're both winners. She's good with numbers, but no one is better than you with customers, both retail and wholesale."

Alexa's whole face glowed. "Thank you for saying that."

Customers started coming in, and soon Amanda arrived after school.

"Homework?" Paula asked.

Amanda made a face and nodded. Paula pointed to the back room, where she'd set up the desk. Amanda rolled her eyes but headed on back good-naturedly. An hour later, she appeared on the sales floor.

"All done?"

Amanda shrugged. "I'm having a little trouble with some math, but I did everything I understand."

"Then come on. Let's go see what we can do about getting you all smart with math again. Alexa, we'll be out in a few minutes."

Once Paula explained the first problem, Amanda was able to do the last three. "You make it seem so easy."

"Well, isn't it?"

"You should've been a teacher," Amanda said as she wrote down the last answer.

"No, I'm right where I should be. I'm afraid if I was a teacher, I wouldn't have any hair left by now."

Amanda giggled. "You are so funny. Can I start working now?"

"Of course." Paula paused and narrowed her eyes. "Are you sure you're done with your homework?"

"Positive." Amanda lifted her hands. "I promise. I have a history test on Friday, though, and I plan to study hard."

"How's your new teacher working out?"

"So much better. She's actually nice."

"Good."

After Paula was sure Alexa and Amanda were okay on the sales floor, she left for the Senior Center. Mildred had everyone on task, and a couple of the ladies had brought snacks, which made the men very happy.

"So how's it going, everyone?" Paula asked.

George Perkins glanced up and lifted a chocolate cupcake. "This is the best job I ever had."

Mildred waved him off. "You'd like digging ditches if someone fed you." She turned to Paula. "Honestly, these people will do anything for food and something to supplement their Social Security."

Paula laughed. "As long as they're happy, I'm good. You're doing an excellent job, Mildred."

The woman grinned as a pinkish color spread up her neck and over her face. "I love working for you. We all do. Our kids even like it since you said we can each have a candle every week. My daughter loves your stuff."

"Our stuff," Paula reminded her. "If you don't need me, I'll leave you to what you were doing."

Paula couldn't believe how well everything was running without her. She didn't know if she should feel bad about not being needed, but she was actually happy.

She called Nick and told him she could be ready early, so he said he was on his way. When he arrived, she flung open the door.

"You look mighty happy," she said as she stepped outside and locked the door behind her.

"That's because I'm with you."

25

*P*aula tried her best to have fun, but knowing Nick would be gone soon dampened her joy. They made the delivery then headed to Channelside, where they had dinner at Tina's Tapas.

"Not hungry?" Nick asked as she nibbled at her food.

She shook her head and pushed her plate away. "Sorry."

"I'll just get them to box it up for us. Ready to go back?"

Paula didn't want to go home, but she nodded anyway, her pent-up feelings confusing her. Lately her whole life was so off-kilter—with both good and bad things happening. Actually, everything was good except the fact that Nick was leaving.

Nick didn't make small talk. Instead, when they were in the car heading back to Tarpon Springs, he finally spoke. "When can you get away to visit me in Texas?"

"How about after the first of the year?"

She watched his profile as he thought about it and nodded. "Makes sense, with the holidays coming up soon. I'm sure your business will boom."

"It already is, thanks to Alexa."

When they stopped for a light, he turned to Paula. "At least having her and Stephie there will give you some peace of mind when you come to see me."

"Yeah, there is that."

"Mama told me to invite you over for the family get-together before I leave. Wanna join us?"

Paula pursed her lips and shook her head. "No, but tell her thanks."

Nick drove her home and walked her to the door. She knew he was hoping she'd invite him in, but she was so miserable she wanted to be alone. Strange how the reason for her sadness centered on his leaving, yet being with him made it worse.

He walked her to the door and dropped a feather-soft kiss on her lips. Her legs nearly gave way beneath her, but she leaned against the door.

"See you around," he whispered. "I'll wait here until you're safely inside."

After unlocking the door, she slipped inside and turned the bolt. She waited until she heard the sound of his car pulling away before turning on the light.

Paula moped around until she was too sleepy to stay awake. When she awoke the next day, she felt like she was simply going through the motions of living.

The next several days brought more misery. Nick stopped by the shop each day, but on the day he was due to leave, he didn't show up. She'd given Alexa the day off to spend some time with Nick. Amanda stayed with her until closing.

As they locked the door, Amanda touched Paula's arm. "I know how hard this is for you. If you need to talk, call me later, okay?"

Paula had to bite back the tears in front of her young employee, but the second Amanda took off she let the flood-gates open. She sobbed all the way home. Nick was probably on his way to the airport, and she wouldn't see him again for at least a couple of months.

After four nights of very little sleep, Paula ached all over. She'd cried at night until she had no more tears. Each morning, she lived on coffee until her stomach rumbled. She ate barely enough to keep going. All her clothes had started to sag on her.

Paula couldn't avoid looking Alexa in the eye anymore. Alexa's eyes bugged. "You have got to quit doing this to yourself, Paula. Nick loves you, and you love him. I don't see the problem."

"Um . . . yeah, I guess you don't." Paula sniffled and looked down. "It's complicated."

"You're both stubborn. And you're both in terrible shape."

"Oh, I'm sure Nick's fine."

"I don't think so," Alexa said. "He kept biting our heads off the night he left, so Uncle Cletus took him to the airport early."

"Sorry."

"Nick said the same thing you just said. It's complicated. But how complicated can it be, really? People fall in love all the time, and they find ways to be together. You and Nick have always had something special. I've never known any two people who are more meant for each other than you guys."

Paula forced a smile. "Thank you, but it's still not that simple. For the first time in my life, I have a home that is solid."

"The same thing goes for Nick. He loves his job, and he doesn't want to be tied down to the sponge or bakery business. Uncle Cletus even told him to find something he loves so he can stay here. No one's gonna try to force him into doing something he doesn't want to do. But they know how much he wants to be with you."

"I'll be visiting him soon," Paula said. "Maybe things will seem clear then."

"Nothing will be clear unless both of you open your eyes."

Paula was about to comment when the phone rang. Alexa took the call and pulled out an order form, indicating it was a wholesale order. She'd be a while.

Each day was busier than the one before, so Paula barely had time to breathe, let alone worry about her feelings for Nick. Amanda agreed to work a few more hours on Saturdays to help with all the extra business.

"What are your plans for Christmas?" Alexa asked.

Paula shrugged. "I'll probably work late on Christmas Eve, go to the late services at church, then go home and crash."

"Wanna come over and spend the night with us?"

"No thanks," Paula said. "I appreciate the offer, but I like to sleep in my own house."

"I just hate for you to be alone on Christmas."

"I don't mind." And she really didn't.

When she was a little girl, her parents always argued on Christmas morning, and her dad would storm out and not return until night. Years later she learned that her dad was seeing another woman, and that was where he went. When she and her mother moved away, Paula spent most of Christmas Day consoling her mother, who sobbed about how lonely she was. Being alone beat both of those experiences.

Paula fell asleep on Christmas Eve praying for wisdom and the ability to bring glory to God rather than feel sorry for herself. It was late, so she expected to sleep in the next morning. However, a loud rapping on the door startled her awake.

She had no idea who'd be at her house at . . . she glanced at the clock and squinted. It was barely seven o'clock. No one she knew would bother her so early.

When she opened the door, she found herself looking at her mother's tearstained face. "Mom!"

"Are you gonna invite me in, or do I have to stand out here and freeze half to death?"

Paula stepped back and pulled the door open all the way. "Come in, even though I don't see how you can freeze in seventy-degree weather." She glanced toward the car to see if anyone else was with her mother. "Where's Mack?"

Her mother sighed in exasperation. "He went to see his kids. Can you believe he'd do that to me?"

"What's wrong with him seeing his kids on Christmas morning?"

"He went last night. I hung around for a while then decided if he could go see his kids, I could come see mine."

"Mom, that's different. His kids live less than an hour away. Does he know where you are?"

She flicked her hand from the wrist. "I left him a note. Ever since he found out I had a private investigator watching him, he's been different. It's like he doesn't trust me now."

"Can't say I blame him."

Her mother shot her a look of disapproval, but she quickly changed the subject. "Whatcha got to eat? I'm starving."

"I picked up a couple of bagels," Paula said. "There's some cream cheese in the fridge."

"I'm in the mood for some eggs. How come you never have decent food around here?"

Paula followed her mother into the kitchen and watched her open the refrigerator door. She pulled out a sack and opened it. "What's this?"

"Leftovers from Tina's Tapas."

Her mother sniffed the contents and made a face. "It doesn't look good."

"If I'd known you were coming, I would have picked up some stuff. You should have called and told me yesterday when the stores were still open."

"How could I have called to tell you when I didn't even know myself?"

Paula thought for a moment then opened the refrigerator. "Do you want a bagel or not?"

"I guess that'll do." Her mother took a step back from the kitchen and glanced around. "Where's your tree?"

"I didn't get one."

"What's wrong with you, Paula? Nothing decent to eat and no tree? What kind of Christmas is this?"

"I went to church last night. It was really nice. The pastor read the Nativity story, and then the children put on a play."

"You didn't pay a bit of attention to me when you were growing up, did you? I tried to teach you all about the important things, and you're living like you came from another planet."

Paula didn't feel like arguing. "Sorry."

"I got your package last week."

"Good," Paula said. "Do you like it?"

"It's very nice. I've always loved cashmere, and you know red is my favorite color. You couldn't go wrong with that."

"Did Mack like the gloves?"

"Yep. In fact, he was wearing them when he left the house."

Paula stood there and tried to think of what to do next. "Want some coffee?"

"Of course."

A half hour later, as they sat at the kitchen table eating bagels and sipping coffee, Paula thought about how her mother hadn't bothered sending anything—not even a card. But she wasn't about to mention it.

"Did you get any presents this year?" her mother asked.

Paula nodded slowly. "Yes."

"Who from?"

"Dad sent me a gift card and a basket of chocolates."

"That's nice. How about Nick? Did he bother with a present?"

Paula reached for the bracelet still in the box on the corner of the table. "Isn't this pretty?"

Her mother lifted it and turned it over. "It's okay. A ring would be better. When are you two getting married?"

"Mom, that's not open for discussion."

"Don't get so testy with me, young lady. I've—"

A ringing sound came from her handbag. She reached in, pulled out her cell phone, checked the number, and groaned as she took the call.

"Did you get my note?"

Paula got up to refill the coffee while she listened to her mother's side of the conversation. When her mother flipped her phone closed, she stood up.

"Mack's mad."

"Because you came down here?"

"No, because he didn't get my note. I'm sure I left one, but he says it wasn't there."

"So what are you gonna do now?" Paula asked.

"I don't know. Everything is just so difficult. I don't get why he's so upset about my coming down here. He should understand."

"Do you think he'll ever get over you hiring the private investigator?"

"I don't know. Like I said, he doesn't trust me now." She shrugged. "He says he understands, after what I went through with your father. But I don't believe he truly gets why I did it."

"Did you ever think about sitting down and being honest with him . . . and having a conversation about your feelings?" Paula asked.

"Men don't understand feelings. They only believe in what they see."

"Not all men."

Her mother snickered. "I've never met one who was different. Sometimes I feel like their only purpose is to drive women crazy."

"Dad used to say the same thing about women."

Her mother cleared her throat. "I might have made a mistake when I left him."

Paula couldn't believe her ears. "Are you serious? I thought you hated Dad because he was involved with another woman. That's what you always told me."

"I didn't really hate him. His relationship with that tramp wouldn't have lasted long if we hadn't left. He would have eventually come back to us."

"I don't know about that." Paula hated discussing her parents with each of them. The couple of times she'd spoken with her dad over the past several years, he'd asked one question after another about her mother. "So where is Mack?"

"Home. And he wants me there."

"Why don't you spend the night and go back tomorrow?" Paula asked.

Her mother hung her head. "If I do, Mack might not be there."

"What?" Paula shrieked. "What kind of marriage do you and Mack have?"

"There are some things I haven't told you."

"Like what? Are you and Mack having problems other than . . . well, the job you never had and the private investigator?"

"Sort of." Her mother pulled a tissue from her bag and blotted her eyes. "Mack is such a frustrating man. He always was, even back in high school."

"Then why did you marry him?"

"I was sick of being alone. After you grew up, I figured I might as well head back to Alabama and be with someone who worshiped me. I assumed he'd want to take care of me and pamper me like he did his first wife." She groaned. "But no, he said he wasn't doing that again."

A phone rang again, only this time it was Paula's house phone. It was Nick.

"Merry Christmas," he said. "I miss you."

"Just a minute." She put her hand over the mouthpiece. "I'll take this call in my room," she whispered to her mother. "It'll only be a few minutes."

Her mother nodded.

After she closed her bedroom door, she chatted with Nick. "Mom appeared unexpectedly, and now I don't know what to do."

"Where's Mack?"

Paula told him a little about what was going on. "I feel like I need to give her some advice, but she doesn't listen."

Nick chuckled. "She hasn't changed, has she?"

"No, I guess not."

"I don't want to keep you long. I just wanted to wish you a Merry Christmas and let you know I'm looking forward to seeing you. One of my buddies has a girlfriend who said you can stay with her when you come."

Paula swallowed hard. "I can't wait."

After she got off the phone, Paula went back to the living room. Her mother tilted her head. "Who was that?"

"Nick."

"I can't believe the two of you still haven't figured out what to do with your relationship. Seems like one of you would have moved on by now."

"To borrow the words you used so many times, it's complicated."

Her mother smiled. "Life is like that sometimes."

"I plan to visit Nick soon, though. He invited me to come to Texas after the holidays."

Her mother's eyebrows shot up. "Well, this is an interesting development. So the two of you are more serious than I realized."

Paula lifted a shoulder and let it fall. "Unfortunately, I can't imagine leaving here, and he loves the Air Force."

"He probably expects you to drop everything and be at his beck and call."

"No, I don't think Nick is like that."

"Oh, trust me, Paula, you're doing the right thing by standing your ground. Don't ever let anyone bully you into doing anything you don't want to do."

Her mother saying that made it sound like she was being selfish. "I'm not—"

Paula's house phone rang again. She gave her mother an apologetic look, but her mother waved her away. This time it was Alexa, calling to invite her over for a late lunch. She mentioned that her mother was there, so Alexa invited her too.

"I'll see if she's interested," Paula said, knowing what her mother would most likely say. Bonnie Andrews was uncomfortable around Nick's family.

"Call me back and let me know, okay? We have something special for you."

"You do?" Paula said.

"Yes, so you have to come, and it would be cool for your mother to be with you."

"Okay, I'll talk to her. See you later, and Merry Christmas."

After Paula hung up, she took a deep breath and slowly blew it out before going back to the living room. "Mom?" Where was her mother? "Mom?"

No answer. Paula walked over to the door and looked in the driveway. It was empty. Her mother's car was gone.

26

Paula pulled her phone back out and punched in her mother's cell phone number. No answer. The voicemail kicked in, so she left a message.

She put the dishes in the dishwasher and tidied up the kitchen then showered. Finally, her phone rang. A glance at the caller ID let her know it was her mother.

"Where are you?"

"On my way home. I decided I didn't need to bother you today, since you have your life here. Just remember that I think you're doing the right thing by not giving in to Nick. You don't want to let him think he can get away with making you do something you don't wanna do. You have to think about number one because no one else will."

After the call ended, Paula sank down in the chair. The very thought of her mother's words chilled her. She never thought about how stubborn—and selfish—she'd been until she heard it from her mother.

But that old, familiar voice kept playing in her head. What if she gave up everything to be with Nick and something went wrong between them? She'd be stuck with a broken heart and dashed dreams. At least she had her business and a home.

She called Alexa back and said she'd be there. "Can I bring anything?"

"Don't go to any trouble. Mama and my aunts have been cooking all morning."

Paula added a Christmas pin to her red sweater and changed into some black velvet shoes. She could at least look festive, even though she felt heartsick.

On her way out the door, Paula lifted one of the poinsettia plants she'd bought to take to the Papadopoulos home. They didn't expect a gift, but it would give her something to hide behind as she walked in the door.

Alexa met her outside, grinning. "Mama's glad you agreed to come on such short notice. And so am I, since it was my job to get you here."

"But why?"

"You'll see. Don't ask questions, okay?"

"Sure." Paula pulled out the poinsettia and closed the car door. "Looks like half of Tarpon Springs is here."

"Maybe so. I think we're probably related to at least half of Tarpon Springs."

Alexa led the way to the house, where Stephanie greeted them at the door. Paula handed her the plant.

A couple of the older Papadopoulos women came out of the kitchen, all smiling and open-armed. Nick's mom was the first to hug her, followed by the rest of them. If she hadn't been around this family so much, she would have been overwhelmed.

"I'm glad you're not spending Christmas all by yourself, Paula."

"My mother came to town this morning."

Alexa's mother frowned. "Why didn't you bring her with you?"

"She left already."

The Papadopoulos women exchanged glances and quickly jumped to action, dragging her into the kitchen. She inhaled the mouthwatering smell of Greek and American food.

"We know how much you like turkey, so we roasted you one."

Paula laughed. "Thank you, but that wasn't necessary. I like everything."

"We know, but we want you to feel at home here, and if you're used to eating turkey on Christmas, then we want to make sure you don't miss it."

Paula refrained from saying that she spent the last two Christmases with her mother and Mack, one of them eating leftover meatloaf in front of the TV and the other packing her belongings while her mother and Mack argued in the living room. She looked around the busy Papadopoulos house and felt at peace. This was how Christmas was supposed to be—extended loving family coming together and celebrating the birth of Christ. And not a single argument could be heard.

Once Phoebe announced that the food was almost ready, her husband Apollo motioned for his brother Cletus to step forward. Paula stood with the rest of the family, watching and waiting to hear what Nick's father had to say. As soon as he opened his mouth, Steph and Alexa gently pushed her forward.

"Paula," Cletus said. "We wanted to do something special for you . . ."

She glanced around at her friends, wondering what was going on. Alexa nodded toward her uncle, so Paula turned back around.

He pulled an envelope out of his shirt pocket and thrust it toward her. "We want you to have this plane ticket to San Antonio so you can visit Nick."

The more outgoing brother, Steph's dad Arthur, took over. "And in case you're wondering, Nick knows about this. He wanted to tell you, but our wives told him he better not ruin your surprise, or else." He wiggled his eyebrows.

Everyone laughed. Paula stood there staring at the unopened envelope.

"Well?" Apollo nodded toward the envelope. "Aren't you gonna open it and see when you're going?"

With all eyes still focused on her, Paula took the envelope and opened it. She looked up at the blur of faces in front of her. "In three weeks? I can't—"

"I'll run the shop," Alexa said. "You even said I was good."

Paula nodded. "Yes, you're very good, but the return ticket is a whole week later. I don't want you to have to work that many hours."

"Oh, but you forget, dear Paula," Stephanie blurted. "I have experience working for you too. Alexa and I have already agreed that I'll open in the mornings, we'll work together during the afternoons, since that's when most of the phone orders come in, and after Amanda gets there I'll leave."

"Does Amanda know?" Paula asked.

"Yes." The voice came from behind Paula. She spun around and saw Amanda, Kate, and Sam.

Steph cackled. "You should see your face, Paula." A flash temporarily blinded Paula. "Thanks, Adam. As soon as he gets home, he'll put the picture on his computer and send it to you."

Amanda took a couple of steps closer. "I have a present for you too." She handed a box to Paula. "Open it."

Paula's heart thudded as she clumsily undid the ribbon and lifted out a mug with the words "World's Best Boss" inscribed on the side. She smiled and gave the girl a hug. "Thank you, Amanda."

Amanda shyly looked down at her feet. "You really are the best boss. Ever."

Out of the corner of her eye, Paula saw Sam slip his arm around Kate. And Kate didn't push him away .

A moment of awkward silence filled the room before Alexa's mother lifted her hands. "The food's ready, everyone. I need some extra hands to set up the buffet."

Paula, Alexa, Steph, and Amanda hung back. After everyone left the room, Steph extended her arms. "Group hug." As they put their arms around each other's shoulders, Steph started a prayer and then Alexa chimed in. Amanda said a few words of thanks, and Paula finished. After they all said "Amen," they straightened up.

"Y'all are the best," Paula said, her eyes stinging with tears. "Nothing could have prepared me for all this."

"Good." Alexa grinned. "We wanted you to be surprised. Now let's go get some food before it's all gone."

Alexa and Steph led the way to the crowded kitchen. Amanda touched Paula's arm. "In case you're wondering, Mom and Dad started dating, and I think they actually like each other now."

"How did that happen?" Paula asked.

"Dad was furious at Mom for some of the stuff I did. He came over one night, and they argued for hours, so I just went to bed. When I got up the next morning, Mom was grinning. She told me Dad had finally come around to understanding her better and that he was joining us for dinner." She smiled and sighed. "And we've had dinner together every night since then."

"Thank you, Lord," Paula whispered, barely loud enough for Amanda to hear.

"Oh, that's another thing," Amanda added. "Mom has been talking about church, and I think Dad wants to go."

"This is a true blessing, Amanda." She hugged the girl. "I've never had a better Christmas."

"So you like the mug?"

"I love the mug, but more important, I love being here with all of you."

"Mom has something else for you," Amanda said as she nodded toward something behind Paula.

Paula spun around in time to see Kate approaching her with a box.

Kate grinned. "Turn around. I have a surprise for you."

"You don't need to—"

Kate took Paula by the arm and turned her around. "Just hold still."

About three seconds later, Paula felt something on her head. She reached up and removed it.

"A cowboy hat?" She laughed. "This is too cool. Thanks!"

"I figured you might need it in Texas."

"How in the world did I not know about this? With so many people in on the secret, you'd think someone would let it slip."

"It was hard," Amanda admitted. "But we all talked about how important it was . . ." Her voice trailed off as her mother gave her a zip-it look. "C'mon, let's go get some food. I'm starving."

Paula sat with Alexa, Steph, and Amanda. The only people missing in her life were Nick and her parents. She managed to put them in the back of her mind and have fun with the people there because they cared enough to make this a very special occasion for everyone.

After dessert, they all helped clean up then gathered in the sunroom and played games. Paula watched as Amanda thrived in the loving environment. When she cast a glance in Kate's direction, she saw tears glistening in her eyes. That touched

Paula's heart, and she had to look away to keep from sobbing with joy.

Paula heard the house phone ring, but she didn't think anything about it until Charlene brought it to her. "It's for you."

As soon as she answered, Nick said, "Merry Christmas! Surprised?"

"What do you think?" She glanced around at all the people pretending not to be listening. "If you can believe this, I was almost speechless."

"I wish I could have seen your face, but Adam said he'd send me the pictures."

"Looks like I'll be there in a few weeks. I have no idea what to wear."

"Wear what you want. But bring a jacket 'cause the weather here is crazy. It might or might not be cold."

Paula had so many things she wanted to say to Nick, but she couldn't with this huge audience. So she told him they could talk later, and he understood.

Once she pressed the OFF button on the phone, Steph glared at her. "Why didn't you tell him how you feel?"

"You're kidding, right?" Paula said. They both laughed.

When she was able to get away without seeming rude or ungrateful, Paula said she needed to go. Alexa, Steph, and Amanda walked her to her car.

When they stopped, Alexa held up her hands. "I've called this staff meeting to inform you—"

Before she had a chance to finish her sentence, they all cracked up with laughter. Amanda was laughing so hard tears streamed down her cheeks.

"Y'all are the best," Paula said as she looked at her friends. "Thank you for everything."

"This is my favorite Christmas," Amanda said. "I don't think I've ever been so happy in my life."

Alexa smoothed Amanda's hair away from her face. "Ya know, I think God had a plan for you to come into the shop that day."

Amanda pulled back and gave her a curious look. "God had a plan for me to steal?"

"Yeah," Steph agreed. "He knew you needed to get caught and disciplined."

"Some discipline," Amanda said with a giggle. "I got rewarded with some of the sweetest people ever and a job I love."

"Discipline doesn't always have to hurt, ya know," Paula said. "Or maybe the pain is there, but you don't feel it."

"That's crazy." Amanda rolled her eyes.

"No, that's Paula." Steph winked at both of them. "She used to tell me that the sooner I messed up, the more time I'd have to straighten up. I think this same thing might apply with what happened to you."

Amanda shook her head, still smiling. "I don't get it, but I guess it doesn't matter."

"Right. The only thing that matters is we have each other." Alexa flung her arm around Amanda's shoulder before turning to Paula. "Okay, we'll see you at work tomorrow. You better get home and call Nick back."

On the way home Paula allowed the tears to flow beneath the cowboy hat, sitting at a jaunty angle on her head. The day had been bittersweet, and she wouldn't have traded it for anything.

As soon as she walked into her house, Paula called Nick back. He answered before the first ring finished.

"Took you long enough."

Paula laughed. "Thanks for ganging up on me."

"No problem. I'm sure it won't be the last time my family does something like this. So are you okay with leaving the shop for a week?"

"Yes, in fact I suspect Steph would be okay if I never came back. She's tired of working at the bakery and restaurant, and while I'm gone they aren't likely to call her in on an emergency."

"I know. She told me."

"Sounds like you talk to your cousins a lot." Paula flopped onto the couch and flung her leg over the arm. "What else did she tell you?"

"Alexa told Steph, and Steph told me that your wholesale business keeps growing with no signs of letting up."

"Since Alexa's been there, it does seem to be heading in that direction."

"She also said that Kate and Sam have been hanging out. Think there's another romance in the works?"

"Today was the first I realized how serious it was," Paula admitted. "I couldn't believe my eyes."

"I think you helping her daughter was the best thing that could have happened to Kate." He paused for a moment. "In fact, she actually sent me an e-mail apologizing for how she used to treat you. I told her she needed to apologize to you."

"She did."

"She said what she used to think was cool was juvenile and what she thought was nerdy was actually really cool."

Paula laughed. "She said something like that to me."

"Which explains why she's suddenly so interested in Sam— the biggest nerd in school."

"Isn't that the most amazing thing?"

"Yeah," he agreed. "It is. I have to admit I was even shocked at that one, and it takes a lot to surprise me."

"So you have a place for me to stay once I get to Texas?"

"Yes. I have a buddy whose girlfriend lives in a nice apartment nearby. She said you can stay with her. In fact, I think she's really looking forward to it."

"Good. I'm excited."

"Would you have come next month if my family hadn't taken the liberties to get your ticket?"

27

*P*aula thought for a moment. "Probably not."

Nick laughed. "Didn't think so. I'm glad I went along with the plan."

"The very sneaky plan."

"Sneaky but smart."

After they hung up, she called her mother's cell to see how she was doing. Her mother answered right away.

"Where are you?" Paula asked.

"About an hour and a half from home. I guess it was pretty stupid to come down there on a whim."

"It's okay to come visit me, but call next time. What if I wasn't here?"

"I thought about that. Did you have fun at the Papadopoulos house?"

"Yes, it was nice."

"Did you like their gift?"

Paula didn't remember telling her mother about going there. "How did you know about that?"

"Nick called a little while ago and wished me a Merry Christmas. He told me about your surprise."

Paula laughed. "I was definitely surprised."

"Just remember what I said. Always remember what you want, and don't let some man try to convince you to do otherwise. It'll make you resent him."

"Is that how you feel about Mack?"

"Yes. He doesn't understand how I feel."

"Have you tried talking to him?"

"Of course. Why do you think I'm so upset all the time? When he tells me to get a job, I tell him exactly how I feel. And even though he says he understands about the private investigator, he still throws that up in my face."

Paula had heard her mother rant before, and if she did that to Mack, he probably tuned her out. "Why don't you tell him you'd like to talk about it sometime when he's not upset with you?"

"Oh, puh-lease. Do you think I'm stupid or something?"

"No, of course I don't. You're not stupid." *Just misdirected.* "Why don't you and Mack go for counseling?"

"You're starting to sound just like him. He said that very same thing a few days ago. Have you talked to Mack?"

"No, but if you want to save your marriage, it's the logical thing to do. Living without trust is hard."

"You need to think about that too, Paula."

Paula swallowed hard. For once her mother had a point. "Will you at least think about going for counseling?"

"I told you I've been seeing a shrink."

"I'm talking about marriage counseling. With Mack."

"I have to go, Paula. The traffic is starting to get heavy."

Avoidance—another of her mother's techniques for dealing with distasteful subjects.

Over the next several weeks, as Paula prepared for her trip, her mother's words about not letting a man determine her future played through her mind. Until now, she'd subconsciously thought along the same lines as her mom—and that made her shudder. It didn't seem wrong to want to stay in Tarpon Springs until her mother talked about standing her ground to get her way. Now it seemed downright selfish.

She loved Nick, and he said he loved her. It wasn't like they'd just met and let the chemistry take over. They'd had years of knowing each other and seeing the differences as well as their similarities.

"Something seems different about you," Alexa said on the morning Paula was leaving for Texas.

"Yeah? How so?"

"You don't seem worried about the shop. I thought you'd be running around with last-minute lists, giving me instructions, and . . ." Her voice trailed off.

"Making you crazy?" Paula added.

"Well, yeah." Alexa gave her an apologetic grin. "But you're acting like you trust me enough to run this place."

"I do."

"I know, but you don't even seem nervous."

"To be honest, I'm a nervous wreck inside," Paula said. "But it's more about seeing Nick than worrying about this shop."

"Good. That's the kind of nervous you should be."

"Do you think I should bring something dressy?"

"Of course," Alexa said. "You know that little red dress you bought for the Chamber of Commerce event last year?"

Paula nodded. "I'm not sure it still fits."

"Go home and try it on. If it doesn't fit, you can borrow one of my outfits."

Paula opened her mouth to argue that she was supposed to work until noon, when Steph was taking her to the airport, but she stopped herself and nodded. "Okay. I'll do that now."

She'd gotten to the door when she heard Alexa call out, "And don't stop by the Senior Center. No one's there. They're taking the morning off."

Man, Alexa sure did have her number. "Okay, okay, Miss Bossy."

"Just wanted to make sure you knew."

⌒⌒

Nick got to the airport early. He'd been pacing like a madman, but his friend Lance shoved him out the door. "You're better off waiting there than here driving me nuts."

"I'll call Beth as soon as we're on our way."

"She knows." Lance pointed toward the door. "Now go."

Waiting had never bothered Nick before, but now that he wanted everything to be perfect, he felt jumpy. He parked in the short-term lot and went into the terminal. It seemed like forever until he spotted Paula walking his way. When her gaze met his, her entire face lit up.

He opened his arms and lifted her off her feet. She dropped her carry-on bags and flung her arms around his neck. "I thought you'd never get here," he said.

"What are you talking about?" she asked as he set her down. She tapped her watch. "My plane was fifteen minutes early."

"Okay, let's go get the rest of your bags."

A half hour later, they were on their way to Lance's girlfriend Beth's apartment. Nick pulled out his phone and punched in Beth's number.

As soon as she answered, he said, "We're on our way."

"Good. Now try to calm down. I know you're excited about her being here, but you have a whole week."

"Okay, I'll try to do that."

After he pushed the OFF button, Paula laughed. "What did you just promise to try to do?"

"Calm down, but it's hard when I'm this excited."

"Why?" Paula asked as she looked out the window. "What are you so excited about?"

"You being here."

"Nick."

He cast a glance in her direction and saw her you've-gotta-be-kidding look. "What?"

"You saw me just a few weeks ago. I'm totally not that exciting."

"To me you are."

She snorted. "Doesn't take much for you then. So are you sure it's okay for me to stay with this Beth girl?"

"Absolutely. In fact, when I mentioned that you might come, she volunteered her place right away. She and Lance met at church. I think you'll like her."

"It's good to know they attend church. Same one you go to?"

Nick nodded. "Yeah, I went to the base chapel until Lance invited me to his small church that meets at an elementary school."

"Interesting."

They chatted about some of the differences between San Antonio and the Tampa Bay area until he pulled into the apartment complex and wound around toward the back.

"These look like nice apartments," Paula said.

"They are. Beth had a roommate until recently. She's living in a huge two-bedroom apartment by herself for now—at least until she can find another roommate. Your timing is good."

Beth stood at the door of her apartment, waiting. Nick waved, and she met them at the car.

"Hi, Paula, I'm Beth. I bet you're exhausted. I have your room ready, so you can relax for a little while until the guys come back and pick us up for dinner."

"Oh, I forgot to tell her." Nick turned to Paula. "We're taking you to this fabulous Mexican restaurant for dinner."

"Sounds good," Paula said.

After Nick carried Paula's bags to her room, he gave her a quick kiss and whispered, "I love you. See you in a couple of hours."

He left, and Beth took Paula on a tour of the apartment. "Help yourself to whatever you want. Nick said you like sweets, so I bought a bunch of stuff."

"You didn't have to do that," Paula said. "But thanks. I just don't want to be an inconvenience."

"Oh, trust me, you're not an inconvenience. We've all been looking forward to meeting the girl who's had Nick's heart for so long."

Paula gave Beth a curious look. "What?"

"We kept trying to fix him up with nice girls, but he was never interested. Finally, last summer, he told Lance that he's been in love with the same girl since high school."

Paula's heartbeat quickened. "He said that?"

"Yep. He not only told Lance and me, he said it in front of our entire group at church." She gestured toward the living room. "Why don't we sit down in there and relax. Want something to drink?"

"Sure," Paula said. "Whatcha got?"

"Lemonade or sweet tea."

Paula grinned. "Sweet tea will be just fine."

Within minutes Paula felt as if she'd known Beth forever. She was from Mississippi, and her background was similar. Her parents divorced when she was a little older, so she and her mother went to live with her grandmother.

"With Granny there to take care of me, Mama went hog wild with the men, if you know what I mean."

Paula nodded. "My grandmother moved to a retirement center, and she didn't approve of my parents getting a divorce, so Mom stuck around to try to keep her happy. After she passed away, my mother and I moved down to Florida to get a fresh start."

"Aren't you glad?" Beth asked.

"At the time, no. I wanted to stay right where I was, with the friends I'd known since I was little. I hated leaving Alabama, but it wasn't hard to make friends in Tarpon Springs. Nick's cousin came up to me the first day of school and asked if I wanted to join her and her friends for lunch."

Beth tapped her chin. "Is that Alexa?"

"No, it was Steph. Alexa is a little bit younger."

"Nick talks about his cousins, parents, aunts, and uncles all the time. We feel like we know them. I have to admit, Lance and I got a kick out of hearing that his daddy's in the sponging business. I never even thought about people diving for sponges. I just thought you went to the grocery store and bought 'em."

"That's what most people think."

"Nick also told us about your soap and candle shop. It sounds like such a fun life."

Paula told her about how she'd always wanted her own business, and when she had the opportunity to rent space from Nick's uncle, she couldn't turn it down. "Alexa works for me now, and she's taking my business to a whole new level."

"It's good that you have someone you can trust working for you. You're able to get away without worryin' about your employees robbin' you blind."

"I know. I'm blessed."

Beth hopped up. "We better start getting ready for our big date. I hope you like enchiladas. The place we're going has the best in the world."

That night was the start of what seemed like a dream vacation to Paula. Nick was the perfect tour guide, showing her around the Air Force base and San Antonio. The more she got to know Beth, the more she liked her and valued her new friendship. When it was time to leave, she hugged her hostess.

"Come back and stay here anytime. Even if I find a roommate, you're still welcome."

"Thank you so much for everything." Paula made a mental note to send Beth a gift basket filled with a variety of soaps and candles.

At the airport, Nick held her in his arms for a long time. Finally, she had to pull away. "I need to go to the gate and check in."

He nodded. "I might come back home again in a few months." He glanced down then looked back into her eyes. "That is, if you'd like me to."

"Of course I want you to." She dropped her bag on the floor and ran back up to him. After kissing him once more, she backed away. "I'll see you then, Nick."

Paula's heart ached from the moment they parted until she arrived at the Tampa International Airport. Steph had pulled up beside the curb to pick her up.

"How was San Antonio?"

Paula sighed. "Wonderful."

"Did you actually see San Antonio, or were you and Nick too busy staring at each other?"

Paula told her all about the trip and her new friend Beth. "I think you'd like her."

"I'm sure I would." She pulled out onto the road leading home. "I can't believe you haven't asked about the shop yet."

"Oops." Paula giggled. "So how's the shop? Still standing, I hope."

"It's doing better than that," Steph said, her voice tightening with excitement. "Alexa just got a huge order from one of the biggest retailers in the country, and my uncle is interested in selling one of his stores at the other end of the sponge docks. I thought you might want to look at it before he puts it on the market." She turned to Paula when she got to a stoplight. "It's about 50 percent bigger than where you are now, and it's a lot brighter."

"Sounds good. Any idea how much he wants?"

"I'm sure you'll get a good deal on it since you're practically family. Oh, and get this. Amanda asked for next Saturday off so she can go to Disney World with her parents."

"That's the most amazing thing ever."

"I know. One day she's a latchkey kid with two totally absent parents, and a couple months later she's having an all-American family weekend."

"God is good, isn't he?"

Stephanie nodded. "He's the best."

As soon as Paula put her things away, she went to the shop to check on Alexa and Amanda. They were deep in discussion over a new product display.

"What do you think, Paula?" Amanda asked.

Paula cut her eyes over to the stand. "Very nice."

"These are the candles you were working on before you left. Mildred got her crew working on them right away so we'd have them when you got back."

"I understand you've been doing well while I was gone."

Alexa told her all about the big order that came in. Once she finished talking, Amanda told her how she was learning to up-sell customers. "When they come in for a candle, I try to get them to buy more. I even show them soap with a matching fragrance. Alexa's been teaching me all kinds of stuff about sales."

"Good job," Paula said. "You're turning into quite a salesperson."

"She sure is," Alexa agreed, pride sparkling in her eyes.

Paula had known the shop would be fine without her, but it was even better than fine. For the first time, she was sure it would run just as well if she didn't even come in.

28

*Y*ou're not gonna believe this!"

Paula snapped her head up to see Charlene walking in. "Hey, Charlene. What's up?"

"Seriously, I have some news."

"Okay, spit it out."

Charlene's eyes were lit up, and she looked as if she were about to jump out of her own skin. "Guess what couple is the hottest item in town these days!"

"Um . . ." Paula tapped her chin. "Kate and Sam?"

Charlene's shoulders slumped. "How did you know?"

"Amanda works for me. Yesterday she said she hopes they fall in love again and get married. I don't think her feet touched the floor during her entire shift."

"Think it's possible?"

"Of course it is. The Lord can make anything happen."

"Yeah, but you have to admit that would be a miracle," Charlene said.

Alexa came out from the back room. "Miracles do happen. Look how God used Amanda's attempt at shoplifting."

"What?" Charlene tilted her head. "Amanda shoplifted? Where?"

"Where have you been all this time, little sis? We caught her shoplifting here."

"So . . . you decided to hire her . . . why?"

"It's a long story, but you'll understand after we tell you. But first, did you know Kate and Sam are going to church now?" Paula asked.

"Another miracle," Charlene said.

"If you'd go to church with the rest of us, you'd know this stuff," Alexa said.

Paula laughed. "Amanda and her mother came as my guests, and last time Amanda visited her dad, she talked him into going with her."

"Wanna hear my other news?" Charlene said, wide-eyed.

Paula and Alexa both looked at her. "Other news?" Paula said. "Like what?"

Charlene looked at Alexa. "You heard Papa talking about it last night, didn't you?"

Paula glanced at Alexa, whose eyes suddenly narrowed. "I can't believe you're blabbing this. It's supposed to be a surprise."

"Oops." Charlene pretended to cover her mouth with her fingertips. "Sorry."

"Okay, what's going on?" Paula said. "Why do I have a feeling this surprise has something to do with me?"

"You wanna tell her, now that you've opened your big mouth?" Alexa said.

"Nick is coming back . . . like very soon."

"He is?" Paula's voice screeched. She'd just spoken with Nick last night. He asked if she'd like to see him again soon, but he'd mentioned months.

Charlene nodded. "He can't stay away."

Paula leaned against the counter. "I wonder why he didn't tell me."

Alexa rolled her eyes and glared at Charlene before turning back to Paula. "I'm pretty sure it was supposed to be a surprise."

"Yeah," Charlene said, looking contrite. "And I blew it."

"Don't worry about it," Paula said. "This isn't the kind of surprise I like."

"That's what Nick said, but Uncle Cletus talked him into not saying anything yet."

A customer arrived, so they went to work. Paula's thoughts swirled all afternoon, and she found herself staring off into space daydreaming.

That night after dinner, Nick called. "I guess you heard the news, huh?"

"Yep. So you were planning to just show up without any warning?" She needed time to emotionally prepare for him.

"I would have told you, but probably not for another week or two."

"How long will you be here?"

"Not long this time. Less than a week. I have something very important to discuss with you."

"Like what?"

"My reenlistment in the Air Force is coming up soon."

❧

Nick stood at the arrival curb, watching for Steph's car. Seeing Paula instead gave him a kick of joy.

"Steph was supposed to be here," he said as he tossed his suitcase into her trunk. He leaned over and gave her a brief kiss then slammed the trunk shut.

"Disappointed?" Paula asked after they got in the car.

He turned to her and grinned. "What do you think?"

She shrugged and cast one of her good-humored but smirky looks at him. "Never know what's going on in that pretty head of yours."

He fluttered his eyelashes. "You probably say that to all the guys."

"Actually, that's the first time I've ever said it."

He rubbed her shoulder. "I know."

"So what's this trip all about?" she asked.

"You."

"Me?" She glanced at him but kept her focus mostly on the road.

"I guess I should have said us. We'll talk later. Did my loyal girl cousins ask you to set aside a couple of nights for me?"

"Yes, of course they did. They even worked up a schedule and told me I wasn't allowed to work more than the hours they had me down for."

He chuckled. "So who's in charge of your shop now?"

"I'm beginning to wonder. But I can't complain. Alexa and Amanda are both very good at their jobs. Steph wants to phase into working more for me so she doesn't have to stay in the restaurant or bakery businesses. The problem is, things keep happening at the bakery, and they need her."

"Sounds like I'm not the only family defector."

"I always thought it would be nice to know my family was there for me with a safety net of established businesses, nice houses, and helping hands."

"Things aren't always as wonderful as they appear." He thought for a few seconds then added, "But I shouldn't complain. My family may have its flaws, but they're good people who have enough unconditional love for all of us."

"Yes," she agreed. "That's a wonderful thing."

"So tell me what nights you'd like to get together with me."

Paula broke into a smile. "I'm free every night while you're here."

Nick pumped his fist. "Yes! The girls came through for their pitiful cousin."

"Pitiful?" She shook her head. "I don't think so."

"I will be if I don't get my way."

"Oh, come on, Nick. You're being silly."

"That's what happens when I'm around you. I get all silly and goofy."

"You are definitely a goofball."

"So tell me more about Kate and Sam. That's one I didn't see coming."

Paula told him all about how Kate started going to church regularly, and Amanda talked Sam into attending after that night when he'd stormed into the house, angry at Kate. Something in the pastor's sermon that week struck a chord in him, so he returned and kept going back.

"Everyone was shocked to see them out and about together."

"It's incredible how things have worked out."

"I guess you can say that Kate and Sam are living proof of what God can do," Paula said.

"Isn't that the truth. I'm happy for Amanda."

"She's doing so well in school she might qualify for some scholarships if she keeps her grades up through next year."

"Amanda's going to college?"

Paula nodded. "She said she wants to run a business just like mine, and I convinced her that college will give her a foundation for it. She'll probably go to the Tarpon Springs campus of St. Petersburg College—at least to start with."

Nick knew that all this talk about Amanda was the easiest way to divert attention from what was on both of their minds.

But that was fine. He had a plan, and now wasn't the time to execute it.

"Where to?" Paula asked as they entered Tarpon Springs. "Who won the privilege of hosting the golden boy this time?"

"I was just here, so they didn't do that. My parents are expecting me."

She dropped him off at his parents' house. After he got his suitcase, he leaned over and talked to her through the window.

"What time will you be ready tonight?"

"How about seven?"

"I'll be at your doorstep at seven sharp."

She laughed as she gave him a mock salute. "Aye, aye, sir."

"Paula. I'm in the Air Force, not the Navy."

"Sorry." She pulled away with a smile on her face, warming his heart and letting him know he'd made the right decision.

❧

Paula tried on three outfits before she decided on something. She laughed as she thought about how much she was becoming like Alexa. That made sense, though, because they'd been spending most of their afternoons together. Alexa was becoming more businesslike, and Paula had gotten more girly. She'd even started going to the mall and ogling handbags. That was a first for her.

The phone rang, and it was Kate. "Ready for your big date yet?"

"Almost. I wish I knew what was going on with Nick. Something seems different."

"Come on, Paula. You know exactly what's going on. That man is pulling out all the stops to make you his."

Paula laughed. "So how about you? Tell me what's going on between you and Sam."

"He started sweeping me off my feet, but then he got scared."

"That's not what I heard."

Kate laughed. "If you heard it from my daughter, there's no telling how the story went."

"So are you and Sam an item now or not?"

"We're trying to be, but there are still a lot of issues. I'm supposed to make an appointment with the pastor for us to work through some stuff."

Paula was happy to talk about Kate and keep the conversation off her and Nick. She asked a few more questions then said she had to go.

"Make sure you listen to whatever Nick has to say with an open mind. I'd hate to see the two of you waste more time. You're not exactly getting younger, ya know."

"Thanks, Kate. I'll talk to you in a day or two."

"You better believe you will. I'm calling tomorrow for a full report."

As Paula hung up, she thought about her unlikely friendship with Kate. Both of them had overcome their insecurities through their mutual faith and Amanda's increasing insistence they all get together. The more she got to know Amanda's mother, the more she realized how similar she and Kate were. They both had absentee fathers and mothers who did the best they could without help from anyone. The biggest difference between them was that Paula's mother had brought her to church that one time, and she'd been pulled into the loving congregation at Crystal Beach Community Church. And now that Kate was part of the same phenomenon, all their lives had changed. Paula wanted things to work out for Kate and Sam so

Amanda would have a stable home. It came sixteen years late, but at least it seemed like there might be hope for them.

Nick was at her door right on time. And Paula was standing there waiting for him.

He looked her up and down. "Still the most beautiful girl in Tarpon Springs."

She rolled her eyes as she pulled the door closed behind her. "We're in Palm Harbor now."

"Palm Harbor too."

She laughed. "And you're still the biggest charmer in town."

"Only when I'm with you. I thought we'd drive over to Crystal Beach before dinner if that's okay with you."

"Sure. You're in charge of our schedule tonight."

He parked the car near the church. After they got out, he gestured toward the path. "Wanna walk?"

Paula was glad she'd decided against high heels in favor of some sequined flats Alexa talked her into buying. "Sure."

They walked about twenty feet before Nick stopped and turned to face the water. "Nothing is as gorgeous as the sunsets here . . . except . . ." he tilted her face toward his. ". . . you."

"Nick." Her breath caught in her throat as he leaned down and dropped a kiss on her lips.

He cleared his throat. "Paula, I've decided not to reenlist."

"What are you talking about, Nick? You love the Air Force. How can you do that?"

"Yes, I do like the Air Force. A lot. But I love you with all my heart, and if I can't have both, I've decided I'll do whatever it takes to have you in my life."

Paula suddenly felt sick to her stomach. "No, Nick, I can't let you do that."

"You don't exactly have a choice."

"Maybe not," she said as she looked into his eyes. "But I won't be part of something that pulls you away from the career you've always wanted."

The pained expression on his face ripped at her heart. "I'm miserable without you."

She was miserable without him too, but she knew if he left the Air Force, he might wind up resenting her in the future. "We can figure out something, but not this."

Nick placed his hands on her shoulders and held her at arm's length as he looked into her eyes. "I want you to know that I'll do anything it takes to be with you. Nothing else matters to me."

But after the honeymoon . . . Paula shuddered to think about the resentment that might follow.

"Let's go to dinner now," she said.

They walked in silence, hand-in-hand, to the car. Paula didn't try to make conversation until they turned off Alternate 19 toward Bon Appetit.

"I've always loved this place."

"Yes, I know." Nick smiled as he pulled into a parking spot. "I wanted this to be a night to remember."

Nick had reserved a table overlooking the water. Paula felt her pulse surge merely by looking at the man across the table from her. If she'd ever doubted his love, she couldn't any longer. That made her want to please him even more.

"Nick, please don't leave the Air Force. I can't stand the thought of you being miserable here in Tarpon Springs."

"I won't be miserable."

"But you won't be happy either."

He tilted his head downward and shut his eyes. Paula knew he was praying.

When he looked back at her, he said, "I still have a few weeks after I get back to the base to let them know my decision."

She smiled. "You're an amazing guy, Nick."

"That's what I keep trying to tell you."

At that moment, Paula knew what she needed to do. But she needed to wait for the right time to make sure Nick wouldn't do anything he'd regret.

29

"Don't breathe a word of it to Nick," Paula said. "And please make sure Lance doesn't slip up and say something."

Beth giggled. "I love surprises—especially when I'm the one doing the surprising."

"I haven't been on this end of the surprise very often," Paula admitted. "But I have a feeling I'll enjoy it."

"Okay, so let me get this straight. I'm picking you up at the airport, and we're coming back to my place. Lance will get Nick to come over with him." She paused for a couple of seconds. "That might be the hard part. Lance said it's getting harder to talk Nick into anything lately. All he wants to do is mope around and think about you."

"Ironic, isn't it?"

Again, Beth giggled. "Yeah, but we have to figure out a way to get Nick here."

"I have an idea. Why don't you have Lance leave his car at your place, so he can tell Nick he needs a ride? Nick is a good guy, so he can't turn Lance down."

"You are brilliant, Paula."

"When it comes to conniving, apparently so."

After they made their plans, Paula came out from the back room and told Alexa everything was confirmed. Alexa pumped her fist.

"Nick will be so surprised he won't know what hit him."

Paula rubbed her neck. "I just hope you continue to like working here. If that ever changes, this whole plan will tank."

"I can't see that happening," Alexa said. "But if it does, at least you have backup with Steph, Amanda, and Kate."

"That's another thing. What made you think Kate would be so good at sales? She sold more during her shift yesterday than I ever sell in a week."

"I dunno," Alexa said as she placed the palm of her hand on her abdomen. "Just a gut feeling, I guess."

"I'm just glad you and I are on the same team. You've been amazing."

Alexa beamed. A small amount of praise went a long way with her.

Paula left to check on the folks at the Senior Center. Mildred met her at the door. "We're already getting applications for the new jobs. I don't think we'll have any trouble filling them. Every senior citizen in Tarpon Springs and Palm Harbor has heard about the perks of working for you." She snickered. "We love our freebies."

"And I love my Mildred," Paula said. "You're doing a great job. I just stopped by to see if you needed anything."

Mildred shook her head. "Not now. When are you leaving for Texas?"

"Next week. I would have liked to do this next month, but there's a time element for Nick. I have to do this before he makes his decision about reenlisting."

"My Frank was in the Army. Career man. Loved serving, and when he got out, we had his retirement to fall back on."

"How did you feel about moving every couple of years?" Paula asked.

Mildred shrugged. "It had its good points and bad, just like everything else. I liked making new friends, but leaving the old ones was difficult. However, many of them showed up at other posts, and I've been able to find the ones who are still around, thanks to the Internet." She put her hand on Paula's shoulder. "How do you feel about all these decisions?"

"Surprisingly at peace about them. Everything has fallen into place so well, I know it's a God thing."

"You're a good girl, Paula. Nick is a fortunate man."

❦

Nick stared at Lance. "Why did you leave your car at Beth's?"

"We went out last night, and after I got there she said she wanted to drive." Lance wouldn't look Nick in the eye, so he knew something was up. "We forgot my car was at her apartment, so she dropped me off here." That was the final hint. Lance loved his car.

"So I need to take you to Beth's place, but not until six o'clock." Nick narrowed his eyes.

"Right."

"Man, this is strange."

Lance lifted his hands. "I know, but Beth said to wait until six and not to get there before that."

So Beth was in on whatever was up too. Nick sure wished he knew what it was, but he guessed he'd find out soon enough.

He left for the gym then came back to the barracks, where Lance waited out by the parking lot. "Ready?"

Lance shook his head. "You're not going like that."

Nick opened his arms and looked down. "I just got back from the gym. Whaddya expect?"

"Take a shower and put on something decent."

This sounded very suspicious. "Is this a blind date? Because if it is, I don't want any part of it."

"Blind date?" Lance cleared his throat and looked everywhere but at Nick. "No, it's not a blind date. Go shower and change, and I'll wait. Just don't take too long."

Nick wasn't falling for something so obvious, so he stood his ground. "No. If you want a ride, I'll take you now."

A look of concern washed over Lance's face, but he quickly recovered. "Okay, whatever."

"Just to make it very clear," Nick said firmly, "I'm not going in."

After they pulled onto the main road in Beth's apartment complex, Lance whipped out his cell phone and speed-dialed Beth. "Meet us outside." He listened then cut a nervous glance over at Nick. "No, just come on out. We'll see you in the parking lot."

Nick rounded the corner to Beth's apartment and blinked. He had to be seeing things. He blinked again. Nah, it couldn't be. So he slowed to a stop and turned to Lance. "Tell me that's not Paula."

Lance shot him a grin. "Can't do that because it would be a lie."

"Paula's here." He said that more for his own sake than for Lance's. No wonder Lance wanted him to shower.

"Yeah." Lance gave him a smug grin. "Wish you'd listened to me and taken a shower?"

Nick slapped his palm on the steering wheel. "I can't believe this." At least he'd known Paula long enough that she'd seen him all sorts of ways—including after his high school football games.

He whipped the car into the closest empty spot and hopped out of the car. Paula walked toward him, slowly, tentatively, until he opened his arms. Then she ran straight for him.

As he lifted her off her feet, she put her arms around his neck and gave him a kiss on the cheek. "Surprised?"

He put her down and gestured toward himself. "What do you think? If I'd known you were here, I would have done what Lance told me to do and taken a shower."

"I don't care. I'm just happy to see you."

Nick cupped her face and kissed her on the lips. "What are you doing here? I'm happy to see you too, but what's up with not telling me?"

"It's my turn to surprise you."

"Okay. What else is going on?"

Paula cast a glance over her shoulder, where Beth and Lance stood watching. She gave them a thumbs-up, and they headed inside.

"Wanna go somewhere?" she asked.

"If you don't mind how I'm dressed."

"I've never cared how you dressed, Nick. You know that."

A surreal sensation blanketed Nick as he drove to the closest park. This was the kind of thing he dreamed about. He bit his bottom lip and winced. Ouch. This wasn't a dream. Then he smiled.

"Look. There's a hiking trail." Paula pointed to one of the brown signs. "Let's go for a walk."

If she'd told him to stand on his head and spin around ten times, he would have. "Okay. Whatever you want to do."

She laughed as she led the way. After a few minutes of asking questions about the terrain, she stopped, turned to face Nick, and took his hands in hers.

"There's something we need to discuss." She let go of his hands and pushed her hair behind her ears with a shaky hand.

He leaned in toward her and wrapped his hands around hers again. "Okay, so start discussing."

"You kept saying you wanted us to be together forever."

"That's right," Nick said. "And that's why I've decided not to reenlist."

"It's not too late to change your mind, is it?"

He narrowed his eyes and studied her. "Are you telling me you don't want me to come back to Tarpon Springs?"

Paula nodded. "That's exactly what I'm saying."

What kind of a cruel trick was this? "This makes no sense. If you didn't want me around, why did you bother coming here?"

"I didn't say I don't want you around. Just not in Tarpon Springs." She let go of his hands and took a step back.

"Okay, so exactly what are you saying, Paula? Stop playing this game."

"Do you miss me?" She placed a fist on her hip and tilted her head, not once taking her eyes off him.

"Why are you doing this?"

"Just answer me, Nick. Do you miss me, and do you still want us to be together for life?"

He slowly nodded. She might be playing a game, but he wasn't going to lie. "Yes."

"Then why don't we do something about it?" She stepped closer to him again. "Let's get married."

She couldn't have said anything more shocking if she'd told him his pants were on fire. "What?"

"I think you heard me."

"Are you serious?"

"As a heart attack."

Nick sucked in some air. He didn't know what to do, but he did know that this was an opportunity he couldn't let go. "That does it. I'm definitely getting out of the Air Force. I didn't expect a proposal to go this way, but now that you've asked, I'm all over it."

"Oh, that wasn't a proposal," she said with a coy expression. "You still have to get down on one knee and do the traditional proposal thingy. But I've never been all that good at subtle hints, and I wanted to make sure we were on the same page."

Nick chuckled. "Okay." He started to get down on one knee, but she stopped him.

"We still have to talk about something before you do this. You're not leaving the Air Force—at least not yet."

"But I don't understand."

"I want to know what it's like to be a military wife."

"Huh? What are you talking about, Paula? You have your business, and you said—"

"That's why I'm here. I wanted to tell you my plan in person. I think it's an excellent one, but I can't take credit for it. Alexa and Steph helped me."

Nick had no doubt his cousins would do whatever it took to get Paula in the family—and as long as a scheme was involved, they were part of it. "Okay, so tell me your plan."

They found a bench on the trail and sat down. Paula explained how Alexa had shown her competence in running the shop and now Steph, Amanda, and Kate were working there. She wouldn't give up the shop, but she didn't have to be there all the time.

"How much longer do you have to reenlist for?" she asked.

"Four years."

"How long before you can retire?"

"Twelve years at the earliest."

Paula held out her hands. "That's not very long. We can go wherever the Air Force takes us—that is, if it's what you still want—and I can do my work long-distance. Alexa is capable of handling almost anything that comes up, and I can fly back if needed." She grinned before adding, "The way the business is growing, I can certainly afford it."

Nick was impressed. "Are you sure you wanna do this?"

"Positive. After the last time I saw my mother, I realized how selfish I was being."

Nick hung his head. "I guess I was being selfish too. It started a long time ago with me, though."

"Both of us had dreams, but there's no reason we can't still follow them. We just have to figure out a way to merge them."

Nick was practically speechless at how much thought had gone into Paula's plan. "I like your thinking," he finally managed to mumble.

"We still have some details to iron out," she said, "but I want you to be as involved in the planning as I am."

"Are you sure you're up to moving every couple of years?" he asked. "Because when the Air Force tells me I have to be somewhere, I don't have a choice. I know how important it is for you to have a home."

She nodded. "My home will be wherever you are, Nick." She looked into his eyes. "That is, if you want me there."

His heart pounded so hard he thought it might explode. "I love you, Paula. I do want you with me."

She reached up, cupped his face, stood on her tiptoes, and planted a kiss on his lips. "I've learned that if there's something you want, you can't wait around. You have to go for it. And I want you any way I can have you, even if it means moving every time we turn around."

Paula was right. He got down on one knee, took her hand in his, and looked up into her eyes. "Paula, I've loved you for as long as I've known you. Will you make me the happiest man in the world and marry me?"

She snickered. "Of course I will. I didn't go to all this trouble for nothing."

30

*P*aula had only been back to Tarpon Springs for a couple of days when the biggest wholesale order she'd ever received came in. As soon as she saw the numbers on the order form, her eyes bugged.

"Hey, don't worry about it," Alexa said in her increasingly calm voice. "It's all under control. This is what we've been working on for weeks, and it finally came through."

"I had no idea it would be this big," Paula admitted.

Alexa smiled as she patted Paula's shoulder. "That's because your mind has been elsewhere. Oh, by the way, Steph said she wants to go ahead and move some of her stuff into your house, if you don't mind."

"That's fine. I'm just thankful you and Steph will rent from me. It's one less thing I have to worry about."

"It's a win-win situation for all of us. You don't have to sell your house or let it sit there vacant, and we'll have a nice place to stay without having to move back in with our parents."

"That wouldn't be so bad, though, would it?" Paula asked.

Alexa gave one of her you've-got-to-be-kidding looks. They both laughed.

"I still can't believe I'm getting married in a couple of months," Paula said. "Everything just seems to be falling into place."

"My family is thrilled to have a project."

"And trust me," Paula said, "I don't mind being their project, as long as it involves food."

"Oh, that reminds me. You need to stop by the bakery sometime this afternoon. Mama wants you to taste one of her new cake flavors."

"I think I can sacrifice the time," Paula said, her mouth watering. "But I think I'll probably go with the almond."

"You haven't tasted the amaretto yet. It's amazing."

"Everything they bake is amazing. By the way, I told your dad I'd let him know what I want on the buffet."

"Let me guess. Avgolemono soup, spanakopita, and lamb stew."

"You know me too well." Paula grabbed her purse and headed for the door. "Mildred called and said she needed me, so I guess I better head on over there."

Alexa's lips twitched, but she didn't smile. "Yeah, I guess you better."

Mildred was up to something, but Paula had been in too big of a hurry to ask what it was. The instant she pulled into the parking lot of their new facility, she had an inkling. All the spots were taken except one by the door with a makeshift sign, her name printed in large block letters.

Paula ran a comb through her hair then got out and headed toward the door. She'd barely reached the top step when the door flew open and a raucous cry of "Surprise!" accosted her. A table with a homemade cake stood off in the corner. Gift-wrapped packages covered the rest of the table and were piled high in the surrounding chairs.

Her eyes misted as she looked around the room at all the senior citizens who worked for her company. These were the people who didn't mind working hard to provide the product for her customers. They never let her down.

"Y'all shouldn't have," she said, her voice barely above a whisper.

"You've been so good to us, Paula," Mildred said. "We're happy to do it." She rubbed her hands together. "Ready to get started? As it is, you'll be here all day."

Since Paula had been living on her own all her adult life, she didn't register for wedding gifts. But these people didn't care. They had enough life experience to know some things she'd need or want without having to be told.

Three hours later, Paula accepted help getting the gifts to her car. Afterward, she made sure she hugged every person there. They each offered some advice on marriage.

"Never go to bed angry," one woman said.

"Take some time for yourself," another offered. "It's hard to be a good wife if you're not rested."

"Communication is overrated," one of the men said. "So try not to talk too much."

Paula laughed. "I'll try to remember that."

"Don't forget to put on lipstick and brush your hair for your husband," another man said. His wife jabbed him, so he shrugged.

With a head full of advice and a car full of gifts, Paula drove home feeling that, in spite of all the unknowns before her, all was right in her world. When she pulled onto her street and spotted her mother's car in the driveway, she tensed up instantly. Her mother stood there shielding her eyes, watching and waiting.

"Mom," she said as she got out. "Why didn't you tell me you were coming?" Paula braced herself for an argument.

"Mack and I wanted to surprise you." Her mother sounded different—more relaxed.

Paula leaned over and looked in the car. "Mack's here? Where is he?"

Her mother pointed. "He went around the house to see if anything needed to be fixed. We have some stuff to give you for the house."

"You know I'm moving to Texas after the wedding, right?"

"Yes, but you also said you were keeping your house, and I know you've complained about not having any gardening tools. You can use them later, after you're settled."

Her mother didn't always make sense, but at least she was being agreeable. "I need to bring some of this stuff inside."

"Good. I'll help."

Something had definitely changed. "Thanks. It'll take more than one trip, even with your help."

"Let's put down this first load, and I'll get Mack to finish unloading. He never knows what to do, so this will keep him busy for a while."

After they dropped the packages in the living room, Paula started a pot of coffee while her mother went to talk to Mack. When she came back inside, she propped her elbow on the counter.

"We need to talk before Mack comes in."

Paula's breath caught in her throat. She hoped nothing else had gone wrong in her mother's life, but that might be too much wishful thinking.

"Okay, so what do you wanna talk about?"

Her mother beamed. "Mack and I have decided to get counseling. We've met with the therapist once, and she says we both have some issues that are hurting our relationship."

Paula could have told her that, but her mother preferred paying money to hear it from a stranger. "That sounds like a good start."

"And I want to apologize to you."

Paula's hand stilled. She slowly looked up at her mother. "For what?"

"For being such a lousy mother. I had no clue what to do with such a smart, independent girl. It sometimes felt like you were the parent and I was the child. I did things I'm not proud of."

Tears sprang to Paula's eyes again, and this time she couldn't keep them from running down her cheeks. "Mother . . ."

In a matter of seconds, her mother crossed the room and pulled her into her arms. "I love you, Paula, and I never meant to hurt you. Will you forgive me?"

"Of course I will. I love you too."

"Hey, ladies. Anything else you need me to do?"

Paula looked up at Mack, who stood in the door of her kitchen looking flustered. "Thanks, Mack. We're fine. Have a seat and I'll bring you some coffee."

"I'll get it," he said as he came toward them. "Our counselor said we both need to do things for ourselves instead of expecting the other one to do it." He turned to Paula's mother. "And while I'm getting my coffee, I'll fix yours too, Bonnie."

"No, that's okay, Mack. I can get it."

"I'll leave the two of you to decide who should get the coffee while I put some of those packages in my room." Paula walked out of the kitchen, wondering how this transformation had come about. Whatever had happened, it was a relief to know her mother was finally accepting some of the responsibility she'd neglected for so many years. And Mack obviously forgave her for not trusting him.

༫ঌ

"Nervous?" Nick's brother Michael asked as they stood in front of the mirror.

"Not a bit." Nick adjusted his collar and turned to face his older brother. "This wedding is long overdue."

Michael nodded toward the door. "Then we better join the other guys so we can get this show on the road."

As Nick stood at the altar, he thought about how long he'd waited for Paula—and it had been worth it. No other woman could make him think or feel the way she did. And she cared so deeply about their spiritual life together.

The music started, creating a stir of excitement in the church. Everyone in the sanctuary had been waiting forever for this to happen. His cousins started the procession up the aisle—first Charlene, then Alexa. Steph was the maid of honor, so once he saw her, he knew it wouldn't be long.

Paula appeared at the door, the sun shining behind her, creating an ethereal glow around her silhouette. Her mother gave her a hug then led her slowly up the aisle. He had to bite back the tears that threatened. Once Paula and her mother got to the altar, her mother whispered something in her ear then turned to Nick and winked before being seated by the usher. Paula's goofy, crooked grin made him smile.

After they said their vows, and Nick and Paula headed up the aisle, he leaned over and whispered, "What did your mother say?"

Paula cupped her hand. "She told me to forget everything she ever taught me and just have a good time being married to the man of my dreams."

He gave his new mother-in-law a thumbs-up as he whispered, "That's the best advice I've ever heard."

Papadopoulos Family Recipes

Phoebe's Baklava

Phoebe's notes: Always have plenty on hand when Paula is around. It makes her smile.

Ingredients:

- 14 sheets of phyllo dough
- ½ lb. butter
- 1 cup vegetable shortening
- 1 cup chopped almonds
- 1 cup ground pecans
- 1 cup chopped walnuts
- ½ cup crushed zwieback
- ½ cup sugar
- 1 teaspoon cinnamon

Syrup:

- 3 cups granulated sugar
- 1½ cups water
- 1 cup honey
- 1 tablespoon lemon juice

Directions:

1. Melt the butter and shortening.
2. Brush a 13 x 9 baking pan with the melted butter.
3. Place a layer of phyllo dough to cover the bottom of the pan.
4. Brush with melted butter.
5. Repeat for 5 layers of phyllo dough.
6. Mix the ground almonds, pecans, walnuts, crushed zwieback, sugar, and cinnamon.
7. Sprinkle the phyllo layers with 1/3 of the nut mixture.
8. Add 3 layers of phyllo and melted butter to the top of the mixture.
9. Sprinkle another 1/3 of the nut mixture over the second layer of phyllo dough.
10. Add 3 more layers of phyllo and melted butter to the top.
11. Sprinkle the remaining nut mixture over the buttered phyllo.
12. Layer the remaining phyllo and butter mixture to the top.
13. Bake in a 350 degree oven for approximately 1 hour.
14. Remove from the oven.
15. Combine the syrup ingredients in a pot.
16. Bring the syrup mixture to a boil.
17. Pour over the hot baked baklava.
18. Allow the baklava to rest for approximately 1 hour.
19. Cut into squares, rectangles, or triangles.

Ophelia's Avgolemono
(chicken-egg-lemon) **Soup**

Ophelia's notes: Perfect recipe for a large crowd. The kids love it!

Ingredients:

- 3 large eggs, separated
- 2 skinless, boneless, shredded chicken breasts, cooked
- 8 cups water
- 6 teaspoon bouillon crystals or 6 bouillon cubes
- 1 cup orzo (rice-shaped pasta)
- Juice of 2 to 3 lemons
- Pepper to taste

Directions:

1. Boil water and add bouillon.
2. Add orzo and chicken.
3. Cook for about 10 minutes, until orzo is tender.
4. Add lemon juice to egg yolks and whisk until blended.
5. Add lemon and egg yolk mixture to the whites and blend on medium speed to soft peaks.
6. Remove the pot with chicken and orzo from the heat.
7. Remove 2 cups of the hot broth from the pot.
8. Slowly add the broth to the egg and lemon mixture, beating on low speed while adding.
9. Slowly pour the broth with egg and lemon into the pot, beating on low speed.
10. Add pepper to taste.

Phoebe's Lentil Salad

Phoebe's notes: Ladies' lunch favorite.

Ingredients:

- 3 cups of cooked lentils, drained
- 1½ cups crumbled feta cheese
- ¾ cup Greek vinaigrette salad dressing
- 1 sliced cucumber
- 1 cup of diced fresh tomatoes
- 1 medium diced onion

Directions:

1. Place lentils in a large mixing bowl.
2. Stir in ½ of the salad dressing.
3. Add feta, cucumber, tomatoes, and onion.
4. Cover and refrigerate for an hour or two.
5. Before serving, add the rest of the salad dressing and stir.

Apollo's Spanakopita (spinach pie)

Apollo's notes: Menu staple.
Popular with tourists and locals.

Ingredients:

- Cooking spray
- 10 sheets of phyllo dough
- ½ cup butter, melted
- 1 pound fresh spinach, washed, patted dry, and chopped
- 2 eggs
- ½ cup chopped onion
- 2 cups ricotta or small curd cottage cheese
- 1 cup grated feta cheese
- Salt and pepper to taste

Directions:

1. Spray a 13 x 8 baking pan with cooking spray.
2. Place a layer of phyllo in the pan.
3. Brush the first layer of phyllo with melted butter.
4. Repeat layering the phyllo and melted butter until there are 5 sheets in the pan.
5. Place the spinach in a bowl and lightly salt. Allow to stand for 10 minutes.

6. Beat the eggs then add onion and cheeses.
7. Fold the spinach into the egg, onion, and cheese mixture.
8. Add salt and pepper to taste.
9. Spread the entire mixture over the phyllo.
10. Layer the remaining phyllo over the top, brushing each layer with melted butter.
11. Bake in a 350 degree oven for approximately 35 to 40 minutes.
12. Cut into squares.

Greek Salad – Tarpon Springs style
(with potato salad)

Apollo's notes: Hide the potato salad beneath the lettuce for the surprise factor.

Ingredients:

- 4 large romaine lettuce leaves
- 8 cups chopped romaine lettuce
- 3 cups potato salad (recipe below)
- 2 medium tomatoes, each cut into 8 wedges
- 1 cucumber cut into 16 slices
- 1 bell pepper cut into rings
- 4 slices canned beets
- 8 cooked and peeled shrimp
- 4 anchovies
- 8 Greek style black olives
- 8 banana peppers
- 4 whole green onions
- ½ cup white vinegar
- ¼ cup extra virgin olive oil
- ¼ cup vegetable oil
- 1 tsp. oregano

Potato Salad:

- 4 large potatoes cubed and boiled
- ¼ cup diced onion
- ½ cup mayonnaise

Directions:

1. Mix the potato salad ingredients and chill.
2. Line a large bowl or platter with large romaine lettuce leaves.
3. Scoop the potato salad onto the romaine leaves in 4 single serving mounds.
4. Cover the potato salad with the chopped lettuce
5. Top with tomatoes, cucumber, bell pepper, beets, shrimp, anchovies, and olives.
6. Add banana peppers and onions to the side of the salad.
7. Mix the vinegar, olive oil, vegetable oil, and oregano.
8. Pour the vinegar and oil blend over the salad.

Greek Lentil Soup

Ursa's notes: Freezes well so always make extra.

Ingredients:

- 1 bag dried lentils, washed
- ½ cup olive oil
- ½ cup chopped onion
- 1 cup chopped celery
- 1 teaspoon minced garlic
- 1 chopped carrot
- 1 tablespoon lemon juice
- 12 cups water
- 2 teaspoon beef bouillon crystals
- Salt and pepper to taste

Directions:

1. Cover the lentils with half (6 cups) the water in a pot.
2. Bring to a boil then turn the heat down to medium. Simmer for 10 minutes.
3. In a skillet, heat the oil and sauté the onions and garlic until the onions are translucent.
4. Add the rest of the chopped vegetables and cook for about 10 minutes on low heat.

5. Drain the lentils and add the remaining 6 cups of water to the pot.

6. Add the sautéed onions and vegetables to the lentils and water.

7. Add bouillon, salt, and pepper.

8. Cook for approximately 30 minutes, until flavors have blended.

9. Remove from heat. Add the lemon juice before serving.

Apollo's Moussaka

Apollo's notes: Make extra for moussaka night. Take some home to family.

Ingredients:

- Cooking spray
- 2 large eggplants
- 1½ pounds ground lamb
- ¼ cup extra virgin olive oil
- ½ cup chopped onion
- 1 teaspoon minced garlic
- ½ lemon thinly sliced (circles)
- ¼ cup fresh chopped oregano
- 1 cinnamon stick
- 1 small can of tomato paste
- 1 small can of diced tomatoes
- ¾ cup feta cheese
- ¾ cup grated parmesan
- ¾ cup bread crumbs
- Salt and pepper to taste

Directions:

1. Peel and slice eggplant to about ½ inch thick.
2. Salt and pepper the eggplant.

3. Pour half of the olive oil into the skillet and fry the eggplant in a single layer until brown on both sides.

4. Place the eggplant on paper towels to absorb excess oil.

5. Pour the rest of the olive oil into the pan and add onion, garlic, lemon slices, and oregano. Cook for approximately 5 minutes or until the onion is translucent.

6. Add the ground lamb, breaking it up. Stir while browning. Salt and pepper to taste.

7. Add the whole cinnamon stick, tomato paste, and diced tomatoes.

8. Simmer until most of the liquid has evaporated and turn off the heat.

9. Spray a 13 x 9 baking pan with cooking spray.

10. Place 1/3 of the eggplant on the bottom of the pan.

11. Spread ½ of the meat over the eggplant.

12. Sprinkle with ½ of feta and ½ of parmesan cheeses.

13. Repeat the layers and sprinkle the breadcrumbs over the top.

14. Bake in a 350 degree oven for approximately 35-40 minutes.

15. Cool for 10 to 15 minutes before serving.

Apollo's Beef Stew – Greek style

Apollo's notes: Always serve in largest bowls available
and fill to the top.
Make enough for seconds.

Ingredients:

- 3 pounds beef stew meat
- 2 tablespoon butter
- 2 onions cut into wedges
- 6 large carrots cut into 1-inch slices
- 4 potatoes cut into bite size pieces
- ¼ cup olive oil
- 2 tablespoon red wine
- 1 tablespoon red wine vinegar
- 1 small can tomato paste
- 2 cloves garlic
- 2 cups hot water
- Salt and pepper to taste

Directions:

1. Heat the butter and 1 tablespoon of the oil in a skillet.
2. Brown the stew meat on all sides.
3. Move the meat to a larger pot.

4. Brown the onions in the skillet. Add to the pot with the stew meat.

5. In a large bowl, combine the rest of the olive oil, red wine, red wine vinegar, tomato paste, garlic, hot water, salt and pepper. Mix well.

6. Pour the olive oil and red wine mixture into the pot with the meat.

7. Add the potatoes and carrots to the pot.

8. Cook on high until it comes to a boil.

9. Reduce the heat to low, cover, and simmer for approximately 2 hours.

10. To thicken the gravy, whisk a small amount of flour and water with a dash of paprika for color. Slowly stir this into the pot and cook until the gravy is the desired thickness.

Apollo's Lamb Stew

Follow the instructions for the Greek style beef stew, but substitute lamb for beef. Add celery and green string beans for extra flavor and nutrition.

Ursa's Tiropitas – Greek-style cheese bread

Ursa's notes: Bring to ladies' lunch when Phoebe makes her lentil salad.

Ingredients:

- 1 package of phyllo pastry dough
- 2 cups ricotta or small curd cottage cheese
- 4 beaten eggs
- 1 cup crumbled feta cheese
- 1 cup melted butter.

Directions:

1. Mix the cheeses and eggs until blended.
2. In a baking dish, layer half of the phyllo sheets, brushing melted butter on each layer.
3. Spread the cheese mixture over the phyllo.
4. Layer the rest of the phyllo, brushing each sheet with melted butter.
5. Tuck the sides around the edges to seal the cheese with phyllo.
6. Bake for approximately 30 minutes in a 400 degree oven, until golden brown.
7. Cool for approximately 10 minutes and cut into squares.

Baked Feta

Ursa's notes: Keeps the men and children from starving to death while they wait for dinner.

Ingredients:

- 1 pound feta cheese
- 2 tablespoon oregano
- ¼ cup olive oil

Directions:

1. Cover a cookie sheet with aluminum foil.
2. Cut the feta into strips and place on the aluminum foil about 2 inches apart.
3. Sprinkle oregano over the feta.
4. Drizzle with olive oil.
5. Fold another sheet of aluminum foil over the feta and fold the aluminum pieces together.
6. Bake in a 350 degree oven for approximately 15 minutes.
7. Serve with crusty Greek bread or pita chips.

Papadopoulos Women's Greek-Style Rice Pudding

Ursa's notes: Keep plenty of rice pudding on hand when Nick is home.

Ingredients:

- 2 cups cooked white rice
- 1 quart whole milk
- 1 cup sugar
- 2 teaspoon cornstarch
- 2 teaspoon water
- 1 egg
- 2 tablespoon butter
- 1 tablespoon grated lemon rind
- 1 tablespoon vanilla
- Cinnamon to taste

Directions:

1. Add the milk to the white rice in a saucepan. Bring it to a boil.
2. Reduce to low heat and simmer for approximately 30 minutes. Stir frequently to keep it from sticking.
3. Whisk the cornstarch in the equal amount of water.
4. Add the sugar, grated lemon rind, and cornstarch mixture.

5. Cook on low for 10 minutes. Remove from heat.

6. Beat the egg in a bowl and gradually add ½ cup of the rice mixture to the egg.

7. Pour back into the rest of the rice mixture.

8. Add vanilla and stir.

9. Sprinkle with cinnamon before serving.

Papadopoulos Family Cucumber and Yogurt Salad

Phoebe's notes: Perfect for a hot summer day.

Ingredients:

- 4 large cucumbers
- 10 fresh mint leaves
- 1 cup plain Greek yogurt
- 2 tablespoon lemon juice
- ½ cup parsley

Directions:

1. Clean and cut the cucumber into bite size pieces.
2. In a blender, combine the rest of the ingredients and mix well.
3. Pour the yogurt sauce over the cucumbers.
4. Refrigerate and serve cold.

Baked Tomatoes and Feta

Ophelia's notes: Perfect appetizer for any family gathering.

Ingredients:

- 3 pounds cherry or grape tomatoes
- 8 ounces feta cheese
- ¾ cup olive oil
- ½ cup fresh basil
- 1 tablespoon minced garlic

Directions:

1. Soak garlic in olive oil for 20-30 minutes.
2. Cut tomatoes in half and place them in a baking dish.
3. Pour olive oil and garlic over the tomatoes and toss. Spread out into a single layer.
4. Bake in 375 degree oven for approximately 10 minutes. Remove from oven.
5. Sprinkle crumbled feta cheese and basil leaves over the tomatoes. Stir.
6. Serve with slices of Greek or Italian bread.

Ursa's Greek Wedding Cookies

Ursa's notes: Any time these wedding cookies are served is a happy occasion. Opa!

Ingredients:

- 1 cup of butter
- ¼ cup sugar
- 1 egg yolk
- ½ teaspoon baking powder
- 1 tablepoon brandy
- 1 tablepoon vanilla
- ½ cup chopped pecans
- 2½ cups all-purpose flour
- Powdered sugar

Directions:

1. Whip the butter with an electric mixer until fluffy.
2. Slowly add the sugar, egg yolk, brandy, and vanilla while still mixing.
3. Sift the flour and baking powder. Fold dry ingredients into the wet ingredients.
4. Slowly add chopped nuts, a few at a time.
5. Scoop tablespoon-size balls of dough and roll into balls.

6. Place the balls on the baking sheet approximately 2 inches apart.

7. Bake for approximately 30 minutes in a 350 degree oven or until golden brown.

8. Cool slightly then dust heavily with powdered sugar while still warm.

Pilafi (rice)

Apollo's notes: Offer with any entrée.

Ingredients:
- 2 cups uncooked rice
- ½ cup butter
- 5 cups chicken stock
- 2 teaspoon salt

Directions:
1. Melt butter on medium in a large pan.
2. Brown the uncooked rice in the butter.
3. Add the chicken stock and salt. Stir. Bring to a boil.
4. Turn down the heat, cover, and simmer for approximately 20 minutes.

Kafes (Greek coffee)

Phoebe's notes: Warn visitors that this is stronger than
American coffee.

Ingredients:

- 4 cups water
- 10 lumps sugar
- 5 tablespoon ground coffee

Directions:

1. Boil the water in a heavy pot.
2. Add the sugar and coffee. Stir.
3. Remove from heat and skim the foam. Put some of the foam to the side for later.
4. Return the pot to the heat and bring to a boil again. Skim the foam and reserve. Repeat.
5. Spoon some of the foam into demitasse cups.
6. Pour the coffee over the foam.
7. Serve with dessert or on its own.

Lemon Roasted Potatoes

Ophelia's notes: Easy to cook. The kids love these potatoes with chicken.

Ingredients:
- 5 large peeled and quartered white potatoes
- Juice from 1 large lemon
- 3/4 cup water
- 4 tablespoon olive oil

Directions:
1. Coat a roasting pan with 2 tablespoon olive oil.
2. Place the potatoes in a single layer on the pan.
3. Mix lemon juice and water. Pour over the potatoes.
4. Drizzle the remaining olive oil over the potatoes.
5. Bake in a 400 degree oven for an hour until the potatoes are brown and tender.
6. Add salt and pepper to taste.

Hummus

Ursa's notes: Don't let Nick see this first, or no one else will get any.

Ingredients:
- 4 cups of cooked garbanzo beans
- Juice of ½ lemon
- Zest of ½ lemon
- 2 cloves garlic
- ¼ cup chopped parsley
- ¼ cup chopped onions or scallions
- Salt and pepper

Directions:
1. Pour all ingredients except the salt and pepper into a food processor.
2. Mix until you have a smooth consistency. If it is too thick, add water 1 tbsp. at a time.
3. Salt and pepper to taste.
4. Serve with pita or any other flat bread.

Pickled Feta

Ophelia's notes: Make this at least one day in advance.

Ingredients:
- 8 ounces feta cheese
- 5 sprigs of fresh thyme
- 8 ounces white wine vinegar
- 2 teaspoon honey

Directions:
1. Rinse the feta and pat it dry with clean cloths or paper towels.
2. Cut the feta into ½-inch cubes.
3. Place one layer of the feta cubes into a jar or deep bowl.
4. Add a sprig of thyme.
5. Alternate layering the cheese with thyme until it is all in the jar or bowl.
6. In a separate bowl, whip the white wine vinegar and honey together.
7. Pour the vinegar and honey mixture over the cheese.
8. Put the lid on the jar or cover the bowl with a couple layers of plastic wrap.
9. Refrigerate for at least one day. Two days is better.
10. Serve on a relish tray with olives, vegetables, and onions.

Fun Facts About Tarpon Springs, Florida

One of the first settlers in the area, Mary Ormond Boyer, named Tarpon Springs after the large fish that came into Spring Bayou and leapt out of the water. She thought they were tarpon, but the fish were actually mullet.

Tarpon Springs had a thriving sponge industry by the late 1890s. In just a few years, Greek sponge divers were brought in from the Greek Dodecanese Islands. They harvested sponges in the Gulf of Mexico off the coast of Tarpon Springs.

There are more than 100 shops along the sponge docks on Dodecanese Boulevard. Tarpon Springs is known for restaurants featuring authentic Greek cuisine.

Tarpon Springs has the highest percentage of Americans with Greek heritage of any city in the U.S.

Tarpon Springs citizens love a good party. Festivals, dining events, parades, and art shows are held on the sponge docks throughout the year.

Every January Epiphany is celebrated in Tarpon Springs with a morning service at St. Nicholas Cathedral and the release of a white dove signifying peace. The Greek Orthodox Church archbishop throws a cross into the water of Spring Bayou. Boys from 16 to 18 years old dive into the water to find the cross. After one of the boys retrieves the cross, he's carried back to the church on the shoulders of his friends for a blessing of the diver, and everyone celebrates with music, dancing, and plenty of food.

Discussion Questions

1. Why is Paula so adamant about staying in Tarpon Springs?

2. Why is Nick so eager to leave a town where he has a family that clearly adores him?

3. Nick was the classic high school football hero, and Paula was more studious. What attracted Nick to Paula? What attracted Paula to Nick?

4. What is the significance of baklava in the story? Have you ever tried baklava? How would you describe the flavor?

5. Paula obviously has a reversal of the parent-child role in her relationship with her mother. How could this have happened, and when do you think it began?

6. Why would Paula continue to give her mother money without more accountability?

7. Do you think Paula's mother and stepfather can work through their issues?

8. After Amanda tries to steal from Paula, what drives Paula to help Amanda?

9. Kate was clearly the "bad girl" from high school. How does this affect her relationship with her daughter? How does this affect her relationship with Paula?

10. Have you ever experienced being labeled "class nerd," "class clown," "the pretty one," "jock," or any other label typically placed on high school kids? Has this affected you for the rest of your life, and if so, how?

11. After Nick retires from the Air Force, do you think he can be happy living in Tarpon Springs?

Inspiration for Sweet Baklava

Q: Where did you find the inspiration for *Sweet Baklava*?

Debby: *Sweet Baklava* is a book of my heart. The story deals with issues I've experienced, features foods I crave, and is set in Tarpon Springs, Florida, one of my favorite places in the world. My dad was in the Air Force and my family moved often, so I wasn't able to establish roots in any one location until I became an adult. People I met sometimes said they envied me because they'd never had the opportunity to travel. I used this experience in creating the theme of the story, with Paula needing roots and Nick longing to see the world.

Q: You mentioned Tarpon Springs, Florida, as one of your favorite places. Can you tell us why that is?

Debby: A delightful Greek community on the Gulf of Mexico, Tarpon Springs has its own flavor and personality that attracts thousands of visitors every month. Walk along the Sponge Docks on Dodecanese Boulevard, and you'll not only smell the aroma of savory food wafting from the kitchens of authentic Greek restaurants, you'll hear the strains of Greek music and shouts of "Opa!" as waiters place delectable dishes in front of guests. Many of the merchants and residents in Tarpon Springs are first- and second-generation immigrants who have customs they've brought to their new home.

Q: How do you hope that readers will connect with the characters of this novel?

Debby: Members of this Greek community are fiercely loyal to those in their immediate families as well as people they've "adopted." I want my readers to get a sense of this through the Papadopoulos family in the story. Nick's parents, aunts, uncles, and cousins won't allow Alabama-born Paula to feel like an outsider. They include her in family activities to give her the sense of belonging that she needs. Of course, they have an ulterior motive of matchmaking, and they do their share of meddling to help Paula and Nick see the love they'll miss if they don't come to their senses.

Q: How were you able to lend authenticity to this story through its setting?

Debby: I show some of the Tarpon Springs culture with a blend of some real places and others I created for the story. The fictional family restaurant and bakery are typical of what visitors will see when they visit the real Sponge Docks on Dodecanese Boulevard, which runs along the Anclote River. The Sponge Docks host all kinds of shops offering souvenirs, Greek apparel, sponges, soaps, candles, and of course delicious Greek food—including baklava (of course!). Visitors can even take a boat ride and a tour of a sponge museum to learn how divers harvest the sponges.

Q: Just how important a part does "baklava" itself play?

Debby: As the creator of this story, I took the liberty of giving Paula a weakness for baklava, which becomes the bait for the Papadopoulos women to bring Nick and Paula together every chance they get. There are as many recipes for baklava as there are Greek families. Baklava takes time to make, but it is absolutely delicious, sweet, and worth the time and effort—just like the nurturing of a loving family.